Merc was right. Craddock had set him up good and proper, and he, Ford Barclay, would never forgive him for it. To catch him out had been Craddock's intention all along. If those two nasty beggars were the kind of friends Craddock had, then he didn't want to be one of them.

As he triggered his remote control Ford did wonder if he was fit to drive after all that drink. But he had no way out of it. Ford drove home very steadily, sweating anew each time he thought about the close shave he'd had. It worried him that he hadn't seen it coming. This rural life had slowed him up and it wouldn't do.

Educated at a co-educational Quaker boarding school, Rebecca Shaw went on to qualify as a teacher of deaf children. After her marriage, she spent the ensuing years enjoying bringing up her family. The departure of the last of her four children to university has given her the time and opportunity to write. *The Village Newcomers* is the latest in the highly popular Tales from Turnham Malpas series. Visit her website at www.rebeccashaw.co.uk.

By Rebecca Shaw

THE BARLEYBRIDGE SERIES

A Country Affair
Country Wives
Country Lovers
Country Passions
One Hot Country Summer
Love in the Country

TALES FROM TURNHAM MALPAS

The New Rector
Talk of the Village
Village Matters
The Village Show
Village Secrets
Scandal in the Village
Village Gossip
Trouble in the Village
Village Dilemma
Intrigue in the Village
Whispers in the Village
A Village Feud
The Village Green Affair
The Village Newcomers

The Village Newcomers

Rebecca Shaw

An Orion paperback

First published in Great Britain in 2010
by Orion
This paperback edition published in 2010
by Orion Books Ltd,
Orion House, 5 Upper Saint Martin's Lane,
London WC2H 9EA

An Hachette UK company

1 3 5 7 9 10 8 6 4 2

A CIP catalogue record for this book is available from the British Library.

ISBN 978-1-4091-1761-2

Typeset by Deltatype Ltd, Birkenhead, Merseyside

Printed and bound in Great Britain
by Clays Ltd, St Ives plc

www.orionbooks.co.uk

INHABITANTS OF TURNHAM MALPAS

Ford Barclay	Retired businessman
Mercedes Barclay	His wife
Willie Biggs	Retired verger
Sylvia Biggs	His wife
James (Jimbo) Charter-Plackett	Owner of the Village Store
Harriet Charter-Plackett	His wife
Fergus, Finlay, Flick & Fran	Their children
Katherine Charter-Plackett	Jimbo's mother
Alan Crimble	Barman at the Royal Oak
Linda Crimble	His wife
Lewis Crimble	Their son
Maggie Dobbs	School caretaker
H. Craddock Fitch	Owner of Turnham House
Kate Fitch	Village school headteacher
Jimmy Glover	Taxi driver
Tamsin Goodenough	Organist
Gilbert Johns	Church choirmaster
Louise Johns	His wife
Mrs Jones	A village gossip
Vince Jones	Her husband
Barry Jones	Her son and estate carpenter
Pat Jones	Barry's wife
Dean & Michelle	Barry and Pat's children
Revd Peter Harris MA (Oxon)	Rector of the parish
Dr Caroline Harris	His wife

Alex & Beth	Their children
Marcus March	Writer
Alice March	Musician
Jeremy Mayer	Manager at Turnham House
Venetia Mayer	His wife
Tom Nicholls	Assistant in the Store
Evie Nicholls	His wife
Dicky & Georgie Tutt	Licensees at the Royal Oak
Bel Tutt	Assistant in the Village Store
Don Wright	Maintenance engineer (now retired)
Vera Wright	Cleaner at the nursing home in Penny Fawcett
Rhett Wright	Their grandson

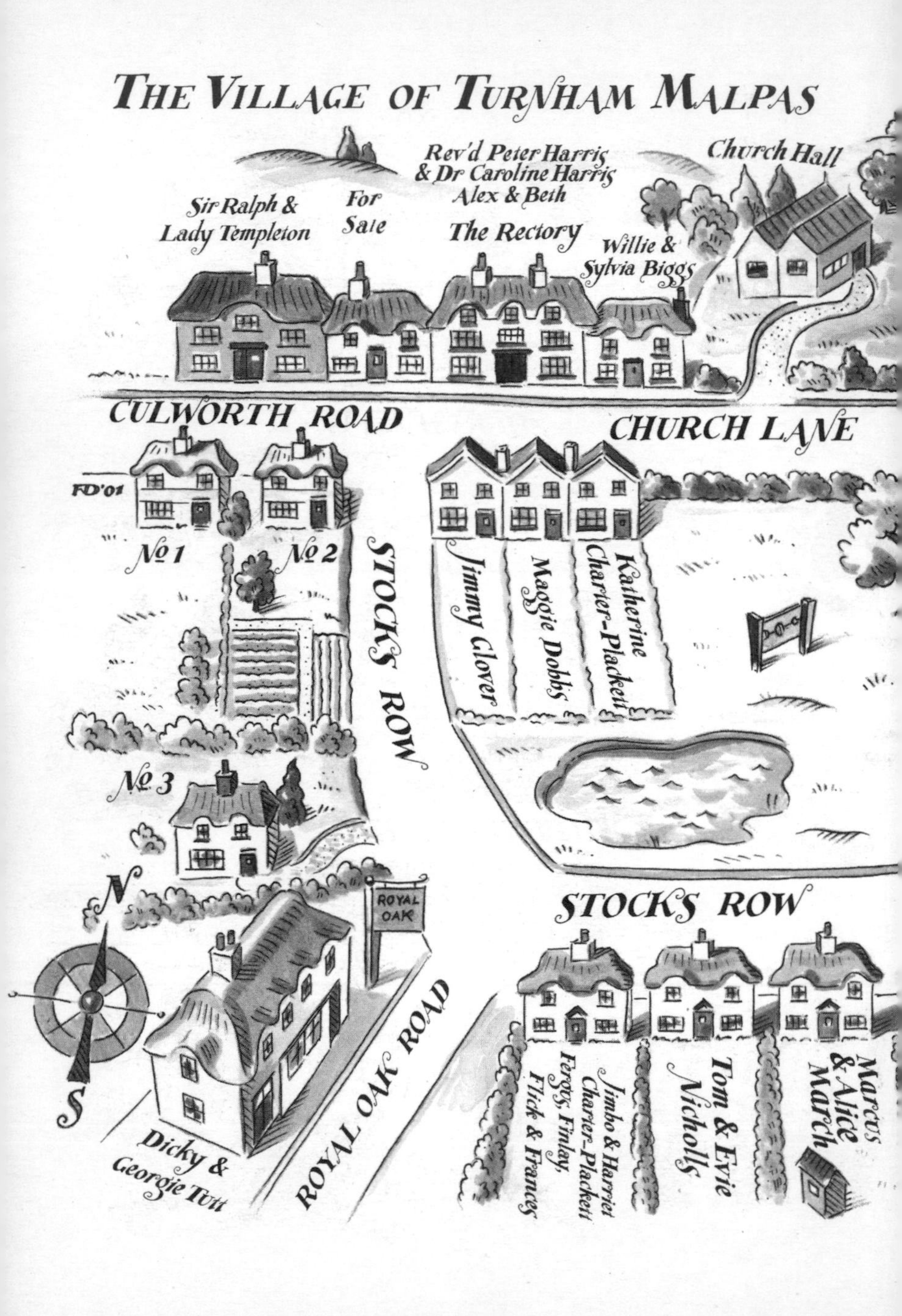
THE VILLAGE OF TURNHAM MALPAS
Rev'd Peter Harris
& Dr Caroline Harris
Alex & Beth
Church Hall
Sir Ralph &
Lady Templeton
For
Sale
The Rectory
Willie &
Sylvia Biggs
CULWORTH ROAD
CHURCH LANE
FD'01
№ 1
№ 2
STOCKS ROW
Jimmy Glover
Maggie Dobbs
Katherine
Charter-Plackett
№ 3
N
S
ROYAL
OAK
STOCKS ROW
ROYAL OAK ROAD
Dicky &
Georgie Tutt
Jimbo & Harriet
Charter-Plackett
Fergus, Finlay,
Flick & Frances
Tom & Evie
Nicholls
Marcus
& Alice
March

St Thomas à Becket
Bel Tutt
Tamsin Goodenough
Ford & Mercedes Barclay
GLEBE COTTAGES
GLEBE HOUSE
CHURCH LANE
Village Store
Swimming Pool
STOCKS ROW
JACKS LANE
Nursery Classrooms
Turnham Malpas School
SHEPHERDS HILL
Gilbert & Louise Johns & Family
pond
Footpath
Alan & Linda Crimble
HIPKIN GARDENS
BECK
TURNHAM
footbridge

Chapter 1

Caroline heard the familiar bang of the front door that told her Peter was back from his prayers and his three-mile run.

'I'm back! Going for a shower.'

He said the same words every single morning, and she wondered why, after twenty-seven years of marriage, he still felt the need to say it. But she still loved him as much, if not more, than the day they married, so, as far as she was concerned, he could carry on saying it until the end of time.

The breakfast table had everything it needed. Ah, no. Beth's muesli. That was another thing that hadn't changed over the years, although the brand was different. At the moment it was Jordans. Caroline smiled. She loved her twins more than life itself. As their grandmother frequently said, 'They are such splendid children.'

The sound of rushing footsteps told her Alex was on his way. Never one for lazing in bed, he appeared in the kitchen at the speed of light, flung himself down on his chair and shook cornflakes briskly into his bowl until there was scarcely room for the milk.

'What's happening today, Mum?'

'Anything you like. It's the last day of the holidays, so it's your choice.'

'Oh, God. Sixth form tomorrow.'

'I don't believe you're not looking forward to it. With results like yours they'll be putting out the red carpet for you.'

'Not just for me, as you well know. They're all so competitive it takes some keeping up to. Getting down to work again will be hard. We've had such a good holiday. Best ever. We loved it in Greece, and being at home. Dad back?'

'He is.' Caroline sat down, poured herself coffee and began eating her cereal.

'Is he free today?'

'I don't expect so, but he'll be down shortly.' They both heard the heavy thud of the morning post arriving through the letterbox.

Alex leapt up and went to the door. There was a pile of letters, mostly to do with Church, so he put those on his dad's desk in his study and took the rest of them, bills and such, into the kitchen.

Curiously there was a letter for Beth and one for him, both addressed in the same unfamiliar handwriting.

His mum began opening the bills and Alex tore open his own envelope, unfolded the sheets of notepaper and looked at the signature at the end. '*With love from your mother*', it said. He knew he should fold it up and read it later, on his own in his bedroom where his mum couldn't see, but he was so torn to pieces by the very first letter he'd had from his birth mother in all his sixteen years that he immediately wanted to see what she'd written. In his excited state of mind he knocked his spoon out of his bowl, spinning cornflakes and milk on to the cloth and down his pyjamas.

'Blast!' He rushed to get some kitchen roll, dropped the letter on the floor and swore as the cold milk soaked through to his chest.

'Alex! Please!' Caroline bent down to pick up his letter and a cold chill circled her heart. The handwriting was a blast from the past and she couldn't think … She put the letter on the table and allowed her mind to wander. Whose writing could it be?

Alex, having cleared up the mess he'd made, sat back down, first carefully putting his letter under his chair cushion, and carried on eating as though nothing had happened. The letter would have to wait.

Peter came down, showered, shaved and dressed for the day in his cassock with his silver cross tucked into his leather belt, his strawberry-blond hair still damp, his face glowing with health and peace of mind.

'It's a Church day then, Dad?'

'It is, otherwise I'd spend it with you. I've got Penny Fawcett market day first as it's Monday, and then on into Culworth for a meeting at the Abbey, lunch with them all and hospital visiting afterwards.'

'You couldn't take Beth and me into Culworth, could you? We'd come back on the bus.'

'Of course, and what's more I'll give you twenty pounds to spend seeing as it's your last day. Save me time if you come to the market with me, though; then we can go straight to Culworth on the bypass.'

'Done. I'll go and tell Beth to get up.' As casually as he could, Alex surreptitiously picked up Beth's letter, took his own from under his chair cushion and went upstairs.

Caroline said nothing until she'd taken Peter's boiled egg from the pan. After she'd sat down she looked hard at Peter, wondering whether or not to tell him what she suspected. He preferred openness so she decided to tell him. Her anxiety made the news burst out of her in a rush.

'I think the children have had a letter each from their mother.'

'From their ... You mean Suzy Meadows?'

She nodded.

'I see.'

'Alex has taken both letters upstairs. He checked the signature on his, then folded it and never read it. I expect they're both reading them right now.'

Peter took the top off his egg and then put the spoon down. 'I see. What makes you so sure?'

'Because when Alex looked at the signature he was so upset he spilt cereal and milk on the cloth and himself, and the letter fell to the floor. I picked it up and put it back on the table, but he seemed to think I hadn't noticed. I couldn't recall whose writing it was, and then I remembered. I'm sure I'm right, otherwise why would he be so secretive?'

The old wounds opened up for Caroline, but she had to credit Peter with his discretion; he never said 'Suzy' but always 'Suzy Meadows', as though to put a distance between them. But it wasn't Meadows any more. Having remarried, she was now Suzy Palmer.

'He'd only be secretive because he didn't want to cause you any pain.'

'I know that. What worries me is what the hell does she want after all this time? No birthday cards, no Christmas cards, nothing. Then a letter each. And not one to both of them but one *each*.'

'In their own good time they'll tell us.'

'They'll tell you and then ask if they should tell *me*.'

'They are both very sensitive about ... well, about me being their biological parent and you not. They're so careful not to hurt you, and it's right they should feel like that. I wouldn't have it any other way.'

'You see, Peter, when they're newborn and completely helpless, and needing love and tenderness and caring, one forgets about them growing up into separate people, actual individuals, and the problems that will bring.'

'You don't regret adopting them? Of course you don't. I'm being ridiculous even to ask.'

'I don't, not for a single second, but this ... They're *ours*, not hers. She has no rights. What's she doing writing to them? What does she want? Sending them letters, right out of the blue ...' Caroline put her finger to her lips then called out, 'Hello, Dottie. Good morning!'

Dottie Foskett stood in the doorway. Now she was not only

doing cleaning jobs but also working with Pat Jones, helping her manage the catering events at the Old Barn, Dottie had put on weight these last two years, having more money for food. But putting on weight had not dulled her hearing, and as she'd walked down the hall into the kitchen she'd caught Caroline's last two sentences.

'Good morning, Reverend. Good morning, Doctor. Wish I'd put a warmer coat on.'

'I think autumn's on the way.'

'Exactly, Doctor. The usual Monday things? Not nothing extra?'

'The usual. Oh! Except the bed linen in Alex's old room needs changing. We had a visitor over the weekend.'

'Righteo. No sooner said ...'

Dottie had strict rules about information at the Rectory. Not a word crossed her lips, much as she was dying to tell people what she knew, because if ever Caroline found out she'd been telling confidential tales that she could have known only through the Rectory, that would be the end of the best job she'd ever had in all her life.

She liked best the days when the Doctor was doctoring all day so she had the Reverend's lunch to make before she left. She loved knocking on his door and calling out 'Lunch, sir' and taking it in, finding a place for the tray on his desk, and him looking up so lovely at her to thank her and her heart melting at his sincerity. And dusting all his books, them she wouldn't understand if she spent a month trying, but she loved the idea of all that learning and sometimes wished she'd paid more attention at school. And that photo of him at Oxford in his cap and gown, looking so handsome and head and shoulders above most of the other students, and him such a lovely man in spite of all that hobnobbing with those toffs.

She began her morning's work by stripping the bed in Alex's old room.

Beth put her head round the door. 'Morning, Dottie. How are you?'

'I'm fine, thanks, Beth. And you? You don't look too chipper today. Not looking forward to going back to school?'

Beth hesitated and then blamed it on the weather. 'We're going into Culworth this morning, she added. 'Anything you need?'

'No thanks, dear.'

So she was right. The twins had got letters from someone, and it had upset Beth and the Doctor, so therefore the Reverend too.

The children didn't have an opportunity to discuss their letters until the two of them were in Culworth in the Abbey coffee shop.

Beth had chosen hot chocolate with foaming stuff on the top. Alex refused to call it cream because it wasn't, he said, not when it came out of a tin. But Beth persisted in choosing it despite his scorn. Alex had chosen espresso, which Beth declared tasted like lavatory cleaner, not that she'd ever tasted lavatory cleaner. Having sorted out their differences, both of them brought out their letters and compared them.

Apparently Suzy Meadows' second husband had died of cancer, and she now lived by herself with time to spare as all three of her girls – Pansy, Daisy and Rosie – lived away from home. This drove a dagger through Beth's heart. Was loneliness a good enough reason for wanting to see them both? Alex's letter told him how like herself Beth was. '*That time when I saw you both at the reunion for the village school's 150th Anniversary, I couldn't believe how like me she was.*'

Beth rapidly folded her own letter and pushed it into her bag.

Alex said, 'I haven't finished reading yours yet. Let me see it.'

'I shall throw it in the first bin I can find.'

'Beth! That's not fair. At least read it and let me read it, please.'

She spooned some of the cream into her mouth. 'All right, then.' She gave him back the letter.

Alex smoothed it out and read on. 'Now we're sixteen going on seventeen, she wants us to stay with her at half-term when she isn't teaching.'

'I read that bit at home. You can go. I'm not. Ever. Ever. Never.'

'She did give birth to us.'

'Yes, and then handed us to Dad as though we were a couple of parcels. We're not, we're real people, not fantasy figures, which is what this letter makes me feel like.'

'Yes, it does feel like that.' He stirred his espresso, now thick with sugar. With his head down he said, 'You and I have Mum and Dad to think about. She doesn't mention their feelings, does she?'

'Typical. Only hers, not even ours.' Beth drank steadily from her glass, and waited for Alex's answer. She knew he'd see both sides of the argument, just as their dad always did. Well, he could do as he liked. She was *not* going. She'd said so and she meant it. She did not want complications in her life which would screw up everything she held most dear. Beth had never forgotten that day when they met this Suzy at the school's 150th anniversary, how she'd been utterly, utterly unable to speak to her. Nor that smooth, softly-spoken man, whom she'd disliked immediately. Everyone had said he had been headmaster at the school for years, which she couldn't believe. Even if he was dead she still wasn't going, and no amount of persuasion could make her. Though she had to agree, she, Elizabeth Harris, looked very much like her, but that still wasn't a reason ...

'Thing is,' said Alex, 'do we tell Mum and Dad about these letters? Mum knows we got a letter each this morning but not who they were from.'

'And she won't ask. You know what she's like about people's privacy.'

'Exactly.' Alex downed the last of his espresso and wondered about ordering another.

'So we could not tell her and save her a lot of heartache. You're not having another of those gut-rot coffees, are you?'

'I'm just wondering about having an early lunch. What do you think?'

Beth answered him with another question. 'What would she mean by a few days? Is that all she can spare? Or is it a sop to our feelings? To make us feel more comfortable that it wouldn't be for long?'

'Both, I expect.'

'Oh, help, there's the Bishop's wife. She's spotted us. She's coming across.' Beth waved enthusiastically, remembering her good manners just in time.

The Bishop's wife dashed towards them with her familiar overwhelming gusto.

'How lovely it is to see you both! Last day of the holidays, eh? My word, Alex, you're going to be taller than your dad. As for you, Beth, you get prettier by the day.' She plumped down on the spare chair and, resting her elbows on the table, said in a low voice, 'A little bird's been telling me how wonderfully well you've both done in your GCSEs. Peter and Caroline must be so proud. What was it – ten As each? Brilliant! What are you hoping to do, Beth?'

Beth shrugged. 'Don't know, haven't decided.'

'Well, there's plenty of time. And you, Alex, do you know yet?'

'I've chosen sciences for my A-levels, so I might choose medicine or scientific research of some kind.'

'Good luck to you both. Your dad's coming in here for his lunch with the others after the meeting. Are you staying? I'm sure they wouldn't mind if you joined them.'

Both Alex and Beth promptly squashed that idea with an emphatic 'no'.

'Very well, then, I'll leave you to it. Enjoy, my dears, enjoy.' The Bishop's wife saw someone else she knew and leapt away, determined they weren't going to escape her.

'I'm going before they get here,' Beth said. 'I can't talk to Dad as if nothing's happened. Let's be off.'

They scuttled out of the coffee shop as fast as they could, ate a sandwich for lunch in a café by the river and then spent the afternoon in the cinema avoiding the issue. Two and a half hours not thinking about it resolved nothing, and with school tomorrow they wouldn't have time. So that was that for the moment. But they promised each other that neither of them would mention it without the other being present.

Monday was a busy day for Dottie. In the morning she was at the Rectory and in the afternoon she was a fully paid-up member of the village embroidery group from 2 p.m. until 4 p.m. Then she called in the Village Store for any bits and pieces, and caught the late-afternoon bus back down Shepherd's Hill – sometimes she walked down if there wasn't much shopping to carry – and to add to the usual there was a business dinner tonight at the Old Barn and she was booked to help out. No need to cook at home tonight.

Dottie had joined the embroidery group more for the company than any particular artistic bent, but after a few weeks she'd found herself enjoying it so much she had become a keen member. At the moment they were all working on a tapestry as part of the refurbishment of a block of offices in Culworth. It was to be placed in the main entrance hall behind glass and its finished length would be eight feet. It was the biggest project they'd tackled and sometimes they got a case of en masse nerves and had to put it away for fear they would make terrible mistakes which couldn't be rectified.

Dottie felt today had been a bad day, and she wasn't entirely sure she was in the right frame of mind this afternoon with this worry about the twins and their upsetting letters. But there was nothing she could do about it, and she certainly couldn't let on about the matter.

She was just on time. Their teacher, Evie Nicholls, had put everything out and Dottie's spirits rose when she saw the wonderful colours of the wools they were using and the part-finished tapestry on its frame. It was a picture designed by Evie, illustrating the kind of work the company was involved in, so there were rivers, boats, cranes and quaysides, men working, men idling, chimneys and smoke. Dottie regarded it as her contribution to the beauty of the world and the only one that would outlast her.

'Good afternoon, everybody! Still cold.'

'It is. Glad you've come, Dottie. I want you to work on that background piece in the duck-egg blue you started last week. It'll have to be done before we can do the next lot of fiddly bits.'

She grinned, did Dottie. 'I always knew I had a place in life: Dottie, the specialist in backgrounds. It'll look good on my epitaph.'

Evie looked crestfallen. 'Oh, I'm sorry. I didn't ...'

But Dottie was laughing and so Evie was relieved.

There were five of them working this particular afternoon: Evie, Dottie, Sheila Bissett, Bel Tutt and Barbara, one of the weekenders. They all worked together very well. The person most likely to cause friction was Sheila Bissett. She'd never been the same since her Louise and Gilbert had lost that premature baby. She'd always longed to be slender, had Sheila, and now she'd no worries for she was as slim as a wand and could wear anything she chose and look good in it, but it hadn't improved her attitude.

'They've moved in,' she said.

'Who?'

'The new people in Glebe House, of course.'

There was a disappointed chorus of, 'No! I never saw the van.' Missing someone moving in? How had that happened?

'The van didn't get here until nearly midnight last night, due to a breakdown, and believe it or believe it not, they unloaded there and then in the dark. Needed the van for another job, apparently, and had to speed off about three this morning.'

Dottie looked up from threading the duck-egg blue on to her very best tapestry needle. 'Seeing as how you live in Little Derehams, how come you know all this and we don't?'

Sheila grinned. She'd always loved being first with the news. 'Because I ran out of milk and came to the Store by half past seven this morning to get some for Ron's breakfast, and *she* was in there buying their breakfast – bacon, eggs, the whole works. So at last, after all the speculation about who had and who hadn't bought Glebe House, now we know.'

The words not spoken were: 'What's she like?' But they didn't need to ask because Sheila was bursting to tell them.

'She's big and blowsy – all money and no taste. Her husband is retired, something big in metal he was, apparently, and has so much money he doesn't know where to spend it next, or so she says.'

'What's she called?' asked Bel, who often worked in the Store and was always mindful that she must remember names because Jimbo liked it that way.

Sheila drew in a big breath. 'She *says* her name is Mercedes and his is—'

'Toyota? Nissan? Skoda?'

There was an outbreak of giggling at this, and Dottie laughed the loudest at her own wit.

Sheila couldn't reply for laughing. When she did speak she said, 'Ford. Ford Barclay.'

Then they really did have to stop sewing, and their peals of laughter could be heard by Zack the verger who was grass-cutting behind the hall.

'Now, just stop it, Sheila, and tell us the truth,' Dottie said.

'It *is* the truth,' Sheila protested. 'He was born in the States and they use the name Ford a lot. It's quite common apparently.'

'So's he by the sound of it. And her!'

This brought more peals of laughter, then Evie suggested she made a pot of tea to give them all a break. They never sewed and drank tea at the same time for fear of a spill, so they all moved their chairs over to a small table they put out for the very purpose of drinking tea.

Evie came back with the tea-tray and as she put it down she said, 'We shouldn't be so cruel, you know. They may be very nice people.'

'You're right as usual, Evie, but even you must admit ...' That set them off again. It was a while since such juicy gossip had come their way and they intended to make the most of it.

'He sings, she says—'

'In the bath?'

'No! Sings, on the stage, and he fancies joining the church choir, she says.'

Evie said she thought that would be lovely, as Gilbert was short of adult male singers. 'I wonder if he's tenor or baritone?'

'She didn't say.'

Barbara the weekender spoke up. 'I bet Ron thought you took a long time getting the milk.'

'He did. He was sure I must have broken down.'

'You did – laughing!'

'You should see her rings! Diamonds as big as peas.'

'Ah!' said Barbara. 'But are they real?'

'They looked it.'

'But then the lights in the Store are very bright; that would make them sparkle.'

'There was one that looked just like Princess Diana's

engagement ring – you know, that giant sapphire with the diamonds all around it.'

Thinking about the new owners of Glebe House reminded Bel of Liz, who had moved out. 'Poor Liz, going all that way to live with her mother, and leaving such a beautiful house, and Neville killing himself like he did. Who'd have thought it? Certainly not me. I wonder how she's going to manage.'

Sheila said, 'I think Neville doing what he did was the last straw for her. I expect she feels so guilty, but then those who are left behind after a suicide always do feel guilty, don't they? Could I have done more? Why didn't I realise? Everlasting questions.'

Bel changed the subject. 'By the way, Michael Palmer died. You know, the old headmaster at the school. Jimbo had a letter from Suzy Meadows-that-was only this morning. Very sudden apparently.'

Sheila said how sorry she was. 'I liked him. A bit old-fashioned but an excellent disciplinarian, wasn't he? Such a surprise when he married that Suzy. I always thought they were a funny match.'

'She'll be lonely, I expect. All her girls will have left home and now him gone, too.'

Dottie kept very quiet but then couldn't avoid answering Sheila's question: 'Dottie, you remember him, don't you? Him and Suzy.'

'Only vaguely. Didn't have much to do with them.'

'Her first husband committed suicide. Funny man. He was all shut in and avoided your eyes. You must remember them.'

'Vaguely, like I said. Anyway, back to work or else it'll be a wasted afternoon.'

Had she got her answer to the riddle of the twin's letters? She wondered. Maybe, maybe not.

Evie knocked on the window to tell Zack that his cup of tea was waiting for him, and they heard him switch off his ancient mower.

Zack, known for being a man of few words, nodded to them all, poured out his cup of tea and gratefully sank on to a chair. He enjoyed watching them embroidering. It seemed so right in an ancient church hall, doing tapestry. It fitted somehow. Peace descended, and that was what Zack liked – peace. No women nattering on.

Then he said, quite suddenly, 'They've bought a plot.'

'Who? A plot of what?' Evie queried.

'Them what've bought Glebe House came round to see me before they moved in to buy a grave. One of the last. They intend staying here for ever, it seems. Going to make some big changes round here, I understand.'

'Oh! So they might think. New brooms indeed! Well, we'll show 'em if we don't like their ideas. Big changes indeed! My eye!' Sheila huffed and puffed her annoyance.

'Been here less than a week and he says he's buying me a new mower for the churchyard. Says it's an antique I'm using. He reckons it was bought before the war. Amazed, he is, that I'm still using it.'

'So are we, Zack. I don't know how you keep it going. It's too much to expect,' Sheila said sympathetically.

'I reckon he doesn't know how expensive they are nowadays, though. I don't suppose such good luck will come my way. He'll never buy it.'

None of them noticed Zack finish his tea and carry the tray into the kitchen for them. They were too busy speculating about what Ford and Mercedes might do with their money. Afterwards, when they'd concentrated on the tapestry for over an hour, Dottie suddenly broke their silence. 'The twins did well with their GCSEs. Never told you with it being holidays right through August. Ten each they got.'

'Ah!' said Barbara. 'What grades, though? Cs Ds? What?'

'All As, both of 'em. They're that bright.' She couldn't help but shake her head in genuine amazement.

Somewhat deflated by this statement, Barbara said, being thoroughly unpleasant as she often was, 'Ah, well. Just goes to show what happens when you can afford to pay for their education, and him only a vicar.'

'He's called a *rector* in these parts. It's their money, so surely they can spend it how they like?' Dottie began to get annoyed.

'It's not fair.'

'Life isn't fair, is it? You've got two houses – what's fair about that when some people have none?'

This comment shut Barbara up, which was just what Dottie intended. Then she made a mistake in her stitching and swore. Evie decided that today was not the day for peaceful stitching and they'd better stop before things got too nasty. You had to be at peace to stitch effectively, she always thought. 'It's only half past three but I think we should stop. We're not in the mood. I'll do some myself during the week to catch up. See you next Monday.'

Dottie stayed behind to help clear up. 'Sorry, Evie, about getting annoyed, but they're such lovely children. Well, I call them children but they're not, are they? More young adults. I only wish they were mine. I'd be so proud.'

'So would I. And they are – lovely, I mean. So well-mannered.'

'Indeed. They treat me like gold, they do, not like a skivvy, which I am, and I can't stand by and see 'em criticised. Sorry.'

'You're not a skivvy, nothing like. Don't worry, Dottie. Can you bring the case with the wools and I'll—'

'Oh no you won't. I'm carrying the frame – it's too heavy for you, slip of a thing that you are. I expect Tom carries it across usually, does he?'

'Well, yes, he does, but he's gone to the wholesalers this afternoon, so I can't ask him.'

'It's dry today, so we'll cross the Green with it. Ready?'

It was far heavier than she'd thought and Dottie was glad to reach Orchid Cottage.

Tatty, Evie's little dog, launched himself out of the door the moment it was opened and greeted them ecstatically.

Evie tried to get past him and couldn't. 'Move, Tatty, move! You silly dog! We can't get in.'

'He's so well since his operation, isn't he? Hardly any limp at all.'

'Exactly.'

'There we are. Is it all right to leave it here? Bye then, Evie. Thanks for everything.'

Dottie left for home, deciding to leave her shopping until tomorrow, and wondering if the twins had worked out what to do about the news in their letters. It had nagged at her all afternoon, and it was thinking about them that had made her so bad-tempered with that Barbara. If she could solve the twins' problem for them she would, because she wouldn't have them hurt, not for the world.

Had she known that they hadn't solved it, or let on about it to either Peter or Caroline, and were facing their first day in the sixth form with it still casting a shadow over them, she would have been even sadder than she already was.

Chapter 2

The following day Peter was in his study making a set of notes about the meeting he'd attended the day before. If he didn't, he'd have no proof of what had been agreed, because the minutes always arrived weeks afterwards and were almost useless by then.

The doorbell rang and he heard Dottie answering it. When his study door opened, Dottie said, 'It's Mr Barclay, Reverend, just moved in to Glebe House. He says is it convenient?'

'It is. Show him in.' He got to his feet, hand outstretched in greeting.

Mr Barclay was almost as tall as himself but twice as wide. His hair was snow-white and stood in a bush around his head as though he'd just been plugged into the mains. There was a slightly swarthy look about his skin, and his eyes were so dark they were almost black.

'Pleased to meet you, Mr Barclay. Do sit down.'

Ford Barclay dropped down with a sudden almighty thud on to the sofa.

'Thank you, Reverend. Most kind, when you're so busy.' He nodded in the direction of Peter's desk, which was covered with piles of papers.

'Everyone calls me Peter, except Dottie who showed you in. I've suggested several times she calls me Peter, too, but she won't have it.'

'Peter it is, then. I've called because we moved in two days ago and this is my first chance. My name's Ford Barclay, and the wife is Mercedes. We're very much looking forward to settling in and taking our place in village life. First, that old mower your ... verger, or whatever you call him, uses. I'm buying him a new one, heard him using it yesterday morning and went to have a word. I couldn't believe what a struggle it was to cut the grass, and it wasn't that long. So, first things first, I'm buying him another one. Bang up to date. Thought I'd let you know. He's too old to be struggling with that old piece of equipment and while Ford Barclay is still breathing he's not pushing it another day. My old lady's busy sorting the house today, so I'm taking Zack to get the mower this very minute. I might even take a look at diggers, too. The clay soil must be the very devil when there's graves to dig. Just a small one, but it may do the trick.'

'I'm overwhelmed. It's more than kind of you, Ford, it's very generous. We've been meaning to buy a new mower but there's always something more urgent to spend the money on. Our previous verger was deeply attached to it, you see, because his father used it for years when *he* was the verger and ... well, he always said it was the best for getting between the gravestones. So we've never bothered about it.'

'Well, to save any friction, don't want to ruffle feathers, we'll keep the old mower for that very job, between the gravestones, and buy the up-to-date one for the big spaces. We're having a grave here for the two of us – when we've done the paperwork, that is.'

'You intend staying, then? For good?'

'Oh, yes. We are. I've taken a real fancy to this place, and we intend putting down roots now I've retired and sold my business.'

'What was it?'

'Metal. Scrap metal. Knew it was the right moment to sell. Copper and lead are fetching small fortunes nowadays. No good selling when the bottom's dropped out of the market, is it?'

'Of course not. So you're a man of leisure, then?'

'Apart from my hobby, horse-racing. Love it. I shall be able to indulge myself any day I like.' Ford smiled as he got to his feet.

'You don't look old enough to be retired!'

'I'm not. I've made my pile and now I'm going to enjoy spending it. Good morning, Peter. Hope you didn't mind me popping in?'

'Not at all.' Peter checked his watch. 'Dottie will be coming in with my coffee shortly. Would you like to have one with me?'

'Thanks, but another day. I want to get off to buy the mower. Very nice to have met you.'

'It's been a pleasure. Give me a knock when the mower arrives; I'd like to see it. I'm in my study all day today unless there's an emergency.'

'In case someone decides it's time to die, you mean, and wants to confess all, eh!'

Peter had to smile. 'Well, I suppose so.'

'Just in case, as you might say, do you do confessions?'

'We're not high church, so we don't advertise confession as such, but I'm always available. And if you have a problem I'm good at listening, and it's always entirely confidential.'

'Right. I'll remember that.'

The persistent sound of the new mower being put through its paces three hours later couldn't be ignored. Finally Peter had to go out to see it.

A small crowd had gathered to watch the inauguration of this fantastic piece of twenty-first-century equipment, and in the front stood Willie Biggs, once verger of the parish until digging graves became too much for him and brought about his retirement.

He gave Peter a nod, but said nothing. Peter knew from

experience that shortly Willie would burst out with a criticism of modern technology.

Ford was marching rapidly up and down the open green parts of the graveyard, energetically cutting the grass. All the cuttings were caught in the superior bag attached to the mower.

'Huh! Nobody bought one like this for me! Oh, no. Daft old Willie Biggs had to manage as best he could, and had all the cuttings to collect up after.'

Sylvia Biggs nudged his elbow. 'Shut up, Willie. You sound just like a grumpy old man. You used to say it made the graveyard look like a superior bowling green it was that good. You were proud of it; you know you were. You should ask for a turn. Where's it come from anyway?'

Peter said quietly, 'Ford's bought it, and I understand a small digger is on order.'

Sylvia smothered a giggle. 'Whoops! One in the eye for old Fitch, then; he's supposed to be the benefactor round here. We'll wait for the balloon to go up.'

Willie laughed. 'But what about that little old mower? It needs overhauling, it does. Thrown it away, 'ave we? Like me, dispensed with through old age.'

'Definitely not, Willie. We're keeping it for cutting between the graves. In any case it was you who wanted to retire, remember?'

'Yes, sir, you're right. Sorry.'

'I'm fancying a turn. How about you?'

'Wouldn't mind.' The temptation was too great. Willie couldn't resist, even though he would have preferred to have his tongue ripped out rather than demonstrate any kind of approval.

Peter asked Ford and Zack if he could have a turn. Ford lowered the throttle and stepped aside. 'Here we are, sir.' Peter took charge and found himself racing along behind a mower he simply did not feel himself to be in charge of. There was a round of applause when he found how to slow it down and come to a full stop. 'My word, Ford, but that's powerful. Willie, come and have a go.'

Willie, more cautious than Peter, went along at a sedate pace, loving its super, up-to-date efficiency. But all he said when he stopped was, 'It's not bad.'

'Not bad?' Ford was very disappointed; it was as though his wonderful gesture was being thrown back in his face.

'Yes, like I said, not bad.'

Ford left Zack to carry on mowing and went to speak to Peter. 'All right, eh?'

'My word it is. I can't thank you enough for your generosity. We should have had it years ago. By the way, "not bad" from Willie is high praise indeed. He's very sparing with his praise, is Willie.'

Ford dug in his jacket pocket. 'Ah! Right. Thanks. Here's the receipt and the guarantee, and I've written on the back to say the mower's the property of St Thomas à Becket Church, so there can be no misunderstanding.'

'I very much appreciate that. Thank you from us all.' Peter shook hands with Ford to demonstrate openly his approval of him. He knew instinctively that Ford, with his lack of knowledge about the delicate niceties of village life, would not easily be accepted in Turnham Malpas, and it concerned him. 'Must get back to work. Thanks again. Our treasurer will be delighted.'

'Who's that?'

'Hugh Neal. He and his brother have offices in Culworth. They're the church auditors.'

'Neal? We bought the house from a Liz Neal.'

'Hugh is one of her sons; he's in charge of the family firm since his father died.'

'I'm looking for an accountant in the area. I might try them.'

'You could do worse. Good afternoon, and thanks again.'

Peter left Ford propped against a grave with a look of extreme satisfaction on his face, watching Zack enjoying his new toy, and Peter wished his self-satisfaction was not quite so evident. That kind of thing got the village annoyed. Yes, they'd accept Ford's generosity, as they'd accepted Craddock Fitch's all these years, but Craddock had learned to keep his self-satisfaction under wraps when he was in public. It was a lesson Ford had better learn, and quickly.

The whole matter was aired in the pub that night, and opinions varied. There was extreme annoyance at the length of time they'd had to put up with the racket the mower made, simply because Zack was enjoying himself so much he was mowing parts of the churchyard that hadn't seen a mower of any kind ever since he became verger. The other side of the argument was if Ford Barclay thought they were all going to fall over themselves with gratitude at his generosity he'd another think coming. If he wanted to throw money about, that was his choice, but he needn't think he'd wheedle his way into their affections by looking so *pleased* with his own generosity.

Willie, always up front with his opinions, said sharply, 'What is it they say in the Bible: "Let not thy left hand know what thy right hand doeth"? Well, he showed us with both his left and his right how wonderful he was for buying that massive machine. Stood there full of himself admiring the blasted thing, he did.' Willie took a long drink from his home-brew and looked about him for approval. Getting no response, he added, 'What they've never thought about is that it's too big to go in the shed!' Willie positively cackled at Ford Barclay's predicament, and all the people sitting at the same table roared with laughter.

Wiping her eyes, Dottie said, 'One thing leads to another ... and another by the looks of it! But it must be heaven-sent to Zack.'

'All right for you, living down Shepherd's Hill. We've got to put up with it, and does it make a racket!'

Vera Wright took a sip of her gin and tonic before saying, 'But it can't take an age to cut the grass. After all, the churchyard isn't *that* big.'

Sylvia said, 'I happened to look at the clock when the racket started and he didn't stop using it for one hour and twenty-three minutes. I know 'cos I timed it.'

'One hour and twenty-three minutes? Did he cut everybody else's grass, too?'

'No,' said Willie, 'but he did cut all the difficult bits that have been growing longer and longer ever since he took over from me. This damn thing does the lot. And if Ford NatWest thinks he's going to ... that was my ankle you kicked, Dottie ... what's up?'

To Willie's horror Dottie was saying, 'Good evening, Mr Barclay. Coming to join us?'

'Uncommonly kind of you, Dottie. I'll pull up another table and join it on to yours, because Mercedes is with me. That'll make it more friendly, won't it?'

Dottie blushed when she found out she was on first-name terms with this huge man who had all the makings of being public enemy number one.

By coincidence, all those at the table were at the point with their drinks when someone was going to have to get the second round in. In the hustle of moving a table and joining it on, and finding two extra chairs, no one offered.

So it fell to Ford to offer. Dottie introduced everyone and as they shook hands they said, 'And mine's a home-brew', or whatever they fancied. As Ford was about to head off to the bar, Mercedes put in an appearance.

It would have been untrue to say she was a fine figure of a woman, because she wasn't. She was scarcely less obese than Ford, and short with it. Sylvia guessed she'd be just over five feet tall, which cruelly emphasised her girth. Dottie judged her make-up excessive, Vera thought her clothes too loud to be permitted, and Vera's Don decided she was common. But she had the sweetest smile, which compensated a little for all her drawbacks. She brought up the subject of the mower while Ford was buying the drinks.

'Ford is so pleased to be able to do a good turn for poor old Zack. He's delighted with the mower, he really is. Always looking for a chance to do good deeds, is my Ford.'

Willie, determined to put the boot in, said, 'Has he realised it won't go in the churchyard shed?'

Mercedes turned her large, slightly prominent hazel eyes on Willie and gave him a huge wink. 'Of course, Willie. You're Willie, aren't you? There's no flies on my Ford. New shed arriving Thursday.' She smiled so sweetly at him that Willie almost knocked over his glass. Sylvia neatly retrieved it for him.

'Oh! Right, well, that's good. I'm pleased he's realised.' And strangely enough, he *was* pleased, because there was something about those hazel eyes that had nothing whatsoever to do with her lavish make-up and her outrageous gaudy clothes. It was almost as though there was a sweet, pleasing, much younger woman behind the lurid façade.

Ford came back with the drinks and handed them out without a falter, as though he'd known them all for years. The time sped by because they were thoroughly enjoying themselves, mostly listening to Ford's tales of his exploits at racecourses all over the country. Don and Willie between them got the next round in, Dottie and Mercedes the next, then Ford happened to mention that he and the wife were going to the races on Saturday. Would any of them like to go?

Within minutes, everyone had agreed.

Everyone ready for the off outside Glebe House at eleven-thirty, right?'

They all nodded.

'Will we be in time for the start?'

'Of course, Sylvia. I'll see to that. You'll love it there. Very friendly and the food – mmwah.' Ford bunched his fingers, put them to his lips and kissed them.

Rather tentatively, Sylvia said, thinking of the expense, 'Would sandwiches be out of place?'

Mercedes said, surprised, 'Sandwiches? When Ford's footing the bill? I think not. You mustn't think of sandwiches. Only the best for our friends, believe me. All you'll need is money for betting and nothing else. My Ford is a generous host.' She squeezed Willie's hand where it lay on the table and gave him another of her smiles.

Sylvia positively steamed at the foolish look on Willie's flushed face. Because of it she almost said they weren't going, but decided that she wouldn't miss the chance of a day at the races because Willie was acting like a fool, so she swiftly changed the expression on her face to one of complete compliance. After all, maybe life in Turnham Malpas had suddenly taken a turn for the better, and why shouldn't she and Willie have a slice of it? The only drawback was just how much this day at the races would cost. After all, there'd be rounds of drinks to get in and they mustn't appear skinflints, her and Willie.

As Dottie told Peter on the Monday morning, they had no worries about money because Ford had taken care of absolutely everything. 'So generous he was, Reverend, you've no idea. Wonderful restaurant there, and we'd a big round table where we could see the races while we were eating, through the big glass windows, you know. The food – well, I can't describe it. I hardly ate a thing yesterday I'd eaten so much on the day. It was so smart, all of it. I was glad I'd got my best suit on, otherwise I'd have felt right out of it. Mind you, neither Sylvia nor Vera nor me could compete with Mercedes. She was utterly splendid, in a bright coral-red outfit with a big white hat, gloves and handbag, and four-inch high-heeled strappy sandals.'

'I'm sure you compared very favourably, Dottie.'

'You weren't there, sir. I know who looked stunning – it was Merc, as he calls her. Ford knows so many people, all looking good and well off. He's very popular. They don't half bet, the pair of them, though. Runs through their fingers like water, but they mostly win so that makes all the difference. I took Ford's advice and won forty-two pounds but Don won a hundred and seventy-five pounds on another race. That chuffed he was! Willie lost ten pounds but Mercedes kissed him and gave him a hug to compensate, and I must say he didn't seem to mind he'd lost, though Sylvia looked annoyed. Must get on. Finished your lunch? I'll be off when I've cleared up. Embroidery class, you see. See yer tomorrow!'

Peter sat for a moment, contemplating Dottie's story about the races. It all made him feel very wary of what was going on at Glebe House with the Barclays. It appeared too good to be true. They seemed to him to be trying far too hard to ingratiate themselves, and he wondered why. It would have been so much better in the long run to move in and take things more slowly. A state-of-the-art mower and a shed, which was twice the size of the original, with a workman coming to lay the base before it arrived and more workmen to put it up, within a week of moving in? He chided himself for being so wary.

But he was, and he was also very wary of Suzy Meadows-that-was sending letters to his children. His all-consuming aim every day of his life was to protect not only them but Caroline, too, knowing as he did that her inability to give him children herself had been the major factor in her decision to adopt his and Suzy's children. The agonizing pain the whole episode had caused him was still as vivid as the day he'd learned that Suzy was pregnant by him, and it the one and only act of unfaithfulness in the whole of his marriage.

Peter picked up the photograph on his desk and studied it. It was a picture of Caroline with the very newborn twins, one in each arm, smiling with such triumphant happiness at the camera that tears came to his eyes each time he looked at it. Today, he wept.

Dottie called out, 'Bye, Reverend, I'm off. See you tomorrow.'

Peter couldn't reply, but Dottie thought he was probably on the phone, so off she went.

The tears made him come to the conclusion that for everyone's sake he would ask the twins about the letters at the first opportunity.

His moment came on Saturday. Caroline was doing an extra surgery and Peter had promised to go to the council tip in Culworth with a load of stuff they'd been clearing out and the recycling things, too. So he encouraged Alex and Beth to come with him and then into Culworth proper for coffee and shopping if they wished.

Beth in particular enjoyed the tip because she loved inspecting the goods laid out for re-sale at one edge of the site. As she always did after she'd been poking about at the tip, she insisted on giving her hands a good wash in the Abbey coffee shop toilets before she sat down at a table.

She'd given her order to Peter before she disappeared, so when she returned her hot chocolate was waiting for her. 'Dad, you're not having that gut-rot stuff Alex drinks, are you?'

'Thought I'd try it for a change, but I think maybe you've given it the right name.'

Alex offered Peter the sugar. 'Might help it down.'

They sat companionably together, drinking and observing people. Lots of people saw Peter and raised a hand or spoke to him. Beth approved of her dad being well liked. He deserved it, she thought. 'Good thing it's Saturday, then the Bishop's wife won't be here.'

Somewhat astounded by Beth's statement, as he'd always found the Bishop's wife very pleasant and helpful, Peter asked, 'What's wrong with her, Beth? She's extremely kind.'

'At the back of her mind there's always the thought that we, Alex and I, need special attention because of our circumstances. She kind of glosses over it without actually mentioning it, but her concern is always there.'

Peter, taken aback by her frankness, said, 'I didn't realise that. She means well.'

'Exactly, Dad, but she needn't because Alex and I are perfectly all right.'

To Peter this appeared to be a heaven-sent opportunity to clear the air. 'Those letters you got the other day, from Suzy Meadows. Are you perfectly all right about *them*?'

Now it was the twins' turn to be surprised. Alex spoke first. 'We didn't know you knew.'

'Mum told me. She didn't *know*, just suspected. On the same day, you see, Jimbo had a letter from her ... Suzy ... telling him her husband had died.'

'She did? Whatever for? Why Jimbo?'

'Why Jimbo? Because he was very supportive of her when her first husband died.'

'Killed himself, you mean.' Beth came out with that remark very abruptly, and there was bitterness in her voice. 'She must be a crazy, mixed-up person, in my opinion.'

'Beth!' Peter was at a loss for words.

Alex said, 'We didn't say anything because we didn't want mum to be hurt. We've not known what to do.'

'Why has she written to you?'

Beth unzipped her bag, glanced at Alex for his approval and gave Suzy's letter to Peter to read.

'Are you sure about this? Because I don't know if I sh—'

'Read it, Dad, and stop being tactful. All this tip-toeing about is getting me down.' This from Beth, who'd reached the end of the road with all the secrecy.

Peter unfolded the two-page letter and began to read.

Dearest Beth,

I know this is a surprise to you because I have never written to you before, but I know you know the circumstances of our relationship and felt you should be aware that my husband Michael died a month ago. It has nothing to do with you but is everything to me, and I thought you should know.

The man I truly love is your father, and I have never stopped loving him since the day I first met him. But with three little girls to feed and clothe, and their father dead, I simply could not manage to work and support two new babies in addition to them, so the answer was to give you to your own father, knowing you were being given the best possible chance in life. As for me, I now have none of my girls at home and no husband, either, which is a desperate state to be in.

Now you are sixteen – see, I know your exact age, I haven't forgotten – and starting in the sixth form and having minds of your own, I've no doubt, I wondered if you might like to get to know me better. I should love more than anything in the whole world to get to know the two of you.

I suggest you come to stay for a few days at half-term. It would be just the three of us. What an exciting time we would have, learning all about each other and sharing our lives! Just think of it!

My address and email address are at the top of this letter. Believe me, it would be the most wonderful thing in my life for you to come to stay. I'm looking forward to hearing from you.

All my love,

your mother

Beth broke the silence. 'All about her, isn't it? That's what strikes me. All about her. No mention of whether or not my mum will find it wonderful. Or my dad. Oh, no! Well, as far as

I'm concerned, I am not going. Full stop. I can't speak for Alex. We're not joined at the hip, so he can decide for himself.' Beth snatched the letter from Peter and tore it into shreds. 'There, that's that.' She concentrated on spooning the cream from the top of her hot chocolate into her mouth and refused to look at her dad.

Peter didn't know what to say. This letter was so unexpected! He'd have to tread carefully. Maybe Alex would want to go.

To Alex, the bit about her loving his dad had been the biggest shock. Two husbands and still loved *him*? Was it reciprocated? he wondered suddenly. No, of course not. Mum and Dad were crazy about each other. He knew every day of his life how much in love they were. Didn't he? A terrible doubt invaded Alex's being.

'Well, Alex, how do you feel about it? Are you going to see her?'

Alex looked Peter full in the face, an unasked question in his eyes, but Peter couldn't read what the question was. 'I shall write a polite letter on behalf of the two of us and say we're not going. She gave us to you and that's where it ends. Her chance has gone.' Alex hadn't brought his own letter with him, so he couldn't make Beth's dramatic gesture. 'When I get home I shall write one letter and tear mine up the minute I've done it.'

'I see. Shall I tell your mum, then?'

'No, Dad. We will.'

Beth protested. 'I'd rather she didn't know.'

Alex said, 'It was you who said the secrecy had to end, so let's do that. Mum must know and then we can all lay a ghost to rest.' But he promised himself that one day when he found the right words, he would ask his father about Suzy and whether he had ever felt love for her, and if he still did.

Chapter 3

'Do you think we'd better tell them at the Rectory that Suzy's Michael is dead? They perhaps ought to know in the circumstances?' Jimbo's voice was muffled as he bent down behind the TV, wondering why on earth they suddenly had no picture at all.

'Honestly,' said Harriet, 'I haven't the faintest idea what to do for the best, Jimbo. I suppose eventually it'll get round to them on the village grapevine.'

'But will it? Pass me the torch. After all, we're every one of us acutely aware that we're talking dynamite, aren't we? Thanks.'

Unaware that Fran had come in, Harriet replied, 'The next time Caroline comes in the Store I shall corner her and tell her. She should know, and the twins should, too. How's that for a promise? There's still no picture.'

'Blast.'

Fran suggested, 'It's Dottie. She'll have caught a cable again when she was vacuuming. Here, let me see.'

Jimbo emerged, tousled and hot, reluctantly admitting to himself that she would most likely solve the problem in no time at all.

Fran tinkered about with the wires at the back and then said, 'There we are. What's the picture like, Mum?'

'Excellent. What it is to have a qualified TV engineer in the house!'

Jimbo grunted. 'Hmm! Luck, that's what, pure luck.'

'Dad! It was me put it right the last time you couldn't get a picture.'

Jimbo feigned memory loss. 'Maybe it was. I don't remember.'

'I don't know why you bother asking him, Mum. Just send for me, OK? By the way, I think they should know.'

'Who should know what?'

'The twins should know that Mr Palmer has died. After all, it will affect their mother.'

'Why should Michael Palmer dying affect Caroline?'

'Well, the twins, you know, *the twins*.'

Harriet, who was more astute than Jimbo at understanding teenagers' shorthand, said, 'What do you know about the twins that I didn't know you knew?'

'Well, that ... well, they're the Rector's and Suzy what's-its, and Caroline's not their biological mother.'

Jimbo moaned, 'Oh my God. I didn't know you knew. You've never said.'

Harriet demanded to know who had told her.

'Oh, for goodness sake! I've known for years.'

Jimbo, still sitting on the floor, looked up at her and said, 'It isn't discussed openly amongst your crowd is it?'

'No, but we know.'

'You never say anything, do you, to Beth? Nor Alex?'

'Give us credit for some sense, please. I wouldn't dream of it.'

Harriet hugged her. 'Of course you wouldn't. It's not our secret, you see.'

'No. But it must have been big news at the time. My God! In a village like this, the gossip must have been flying round the tinned soup shelves like fury. Just wish I'd been old enough to know. People like Sheila Bissett must have had a field day.'

Jimbo and Harriet exchanged glances, both of them reflecting on the accuracy of Fran's comments.

Harriet, who fully understood Caroline's motives in being willing to adopt the twins, found it harder to forgive Peter. She decided to change the subject.

'Right, well, I'm going for a box of chocolates that have been in the cupboard a whole week and never been touched. Don't you think I've been good? They're Belgian chocolates from the smart shop in Culworth, present from a grateful client.'

These diversionary tactics on Harriet's part cut no ice with Fran. At fifteen there wasn't much that got past her because she loved gossip as much as her dad did. In fact, she was better than him at picking up the latest news now she worked in the Store on Saturdays. She had her wilder moments when she planned how she would expand the business by starting another Store in another village. How she'd love to be in charge of it all by herself.

The three of them sat very comfortably, eating the chocolates and watching TV for at least an hour, when the doorbell rang. Jimbo got up to answer it.

Standing on the doorstep were Ford and Mercedes Barclay, dressed to kill.

'Good evening. We're Ford and Mercedes from Glebe House, just moved in. It's not a social call. It's business. May we come in? We know it's late but we've been out all day and made a decision, and we want to sound you out about it.'

'Certainly. I'm Jimbo Charter-Pl—'

'Yes, we know, that's why we're here.' This was Mercedes speaking. 'Can we come in?'

'Oh! Sorry, I beg your pardon. Yes, please do. Shall we sit in my study or—'

But Ford was already in the sitting room greeting Harriet. 'My dear Mrs Charter-Plackett. I understand you are a cordon bleu chef. I'm honoured, yes, *honoured*, to meet you.'

'Ah! Right. You must be—'

'Ford Barclay. And this is—'

'This is Frances. We call her Fran.'

'What a very pretty young lady. Do you work in the business?'

'I'm the Saturday girl, that's all. I'm still at school, you see.'

'Ah! Young ladies grow up so quickly now. This is the wife, Mercedes.'

They all shook hands, then Jimbo offered them a drink.

'Thank you. A gin and it for both of us.'

Harriet suggested they sat down. By the time the drinks had been served Mercedes was quizzing Fran about school. 'I loved school. Do you love school?'

'Yes, I do.'

'What's your favourite subject?'

'Well, I'm best at French.'

'Oh! Hear that, Ford? Fran is best at French. She could come in useful when we go to our gite in the summer. Have you been to France?'

'Yes, several—' But she got no further because Ford interrupted her, so anxious was he to get on with the business he had in mind.

'Now see here, Jimbo. I've heard on the village grapevine that you do catering.'

Jimbo almost choked at being reduced to 'catering'. It seemed rather to lower his treasured gourmet standards. He nodded.

'I understand you own the Old Barn on the estate belonging to that old man ...' he snapped his fingers while he tried to remember the name, 'Craddock Fitch, and you have parties there – balls, smart lunches, weddings. That right?'

'It most certainly is, yes. You name it, we organise it. I have the highest standards ...' Jimbo intended expanding on the idea but was stopped by Ford.

'Well, I have this idea, you see. Now I'm not working I've got time to spare thinking up original ideas and I've come up with one.'

'Right!'

'It's soon to be our twentieth wedding anniversary and Mercedes wants us to have an Elizabethan banquet. Different, you see, from the usual wedding anniversary party. How do you feel about it? Of course, we'd have to see the Old Barn, decide if it's suitable for what we have in mind.'

Jimbo, ready for anything, cut in. 'It was a Tudor barn originally; we've kept all mod cons as discreet as possible. Last year we had a whole cow roasting on a spit. It gave the guests a real thrill. They had roast beef for the meal but not all of it from the cow roasting outside, obviously. Logistically that wouldn't have been possible. We served—'

Mercedes burst in. 'Could we have serving wenches with all their bosoms showing? I'm very keen on that – makes it realistic, you see.'

By this time Harriet was almost in hysterics. Jimbo's mind was too busy encompassing the whole idea to take in what Mercedes had said, but Fran had to leave the room before she made an exhibition of herself.

The plans were discussed for a whole hour and a half with Jimbo busy making notes, and Mercedes coming up with even more surprising ideas. Eventually Jimbo grew too tired to care. There was so much to take in. 'Look, before we go any further, come tomorrow at 9 a.m. to see the barn and judge for yourself if it's OK. We have a business lunch on so we must be there on time. The staff need to lay tables etcetera, because my clients have drinks at eleven-thirty and lunch at twelve. So, 9 a.m. sharp, right? In the meantime I'll have a think. We're well booked up, so any decisions have to be made pronto. Lovely to meet you.' He stood up to shake hands, and finally the pair of them made their way to the door. Mercedes was still coming up with ideas as they were leaving.

Afterwards Harriet fell back in her chair exhausted. 'God! What a pair! I need a drink after all that. Are you willing to fall in with their plans?'

'Oh, yes! It's the ideal venue. We'll have Ford as the Earl of Leicester and Mercedes as Queen Elizabeth. They'll love it. Could have some "strolling players" coming in to entertain them, couldn't we? Mead by the gallon, though it's very potent. We'd have to ration it as she suggests serving wenches. The whole idea is brilliant. Afterwards we could do them for the general public. Eh, what?'

'You're over-reaching yourself. Let's do this first and see if it's successful.'

'*See* if it's successful? What does that mean? Of course it will be successful. How can it be anything else?'

Harriet leant across and kissed him. 'You're right. I'm going to bed with my gin. Goodnight, darling.'

'You'll never sleep.'

'Try me. And don't start talking to me when you come to bed. I need my sleep even if you don't. Write your ideas down and I'll read them in the morning.'

On her way upstairs Harriet put her head round Fran's door to find her still reading. 'Fran, you really must get some sleep. It's awfully late.'

Fran laid her book on the bedside table and snuggled down. 'Mum, they're not quite us, are they?'

Harriet thought about this. 'No, not quite, but it doesn't mean to say that diminishes them. They are very worthwhile people, even if they don't sing from the same hymn sheet as we do.'

Fran giggled. 'Mum, you sound just like Peter. He sees the best in everyone.'

'Well, he's right, isn't he? Everyone has their slot in life, you know.'

'I can't stand snobs.'

'Do you think I'm a snob?'

'No, but Dad is.'

'Fran!'

'When she said about serving wenches and could they have all their bosoms showing, I thought I'd die laughing.'

'Fun way to go! Goodnight, darling.'

*

At 9 a.m. sharp Jimbo was pulling up at the Old Barn, but Ford and Mercedes were there before him.

'Early bird catches the worm. We decided not to go in until you arrived. Lovely morning, isn't it? We can't wait to see the barn.

'Is it really, really old, Jimbo? Genuine?' Mercedes asked, staring up at the old redbrick walls.

'My word, yes. It really was an old barn, the biggest in the area. You should have seen it. There was a lot of work to do. We did a very sympathetic conversion, you see, which takes time. Let's go in.'

Rather than let them in through the side door which the staff used, Jimbo opened up the huge main doors so they got the very best impression as they entered. It gave him a lift each time he walked in, so he knew the impact for them would be tremendous.

It silenced them, as he guessed it would. They stood open-mouthed, staring first at the soaring height of the roof and the wonderful ancient beams that supported it, the sun gloriously pouring in through the roof windows, the long, gleaming tables. Mercedes trailed appreciative fingers along the panelled walls. 'Is this wall real? Not modern tarted up to look old?'

'Tudor panelling taken from an old place in the City that was being pulled down to make way for a road. Criminal, really.'

Very tenderly Mercedes stroked the panelling to show her delight at its authenticity. 'No! That *is* criminal. It's so very beautiful.'

Ford was fascinated by the huge wrought-iron sconces placed strategically along the walls. 'These candles are lit when you have a do?' he asked.

'Yes, we have no electric lights in this part. They'd have been intrusive.'

'I don't think we'd have enough friends to fill all these long tables, would we, Ford?' said Mercedes nervously. 'How many does it hold, seated and having a meal?'

'One hundred and fifty at a pinch,' Jimbo replied. 'One hundred more comfortably, and certainly no more than that if you want a performance of some kind.'

Mercedes gasped. 'A performance?'

'Well, I thought about having some strolling players, wandering in to sing and dance and things, appearing to have arrived by chance, as they perhaps would do in the olden days ... except organised, if you get my meaning. In costume, like they used to do, strolling from one town to another and giving performances to entertain the lord's guests. And I did think of you being Queen Elizabeth, and you, Ford, as the Earl of Leicester, with all your guests in costume, too. Perhaps Mercedes could knight someone for bravery or something.'

Ford almost burst with pleasure. 'Capital. Absolutely capital. What a brilliant idea. Amazing I hadn't thought of that.'

Mercedes crumpled with disappointment. 'But it's no good, Ford: we couldn't fill it, could we? Half-full would spoil the whole thing. Very depressing, half-full.' Her shoulders slumped, her face lost its glow, and Jimbo could see she was on the verge of forgetting the whole thing. He couldn't have that. Very craftily he shaped a remark in his head, tried it out on himself in silence and decided to go for it.

'When we cater for big parties up at Turnham House, Craddock Fitch invites all the villagers as well as his own guests, gives them a good night. It pays dividends as far as relations with the village go. Of course, that would mean a very expensive evening all told, so it might be too much for you. These kinds of things don't come cheap.' He wandered away as though checking everything was as clean as could be, running a finger along the tables looking for dust, checking the sconces were standing straight and the candles firmly in place, head back to look at the roof windows ...

'Jimbo! A word.'

Jimbo swung round as though he was surprised they were still there. 'Yes?'

'Cost it out. The whole works – one hundred guests. Strolling players. The lot. Appropriate menu, drink, whatever. Let me know a.s.a.p.'

'You won't regret it.'

As Jimbo drove away, uppermost in his mind was where on earth he could get the strolling players from. Really talented ones weren't round every corner waiting to perform just because he wanted some. He was such an idiot, promising the earth without the first idea of how to make it all happen. But he'd never fallen down on the job before and he didn't intend to begin now. Because although Mercedes was without doubt common, the way she appreciated the panelling told him volumes about her. Underneath there was something rather beautiful about her inner being. God! He must be going crackers! He'd better not tell Harriet that, or else ... then he had an idea. Morris dancers! Gilbert Johns. They could dance outside under floodlights as the guests were arriving. Of course! Gilbert might even know some singers, seeing as singing was his hobby – well, rather more than that with him being a highly successful choirmaster at the church.

And if it worked well there was still time for him to organise one for the general public right before Christmas. With everything already set up it would be a doddle to organise. Elizabethan banquets for the general public could become a nice little earner. The whole business of setting up the Old Barn had cost him far more than he had ever anticipated, mainly because he wanted it absolutely right, and it was time he got some of his investment back.

Gilbert might be a very busy county archaeologist but he did appear to have flexible working hours, because he arrived very promptly at four o'clock that same afternoon. He'd never been inside the Old Barn and he was enthralled by the beauty of it. 'My word, Jimbo, you certainly know your stuff. This is spectacular. Doesn't everybody say that? They must!'

He wandered about, peering up at the beams, admiring the sconces, stroking the panelling, just as Mercedes had done, absorbing the atmosphere, and finally looking up at the minstrels' gallery.

'Musicians up there?'

Jimbo nodded. 'If you prefer, yes.'

'Such an atmosphere. It would be a joy to perform here.'

'In the first instance it's for a wedding anniversary party for Ford and Mercedes Barclay.

'And then?'

'I have wondered about doing it for the general public to make some money, get my costs back.'

'A regular event? Summer and winter?'

Jimbo nodded, but remained silent. He knew, just knew, that he had Gilbert in the palm of his hand.

'Thrilling idea.'

'Yes.'

'But why couldn't the Morris dancers perform inside? If you limit it to a hundred punters, there'd be enough room.'

'I expect they could, at the start, but outside in the summer?'

Gilbert nodded. 'Right, you're on. The singing ... no good being all classical. You'll need bawdy songs to get them going. Perhaps the odd sentimental love song to twang the heart-strings ... Elizabethan musical instruments: flute, hurdy-gurdy, sackbut, recorder, lute, drums, virginals ... Count me in.'

They shook hands on it. 'I'll try to get back to you in a week with something concrete,' Gilbert added. 'I have some chaps in mind who'd be delighted to earn a crust getting their music in the public eye. Can't be mean with the wages, though. We must get the best of the best. Second-rate would be no good at all in this place, now would it?'

'Know something?'

'What?'

'You're in the wrong job, Gilbert.'

Gilbert laughed. 'Oh no I'm not. The Barclays are the ones who've bought Glebe House from the Neals?'

Jimbo nodded.

'What are they like?'

'Plenty of money, no taste, but kindly people, determined to make their mark in the village. All your children OK?'

'Fighting fit, thanks, and lovelier by the day. Be seeing you.'

Gilbert roared away in his dilapidated estate car, his head full of ideas for the banquets and longing to get down to the nitty-gritty of choosing the songs, finding the instrumentalists and becoming closely involved. Louise would love helping, because organization was her forte, as she'd proved with the upbringing of their five children. God! What an exciting bunch they were.

The table with the old wooden settle in the bar of the Royal Oak was fully occupied by the usual crowd that evening. Willie Biggs had got in the first round and was handing the drinks out to Dottie, Sylvia, Jimmy, Vera and Don, before taking the first sip that day of his favourite home-brew.

'You know, I thought old Bryn's home-brew was good but I do believe that Dicky's is better. Bucks me up no end, it does.'

'Well,' said Don, 'and how's this magnificent mower that we've all heard about? Still driving you mad?'

Sylvia got in a reply before Willie had a chance to grumble about it. 'Zack's doing an almighty good job with it. The churchyard's never looked better and we've to be grateful for it. Even Willie agrees he's making good use of it, don't you, Willie?'

He had to agree. 'Yes, I have to admit that, and he doesn't

use it on and on like he did that first week. What's more, the shed's good. On the big side but at least Zack can get all his tools in there, as well as a chair and a little stove for making tea. Talk about all mod cons! I was in there yesterday having a cup of tea with him. In the winter it'll be real cosy.'

'You'll be fancying your job back if you go on like this,' Jimmy suggested, knowing full well that Willie wouldn't.

'No, thanks. I'm too busy to have a job.' There was a mysterious air about Willie when he said that, and Vera couldn't resist asking him what on earth he found to do all day to keep him too busy.

'Surprised no one's seen me at it.'

'At it? At what?'

'Got myself a hobby.'

They were agog to hear what hobby he'd found at his age.

'Well, I went to the tip with some gardening stuff, clearing up for the winter, yer know, and in that re-sale bit along the end wall I found one of them metal detectors. All complete and singing like a bird when I tried it on that heap of scrap metal. So I bought it for a song and ...' He paused for effect.

'Yes?'

'Yesterday I found three pound coins in a plastic bag in our garden, about five inches down from the top. Nothing to do with Sylvia and me, and we don't know how they came to be there.'

'Ones you can't use?'

'No, new. Anyway, it's helped to pay for your drinks tonight. Heard the latest news?'

His answer was a chorus of curious no's and a coming together of heads all the better to hear.

Willie glanced round to see if anyone was eavesdropping. 'He's asked Jimbo for a quote for a party for his wedding anniversary, and he wants an Elizabethan banquet at the Old Barn. No expense spared. There's going to be singers and that, like an entertainment. Mercedes' idea.'

'Oh well!' said Sylvia in a sarcastic tone. 'If Mercedes thought it up it'll be OK by you, won't it, Willie?'

The tone of Sylvia's voice caught their attention, obviously there was something going on between Mercedes and Willie. But what for heaven's sake?

Somewhat defiantly, Willie said, 'Underneath all that make-up and fancy clothes she's a lovely woman.'

'Who told yer?'

'About Mercedes?' asked Willie, wishing that wouldn't be what they wanted to know.

'No! About the banquet?'

'Oh, that. They were in the Old Barn discussing it with Jimbo while Pat Jones and her lot were getting ready for a lunch. Apparently they want serving wenches with their bosoms showing, just like it used to be.'

Sylvia said, 'That is disgusting. I knew they were common the minute I clapped eyes on 'em.'

But Jimmy and Don asked, rather too eagerly, 'Can anyone go?'

There was an outburst of loud protests from the ladies, except for Dottie, who thought it might be good fun.

'It's a *party*, and not for the public. By invitation, I expect.'

Jimmy and Don looked quite disappointed. Jimmy said, 'I've heard of them banquets; they're really good fun. Free mead and that's potent, I understand. Three glasses and you're under the table. Pity. It'll cost a packet. He must have some money.'

'Now we've got two benefactors in the village. Can't be bad, can it?' said Dottie. 'I shall be helping Pat behind the scenes, but you two could always offer your services in the serving wench department for this 'ere party, Vera, and you, Sylvia, you're both well ... endowed.'

Briefly both Vera and Sylvia did wonder about volunteering and then both thought better of it.

Dottie nudged Vera. 'Think of the money!'

'Think of the embarrassment. I have heard,' Vera bent a little closer to Dottie, 'at those sort of parties the punters push five-pound notes down the front of the wenches' ...' and she indicated her cleavage with a discreet finger.

Sylvia blushed and Dottie roared with laughter. 'Better not, then. It wouldn't be decent, would it?'

'Don't you volunteer, Sylvia, I won't have it,' Willie said.

'Don't be daft. It's not women my age they'll want, though I'm flattered you think I might qualify.'

Right then, in wafted Ford and Mercedes, and they headed straight for the table where they were being gossiped about. Sylvia shuffled along the settle to make room for them.

'Good evening, everyone.' Ford sorted out somewhere for Mercedes to sit and promptly volunteered to buy a round, an offer no one at the table refused.

They couldn't resist asking Mercedes about the banquet, and Mercedes was thrilled they'd mentioned it. 'My idea, actually,' she said eagerly. 'You're all invited. Will you come?'

There was a momentary silence round the table, and then they all burst out with their thanks. Mercedes glowed with delight. 'Oh! That's wonderful. Nothing's settled yet. I mean, we're doing it but the finer details haven't been organised. Jimbo's come up with some marvellous ideas. We're so looking forward to it.'

'That's how many years you've been married?'

'Twenty years and it feels like only yesterday.' She blushed rather naïvely. 'You see, we're still in love. My heart dances when I see him.'

Willie patted her hand, thinking there was that vulnerability he sensed about her.

Vera thought about her Don and decided no, her heart definitely didn't dance when she saw him, and Sylvia decided that perhaps hers did dance a bit when she saw Willie but then they'd not been married as long as some.

Ford came back with the drinks and passed them round. Then he sat down at the table, took a long swig and decided to put forward an idea he had for the Turnham Malpas lunch club.

'I've been thinking, this lunch club you have, once a month, do you ever go somewhere different from the village hall?'

They all shook their heads. 'Why?' asked Sylvia, who was involved in the organizing of it.

'Just thought it might be fun to go somewhere else.'

Sylvia said, 'Trouble is, most people can't afford the price of the lunch and a trip out. But if you're in a charitable frame of mind, Ford, it's the youngsters round here who need money spending on them, not the old folks.'

There was a great deal of chuntering then along the lines of 'Why not the old folks?' All of them conveniently forgot that they were old folk themselves.

Ford asked, 'In what way, Sylvia?'

'Well, we have the youth club run by Kate Fitch and Venetia Mayer. They do have fundraising efforts but they never quite raise enough, and what they need is to be able to go somewhere exciting. They're all worthwhile young people, not tearaways, and they deserve something going on in this village, and out of it. You'd be doing them a real service if you could come up with some funds. They deserve it more than the old people, believe me. They *need* it more. Country life for young people nowadays isn't, well, isn't exciting enough.' Sylvia glared round the table, eyeball to eyeball, daring anyone to disagree.

Mercedes lit up at the prospect. 'I see what you mean. Bless 'em.' There sounded to be real feeling in her voice when she said that, and they all wondered why it was so heartfelt.

Ford said nothing.

He got a nudge from Mercedes but still he said nothing.

To fill the silence someone mentioned the date of the end-of-season cricket team dinner, and were they ...

Ford burst into life. 'Where do I find these people? This Kate and Venice whatever she's called?'

Sylvia began singing inside. 'Up at the Big House – Turnham House. It's a training college for Mr Fitch's staff, for his business. Venetia's the sports person and Kate, of course, lives in the flat.'

'Will they be in?'

'Worth a try,' said Sylvia, staggered by Ford's decisiveness.

'Right! I'm going up there. Coming, Merc?'

Chapter 4

They found Venetia supervising the swimming pool. She was languidly resting on a white plastic lounger, idly admiring the young men showing off their prowess.

She sprang to life when she spotted Mercedes and Ford stepping along the edge of the pool towards her.

'Good evening. How may I help?'

'Venetia Mayer? I'm Ford Barclay. This is my wife, Mercedes. We've come specially to see about the club for the young people you run on Friday nights.'

Venetia had really gone off obese men since she'd got her Jeremy down to an acceptable size and didn't find Ford at all appealing, so she didn't bother to fluff up her blacker-than-black hair, or to get up from the lounger. Behind his innocent question he'd only be wanting to join the leisure club and it wasn't for the public.

'I see. I run the youth club along with Kate Fitch and a committee of the young people in the village – well, villages, because we include Penny Fawcett and Little Derehams, too. Do you have children of an age to join, then?'

'No, no. Someone called Sylvia in the pub just now suggested the club might be in need of funds.'

'Always in need of funds.' Venetia glanced at her watch and took her mobile from the pocket of her pink linen shorts. 'It's nine, so Kate will have finished their evening meal. I'll give her a ring, see if it's convenient for us to go up to their flat. She's Kate *Fitch*, you see.'

She was in and yes, anyone with money to spare for the youth club was more than welcome. Venetia closed her mobile, swung her long, slender legs off the lounger and stood up. Mercedes almost fainted when she saw her figure full-length. She admired the devotion needed to maintain a figure like that, taut and neat-bottomed. She'd need to watch Ford; he was passionate about neat bottoms.

They reached the main hall of the Big House with its original Tudor panelling, exquisite flower arrangements, and beautiful banisters, along which Mercedes trailed her fingers in delicious enjoyment of the old wood. She was overwhelmed. Her mouth was dry and her legs were shaky; she wouldn't speak, that was the easiest. Not a word. She'd leave it all to Ford.

The luxuriousness of the furnishings and the hangings in the sitting room in this Mr Fitch's flat alarmed Mercedes. Such taste! It was straight out of one of those smart magazines that Ford kept buying her in the hope that some of the style would rub off on them both. Mercedes shook the hand he offered her and trembled all over. He frightened her. But Kate was an entirely different matter. Obviously she must have misheard; she must be his daughter, not his wife. She was much more down-to-earth.

Mr Fitch served drinks from a thing like a cocktail cabinet, except it was too old to be called that, and finally, when they were all seated, drink in hand, Ford launched into his ideas.

'I was thinking about perking up the lunch club for the old folk but instead someone mentioned that the youth of the villages were in need of some excitement, so I've changed my mind. What ages do you cover, Kate?'

'Thirteen to eighteen.'

'Right. They'll need something exciting, won't they? Weekends away, camping or in hostels, trips to Go Ape – expect there'll be one somewhere within reasonable distance – their own gigs, sport of some kind. The list is endless. Brighten everything up, we shall. How about it, Venice? Are we on the right lines?'

Venetia appeared extraordinarily at home in this room, and Mercedes wondered why that should be because she was common, no doubt about that, and didn't really fit in. She waited to hear what she had to say to Ford's proposals.

Venetia unravelled her gorgeous legs, fluffed her hair and said, glancing coyly at Mr Fitch, whose cold eyes didn't appear to be the least bit impressed, 'It all sounds brilliant, doesn't it, Craddock?'

That she should feel free to use his first name surprised Mercedes; it didn't ring quite true somehow.

Mr Fitch froze her with a steely look and addressed Ford. 'Sounds to me just right for these young people.' He turned to Kate. 'What do you think, darling?'

Mercedes thought, darling? To his daughter? Well, she couldn't be his wife. Heavens above, he was old enough to be her father.

'Well, we have about sixteen regulars, more occasionally, but with activities like you've mentioned I'm sure there'll definitely be sixteen, and that means an awful lot of money.'

'Well, I was thinking about that on the way up here. If it was a big project like a four-day trip somewhere after GCSEs or A-levels then they'd have to match me pound for pound. Say it cost a hundred pounds for four days in a hostel, I'd offer fifty pounds and they'd have to find fifty plus their spending money. Would that be any good? Can't always hand it to them on a plate, can we?'

'For some of them that's a lot of money,' said Kate. 'Believe me it is. Hardly any of them are earning, you see. And there's transport, too, isn't there? That's expensive nowadays.'

'I would pay the transport costs,' Mr Fitch suggested.

But Ford positively disagreed. 'No, no. It's my project. I'll pay for the transport.'

This well-intentioned offer was made kindly enough but Mr Fitch was having none of it.

'Absolutely not. I'm the benefactor round here and I shall pay for the vehicle, as often as needed. That's settled.'

Kate knew before Ford replied that he was about to drop the proverbial brick.

'No, I'm sorry, it isn't. I can't allow you to feel you have to chip in. It's not right, and you retired and living in this rented flat.'

A slight flush flooded Mr Fitch's cheeks and in the iciest tones any human being could have summoned he said, 'I don't think you realise who I am. I *own* Fitch Enterprise Europe. The construction company. If I say I shall pay for the transport, that's exactly what I mean.'

Ford, who hadn't heard of the company, was only briefly fazed by this revelation. He quickly recovered and thanked Craddock profusely for his generosity.

Kate interrupted him. 'Look, Venetia and I will discuss all this with the members this Friday and see how they feel about it. I agree they should make some effort to pay for these trips, if only on a character-building basis, and perhaps we could hold fundraising events to help them all, especially the ones whose parents can't afford such expense. How about that, Ford? Would that be a good idea?'

Ford nodded his approval, and Kate asked Mercedes what she thought.

'That's fine by me. I don't have anything to do with his charitable … efforts, I leave it all to Ford; he loves getting involved.' Then Mercedes saw Mr Fitch's reaction to what she'd said and sank back into her chair, vowing not to say another word.

'You're in the habit of giving a lot to charity, then?' Mr Fitch said.

Kate heard the hint of sarcasm in his voice and wished she could think on her feet and divert the conversation to something less confrontational, but she didn't. In fact, she hadn't a chance because Ford plunged immediately into listing his recent donations, mentioning in particular the purchase of the state-of-the-art lawnmower for the church.

Mr Fitch almost jerked with surprise; he'd not heard a word about that. 'A lawnmower for the church! I didn't even know they needed one.'

'Oh. Yes, the old one nearly killed that Zack the virgin. I saw to that pronto. You see, I feel I need to give something back.'

'Back? To what exactly?' Mr Fitch said sharply.

'I beg your pardon?'

'Why do you feel the need to give something back? To what are you going something back?'

'Well, I've been lucky, you see, and made pots of money, so I give it back as a thank you.'

'What are you, then?'

'A philanthropist, I suppose.'

'No, no. How did you earn your money?'

'I've sold my metal business outright,' Ford replied with a hint of pride in his tone.

'You mean you were in scrap metal?'

Ford loathed that description, and began to lose his temper. Mercedes wished she could curl up and die. She slowly slid her foot over the carpet towards Ford's ankle and kicked it slightly but it was all too late.

'I describe myself as having dealt in metal. The phrase "scrap metal" makes the whole business sound seedy and illegal, thank you very much, Craddock ...'

It was the spine-chilling look at the use of his first name that stopped Ford in his tracks. Who the hell did this Mr Fitch think he was to be so scornful of the pride of his life's achievements. 'Do you have a problem with that?'

'None at all. It's just that "scrap metal" seems to me to be common usage, surely?'

There was no doubting the underlying scorn in Mr Fitch's voice, and Ford wasn't going to put up with it for another moment. He searched feverishly in his mind for a cutting reply. Too late.

'My paying for the transport for your … little enterprise … isn't going to take anything away from your charity work, now is it? It's simply a small helping hand.'

'Well, I won't spoil our concept for the sake of a man who can't take no for an answer. Between us we should be able to do something constructive for the young people in the villages, and that's what's important.'

'Indeed it is.'

Kate and Venetia sighed with relief.

Then Kate launched herself into cementing the relationship. 'We would be delighted to have your support, and, as I said before, we shall discuss it with the members on Friday, won't we, Venetia? Another drink, anyone?'

But Mercedes had had enough and began gathering up her smart Chanel handbag from the luxurious carpet and making ready for a rapid retreat.

However, Ford had other ideas. 'Thank you. I'll have another gin and tonic, please.'

Whether it was the second gin – though two gins were only starters as far as Ford was concerned – who knew? But Ford came out with the remark to end all remarks, and Mercedes almost fainted when he said it.

'I think it's wonderful for your daughter to give time to the village young people. She deserves support. And you, too, Venice.'

Ford blithely carried on sipping his drink, totally unaware that Mr Fitch was on the verge of an apoplectic fit.

Visibly taking a grip on himself, Craddock said graciously, though tight-lipped, 'Kate is my wife.'

After this the conversation was sustained only just long enough for Ford to finish his second G and T. Then Mercedes actually stood up ready for the off and he had to leave.

Kate saw them to the front door, and then raced up the stairs back to the flat, to find Craddock storming about the sitting room like a maniac.

'I'll sort something out for *him*. Settle him once and for all. My daughter indeed! I'll give him what for. The bloody little upstart!'

'Craddock! Really!' Kate laughed. 'I don't care. *We're* the ones having a wonderful life married to each other and loving it, and no one can take that from you or from me, whatever they say or think.'

Craddock put his arms round her and kissed her. 'How right you are. We're the winners in this, aren't we?'

'Exactly.' She kissed him back, glad the hurt was resolved.

'But ... coming here and throwing his money in my face. Who the hell does he think he is?'

'Someone doing the youth club a very good turn. He's being generous in the only way he knows. You were unfair.'

'Do I go round telling everyone, quoting figures, how much money I've given to this village? No, I do not. It stuck in my craw listening to his list.'

Kate began laughing. In fact, she rolled about in her chair uncontrollably. Finally she managed to speak. 'You did used to, before I appeared on the scene. You've learned since that giving quietly but with purpose earns you far more Brownie points than making a song and dance about it. You know that, don't you? Look how much more acceptable you are to the village nowadays. Far more than ever you were. They're even growing quite fond of you.'

'Well, he'd better learn fast, or else ...'

'Or else, what? She's nice. A gentle person really.'

'She rivals Venetia in the taste department.'

'Now that is cruel. She's very nervous of you. She has lovely eyes and just needs a little—'

'OK, OK. But don't make them part of our social circle or we could come to blows.'

Mercedes didn't speak all the way home in the car. The whole evening had been torture for her. From a poor working-class background she'd been thrust by Ford's success into being wealthy and hadn't yet managed to feel comfortable with it. Glebe House alarmed her for a start. They ought never to have bought it. A nice cosy cottage with a thatched roof and small rooms would have suited her better. She imagined a cat sleeping on the hearth-rug and a bathroom small enough to feel warm instead of that glistening, barn-like bathroom she had to use that was part of the 'step up' Ford had dreamed about. She knew he deserved a better home than they'd had, but it had been close to friends, within walking distance to the shops, and was familiar and comfortable. But here!

In their old house, she'd opened the front door and there was the narrow passage with the old Victorian tiled floor in soft browns, ochre and dark red, and the picture rail with the prints and the narrow hall table with the bowl of dried flowers on it. What had she got here? A huge hall twice as big as the front room in the old house, a shining, glossy parquet floor, definitely not laminate ... She'd never feel at home in it, not in a thousand years, and couldn't understand why Ford liked it so much.

At the house, as she switched the kettle on, Mercedes said, 'He very nearly thumped you.'

'*Me*? Thumped *me*? I thought we'd hit the right note.'

'When you said about his daughter, I could have crawled away.'

'Well, I thought she was – she's too young for that old man. I mean!'

'You didn't see the huge diamond engagement ring and the thick gold wedding ring, nor the wedding photo on the table?'

'No.'

'Well, *I* did. I'm having my hot chocolate in bed, in that huge master bedroom you're so proud of. You know, I much preferred our little bedroom with the furniture you put together for us.'

'But look at the wardrobes you've got here! Massive, they are, plenty of room. Those wardrobes I built were as cheap as chips, and almost too narrow to take hangers, which was a big mistake on my part, I admit.'

'So? I liked them.'

'You've got to grow into this new lifestyle, Merc. Move on. Move up.'

'That Mr Fitch. Don't ever use his first name again, and don't make the mistake of thinking he's a small-time man. I've an idea that our bank balance will be a drop in the ocean compared to his. He's got power, has that man, and he's ruthless if he puts his mind to it. He could ruin you in a second, and don't think he won't if the thought occurs to him.'

Ford put on his sceptical look when he heard this. 'Now, honestly, how could he?'

Mercedes nodded bleakly at him. 'You know full well how.'

She marched up the sweeping staircase, carefully gripping her mug of hot chocolate in fear of spilling it on the thick ivory carpet, sat on the edge of the bed and put the mug down on the mat she had there for that very purpose. Her alarm clock was round and comfortable, big and made of brass, old and traditional, and, after she'd put the alarm on, she held it to her chest, loving the comfort of it and wishing ... how she wished ...

Downstairs in his posh study Ford sipped his hot chocolate, his feet propped on the desk. He looked round and admired his pictures of famous racehorses which now lined the walls instead of the cold, bare, unimaginative pictures that had belonged to Neville Neal. Red Marauder 2001. My, what a horse! Bobbyjo, Papillon in 2000, and last but not least Red Rum in the seventies.

Three times he won the Grand National, three times! Lovely horse. He could name every horse in every picture, and was proud to do so. When he thought about his miserable start in life, and where he stood now, he brimmed with self-satisfaction.

Niggling at the back of his mind, though, was Mercedes' comment as she was setting off up that beautifully impressive staircase, which was what had sold the house to him. He was always of the opinion that Merc was not as bright as himself, then she came out with a remark like that and it floored him. He could only describe it as hitting the nail on the head, because she'd guessed correctly what kind of a man Craddock Fitch was. He, Ford Barclay, thought he had the measure of him, but he hadn't. Fitch had sneered at him. He'd despised him for earning a living in scrap metal, which was indeed the correct name for his business. He, Ford Barclay, would show that Fitch the way to go home with his Elizabethan banquet. It was going to be the highlight of the social year.

Ford tipped the rest of his drink down the sink, and left the mug on the draining board. Upstairs he found Merc had already fallen asleep. All the same he nestled against her, hoping she'd wake and they could talk for a while, but she didn't, so he rolled away to the other edge of their vast bed and it took him all of two hours to get to sleep. She'd upset the applecart with that remark, just when he was beginning to feel safe.

Chapter 5

'Pass the teapot, please, Alex,' Peter said at breakfast.

'Dad! You've drunk coffee for breakfast for years.'

'I know I have.'

Alex passed him the teapot. 'Here you are.'

'I decided I'd got into a rut, so drinking tea is my attempt to brighten up my image.'

Alex laughed. 'Honestly! Do you feel you're in a rut?'

'Yes. Time I moved on.'

'Literally? Move away?'

'Been thinking of it. New challenges, you know.'

'So long as it's not Africa, Dad. I don't think any of us could cope with that.'

'No, I wasn't thinking of Africa, more Culworth, but not yet. Can't do anything drastic until you and Beth have finished school. Anyway, for the moment I need to stay in my comfort zone.'

Alex laughed again. 'Just think: when, or if, Beth and I go to university you'll be able to move anywhere. Anywhere at all.'

'You're right there. I shall. Now where do you recommend?'

'Canterbury?' Alex's wicked grin made Peter smile.

'Definitely not. I'm not into corridors of power.'

'York?'

'Mmm. No, not York.'

'I know! The East End!'

'That would be a real shake-up. New challenges writ large.'

They both heard Beth clattering down the stairs.

'Morning, everyone! What are we doing today?'

'Prep?' Alex suggested.

'Certainly not. I've loads to do but it can wait. I'm dressed for Culworth.'

'If we rush we can catch the bus. Twenty minutes?'

'I'm game.'

'So am I. Here's your tea.'

Beth slurped a mouthful of tea. 'Mum gone already, Dad?'

'Eight-thirty clinic.'

Beth moaned. 'I wish she didn't work on Saturdays. I used to love Saturdays. It's the only day in the week when we're all free.'

Peter protested. 'It only happens occasionally. Be fair!'

Alex pointed at her cereal bowl with his knife handle. 'Eat,' he commanded.

'You're a bully, you are.'

'Hurry up. I'm going to clean my teeth.' He raced up the stairs, eager for the off. He had two CD tokens and £10 in his pocket, and he intended spending it all, though it wasn't very much cash, not nowadays.

Twenty minutes later they ran out of the Rectory, across the Green and arrived at the bus stop outside the Village Store to find a queue of six waiting. They were teased for being out of breath after running such a short distance. But they hadn't time for much more because the bus came groaning up Shepherd's Hill and they all piled on as fast as they could because the driver was so impatient.

'He's almost always late. Today he's early and he still wants to be off sharpish. We can't win,' someone said.

Alone in the house, Peter decided that this was his chance to catch up on some reading. So once he'd tidied the kitchen, cleaned his teeth and read his post, he settled down to read a revolutionary book he'd been longing to begin for over a week, *Is God For Me?*

An hour later and he was deeply involved. He was oblivious to the people going by his study window, the sound of a group of horses trotting by on the regular Saturday morning hack, and the cars pulling up for the Saturday morning coffee hour in the village hall. His book was totally absorbing and well up to what he had hoped it to be.

When the doorbell rang, he went to answer it with his mind very much elsewhere.

Standing on the doorstep was someone he knew but couldn't quite place. She was possibly now in her early fifties, like himself, more plump than he remembered, very fair-haired, with round pink cheeks and looking remarkably like ...

'Peter! Good morning. You don't change. Still that lovely youthful look.'

'I'm sorry I don't ...' Oh God! Oh! God! It was her! It couldn't be. *It was.* Hell! 'Why, it's Suzy ... Meadows. No, Palmer. Of course it is.'

'Yes.'

She looked intently at him, remembering every inch of his handsome compassionate face, his thick strawberry blond hair, knowing she'd done the right thing coming unexpectedly, he'd never have said yes otherwise. 'Can I come in? The whole village will gossip if ...'

'Of course.' Peter opened the door wider and invited her in. What the blazes ... Thank God Caroline was out. And the twins. What was she thinking of coming here uninvited?

'I knew you wouldn't mind. Did the twins tell you I wrote?'

'Eventually.' Peter didn't know whether to go in the study or invite her into the sitting room. 'Shall I make us coffee?'

'Yes, please. It's been a long drive.' Her acceptance solved the problem of where to sit. She followed him into the kitchen admiring his back view as much as she had admired him face to face. She remembered him physically so vividly, and still without a single white hair. Bless him!

He suggested she sat on one of the rocking chairs Caroline always had by the Aga. He was making instant. Ground coffee was beyond him right now. His hand shook as he spooned the coffee out into the mugs. She should never have come. What was she thinking of? 'Milk? Sugar?'

'Both, please. I still have a sweet tooth, you know.'

How could he know that after all these years? He didn't know it when she lived in the village.

He handed it to her, placing it carefully, as Caroline would have done had she been here, on the corner of the Aga, her favourite place for her morning coffee. It was no good, he'd have to ask straight out, with no beating about the bush or polite conversation for conversation's sake. 'Why have you come?'

Suzy observed him over the rim of her mug. 'You ask *me* that?'

'Yes, I do.'

For a while Suzy remained silent, sipping the coffee. It was too hot, too sweet, his abruptness too horrifying. This wasn't the gentle Peter she'd kept close to her heart all these years when remembering their moment of heart-stopping passion.

'Well? It's no good coming and saying nothing, or is that the whole point of this sudden arrival? Silent accusation?'

He'd become harsh and inconsiderate; this wasn't like Peter. All these years with Caroline had obviously taken their toll. 'The twins, are they at home?'

'No, they are not.' He didn't add 'thank God', which he would have liked to have done.

'Caroline?'

'No.'

'That's a pity. I would have liked to see her again. I've chosen the wrong morning. I thought we could all have a talk together, make arrangements, you know. It's simple: I want to get to know my twins. Now they're older they can make their own decisions, can't they? If they see me I'm sure it will have more impact than the letters.'

For one brief moment Peter recalled the sensations he'd felt that fateful morning, when ... but the attraction wasn't there now, that overwhelming need for her body which had scuppered – well, almost scuppered his marriage. If it hadn't been for Caroline's profound love for him ...

'What you are doing right now is quite simply grossly unfair,' he said.

'Not at all. I gave birth to them, they were mine, and now I want to see them. I'm not taking them away from you – I can't, legally – I'd just like a share of them. I got Alex's letter, but of course he didn't mean what he said in it. Reading between the lines, it was a plea for recognition. How could he not want to see his mother? Obviously he was being influenced by Caroline.'

'Caroline had nothing whatsoever to do with the writing of that letter. It was entirely what he and Beth both felt. Had you seen their distress when they read your letters you wouldn't be here now. You are deliberately confusing their loyalties.'

'All I'm asking for is some time set aside for me to see them. I'm not asking them to come to live with me, though that—'

'Stop it right there. This minute. I would do all I could to stop that ever happening. I will not allow their present happiness, their present deep security to be dragged away from them by someone they don't even know. I will not have it. I want you to go. Now! No ifs, no buts. Now. Right away.' Peter got to his feet, put his mug in the sink so sharply that it smashed against the tap and broke. He paused for a moment, gripping the edge of the sink, battling to keep a hold on himself. 'I will not have their lives disrupted because of a *whim* of yours.'

Suzy pressed on with putting her case. '*Whim*? This is all Caroline's doing, I can see that. Though she was grateful enough at the time. Remember her joy? Her joy brought about by my sacrifice? Surely it's not too much to ask – to see them, to talk with them. Things shouldn't be like this. I want to be able to get to know them, to kiss them goodnight at bedtime sometimes. Is it so terrible to feel like that?'

'Yes. No, it isn't. Yes, it is. The decision is entirely theirs and is not influenced by either myself or Caroline, you must understand that. You were glad to give them away when they were born. We were very useful. Just you remember that, please.'

Suzy stood up. She didn't even come to his shoulder, but he felt her strength, her animosity and her shattering disappointment. 'It took two of us. It wasn't a virgin birth. My offering the two of them to you, their father, saved Caroline's sanity, remember?'

She was right about that, for Caroline was full of pain at the time knowing she would never be able to give him children, so much so she'd offered to divorce him so he would be free.

'Yes, I do remember. She offered to adopt them for my sake and I refused at first. I couldn't bear the thought of having the evidence of my infidelity in my own home every single day. My unfaithfulness to her was one of the most distressing, turbulent, horrifying things that has ever happened to me.'

Suzy interrupted him. 'It was one of the most wonderful things for *me*. It was only my desperate financial state that made me know I could never keep the pair of them, not when I had to work to keep a roof over my girls' heads, to buy the very food on my girls' plates. How could I have kept them? I couldn't. It broke my heart giving them away, but there was no alternative.' She drew closer to him. 'Wasn't that day wonderful for you? The two of us? Together? You both got your heart's desire, didn't you? Say you did, or my sacrifice will have been worthless.' There came a gentle, pleading note in her voice in those last words and Peter's flesh crawled with dismay. Or was it revulsion? Had she forgotten she was compliant, a co-conspirator? Eager for him?

'There is nothing else to be said. Please, just go.'

He strode out of the kitchen, unable to cope any longer. He flung the Rectory door wide open and stood breathing heavily, waiting for her. She was more right then he was prepared to give her credit for. Of course they were glad to have them, both of them were glad, but would she never go? Where had that sweet, pliant person gone? Had he, Peter Harris, never regretted anything he'd done? Wished he could turn back the clock? Of course he had. The matter which had brought about the twins' very existence was the biggest regret of his life, but he couldn't turn the clock on that and neither could she.

It felt like an age before she finally appeared in the hall.

Her beautiful blue eyes, Beth's eyes, were flooded with tears. He wouldn't give in, not at this moment. He mustn't. But he felt his determination beginning to wither away.

'Please, Peter, put a word in for me with the twins, especially Alex. I expect he has your kind of compassion and at least he would be a part of you which—'

'Believe me, no part of me is yours. We both, tragically, made a horrific mistake in what we did. I prayed to God for years for forgiveness and don't know if I have it even now. Selfishly perhaps, I am completely safe in Caroline's love and so are the children, and I want it to remain that way. Now, please, leave. I haven't anything more to say. Let's part amicably.'

Suzy rested a hand on his arm. 'You're still a very attractive man. I shall love you to the end of my days, Peter. That's how I feel. But I shan't let this rest. I am determined to get to know our children.'

He heard himself saying brutally. 'At whatever cost to them?'

'There won't be a cost to them, simply an enrichment of their lives. I'm not a bad woman, but I am a loving one.'

Footsteps approaching the Rectory alerted them both. It was Ford Barclay, seeing Suzy's hand on Peter's arm he concluded …

'Good morning, Reverend,' he said. 'Good morning to you, madam. You must be the Reverend's wife. Nice to meet you. The name's Ford Barclay. Beautiful morning, isn't it? Makes you glad to be alive.'

He offered his hand to Suzy and she shook it saying, 'Nice to meet you. I'll leave you with Peter.'

Stunned by her obvious attempt to pass herself off as his wife, Peter hurriedly explained, 'This lady is a parishioner from years ago, just passing by.'

'Oh! Sorry. Didn't realise. I'll call back on Monday, then. It's not urgent. Will you be around?'

'In the afternoon I shall.'

'Fine. That'll do nicely. Good morning to you both.' He smiled at them both and left, and Suzy smiled back. For one brief moment she imagined she really was the Rector's wife. She looked up at Peter and saw the disappointment in his face; she convinced herself that the disappointment she saw was because of his regret that she wasn't the Rector's wife, so the truth really was that he would have preferred for that man to have been right. Well, she certainly wouldn't have any problems with that.

Then Suzy reached up on tiptoe, kissed Peter, patted his arm and gave him a tremulous, loving smile, which took away the past years from her face and made her young again.

As the door slammed behind her, Suzy smiled to herself. Obviously she'd caught him on the raw. Still, he'd come round. Well now, what was there to stop her going for a coffee in the village hall? Quite a normal thing to be doing in Turnham Malpas on a Saturday morning, surely? There'd no doubt be a few people there who remembered her.

The twins rang at twelve to say they were staying on in Culworth to see a film so they wouldn't be back until the teatime bus. 'All right, Dad?' Alex asked. 'Your voice sounds odd.'

'I'm OK. That's fine. Are you both OK?'

'Of course.'

'All right for money?'

'Yes, thanks. Beth's found a ten-pound note she'd forgotten she had, so added to mine we shall be all right.'

'Right, then. Be seeing you. Enjoy.'

It was Suzy's determination to have 'a share', as she called it, of the twins that had upset Peter. Just how ungracious was he being by saying no to her? Come to think of it, though, it was Alex and Beth's decision and he'd no business to interfere. But her visit had shaken him to the core. There was no doubt he had to tell Caroline. A glance at the clock told him that she would be back in half an hour at the earliest, depending on when the clinic ended.

They'd have lunch, just the two of them, in the dining room. He'd lay the table with the best china and open a bottle of wine, heat up the quiche, use some of the salad in the fridge. Or would that appear too obvious? It well might. No, in the kitchen would be better.

He heard her footsteps in the hall and the sound of her voice calling, 'Darling! It's me! Lunch ready? I'm starving.'

They always kissed when either of them got home, and this morning Peter kissed her more fervently than usual.

'Rector! You've missed me! And I've missed you, too.' She stood back and looked at him. 'What's wrong? Something's happened.'

'It's all ready. I'll get the quiche out. Sit down.'

Caroline gave her hands a thorough wash under the kitchen tap then sat down. 'I don't like the look on your face. What is it? Peter?'

'Bread roll? Butter?'

'Thanks. Well?'

'Get started. Wine?'

'Oh! That's nice. Just what I need. It's been hectic at the clinic today. I'm worn to a shred.'

'Beth doesn't like you working on Saturdays. She claims it's the only day in the week we have together.'

'Well, it is only occasionally, and if that's all she has to put up with ... it's nothing compared to what some children have to tolerate.' Caroline shrugged, spooned some salad out of the bowl and began to eat. 'I had three retired people in this morning, when the clinic is supposed to be for people who work and can't get in without taking time off, and you'll never guess, they—'

Peter laid down his knife and fork. 'I had a visitor this morning.'

Caroline looked up, alarmed by the tone of his voice. 'Yes?'

'Unfortunately it was,' he paused, 'well ... it was Suzy Meadows.'

'Suzy Meadows, *here* this morning? I knew there was something very wrong. What the hell did she want?' Her knife and fork dropped on to her plate. The idea of her here in their house shocked her. She sat back, ashen-faced. 'I can't believe this. Did you know she was coming?'

'Of course not, otherwise I would have said absolutely no. She, well, she wants ... she wants to see the children.'

'I hope you said no to *that*!'

'I did, but she didn't appear to hear.'

'Doesn't *want* to hear, you mean.'

'Both. I more or less turned her out. Flung the door open and stood there waiting for her to go. I'm ashamed of myself for that but—'

'But nothing. Where did you sit?'

'In here and had a coffee.'

'I see. There was not one jot in the adoption papers about access and as far as I'm concerned, that's it. I will not have the children upset. Nor me for that matter. How dare she? How *dare* she just arrive uninvited.'

Caroline began pacing the kitchen. 'Who does she think she is? Just who?'

'What do you think? She claimed she was their mother and had rights.'

The truth hit home. Caroline slumped down on to her chair and glowered at him. 'That was a very hurtful thing to say.'

'I'm so sorry. I didn't say it – she did. I lost all my ability for reasonableness and seeing the other's point of view. I could have been really nasty to her. In fact, I think maybe I was. The shock made me speechless. When I answered the door I couldn't for one blind moment think who on earth she was.'

'Does she look older, then?'

'Plumper, I think, and yes, older, of course. When I said that she would be pulling the children's security right from under their feet and how did she feel about that, she more or less claimed she had a right and what harm would it do. Finally she left me with nothing to say. That was when I opened the door and waited for her to leave. Then of course—'

Caroline groaned, 'Don't tell me! Someone saw her.'

'Ford Barclay, coming with a message.'

Relieved, Caroline remarked, 'Oh! Well, he wouldn't know who—'

'He assumed she was the Rector's wife. I had to explain.'

'Well, thank goodness you put that right.'

'Not before she shook his hand as though she was.'

Caroline stopped all pretence of eating her lunch. 'My God! Has she gone mad? Is that it? She must have done. Being widowed twice has finally made her crack.'

Peter too had stopped eating. 'When all is said and done, the children have the right to say what their wishes are, and we have the right to defend their decision. And I'm sure they won't want to bother with her. Aren't you? Beth was quite vicious the way she tore up Suzy's letter. I didn't see Alex's reply but he did write and I know from her attitude that it was a refusal.'

'When you told me what happened when you mentioned her letters to them, I was absolutely sure, but her coming like this ... On the other hand, what are we afraid of? There is nothing to be afraid of, but God, it hurts!' She wiped her eyes then picked up her glass. 'Let's cheer ourselves up. A toast to our children and our family life being secure and inviolate.'

On Sunday morning Caroline had those very words brought to mind when, quite by chance, she overheard a conversation behind her outside the church. She swung round to face who was gossiping about the events at the Rectory and found she was facing Valda Senior, who had a very attentive audience. Their eyes were glued to Valda, mouths agape.

'... I saw her with my own eyes at the coffee morning. Dressed to kill, she was, wanting to make an impression, and did she? She did. Fortunately,' Valda paused for effect, 'the Doctor wasn't there. If she had been I daresay the balloon would have gone up. Suzy Meadows-that-was said very positively to *me* that she was having the twins to stay. Would you believe it? So it's true what we all thought – the twins *are* his and hers.'

Valda, unaware that Caroline had heard every word, stood back, looking positively triumphant at being the centre of attention and having such news to impart. Two people from down Shepherd's Hill who came to church only intermittently were standing, their mouths hanging open, but Dottie, who had also been treated to this outrageous tale, was bright red with anger.

'And do you believe that? That they'll want to go and stay with her?' she asked.

'Naturally. First real confirmation we've had that the twins are the Rector's and hers, isn't it.'

'Well, you can keep your nasty, spiteful gossip to yourself. I can tell you that the decision will be made by Alex and Beth and no one else, and I bet my bottom dollar that it's all wishful thinking on her part.'

'Oh! Gone all hoity-toity, have we, now we work at the Rectory? Well, I'm telling the truth, believe me I am. I heard it with my own ears. I can't think that you as the cleaner—'

This was one step too far for Dottie. Caroline never called her a cleaner. It was always 'Dottie keeps house for me' if she introduced her to someone. She swung her handbag well back and slammed it against Valda's head. Thelma Senior tried to intervene on her sister's behalf but, as always, her reactions were far too slow and the handbag landed fair and square on the side of Valda's head.

The commotion couldn't go unnoticed. They all saw Dottie incensed and they all wanted to know why. Zack the verger rushed inside the church to tell Peter, who was in the vestry removing his vestments.

Zack looked him square in the face and said, 'Better go see what's up, sir.'

So Peter went out. One look at Caroline's face and he guessed what the trouble was about.

Dottie left him in no doubt. 'Reverend! She's spreading unfounded gossip, she is, about Suzy Meadows and Beth and Alex going to live with her. I'm that upset.'

But Dottie didn't stay to hear his reaction to this as she'd spotted Beth racing for home. 'Blast it!' she said under her breath and set off after her. She caught up with her just as Beth was fitting her key in the lock.

'Now, Beth, take no notice. That daft old cow has gone senile, believe me. Come in the kitchen and we'll have a drink. What do you fancy?'

'Oh, Dottie!'

Dottie opened her arms wide and took hold of poor Beth, whose tears wouldn't stop coming. Her sobs tore Dottie apart. They stood gently rocking together until Dottie could find her voice. 'My little love! Now come on. You mustn't take on so. Look, here's a tissue. That's a good girl, blow yer nose. I wish you'd never have heard her, the old cat. I know she can't hear you, but you stand there and call that Valda all sorts of disgusting names, really loud. Shout them out, the worst ones you can think of right this minute, and you'll feel a lot better. Go on.'

So Beth did. Some rather shocked Dottie; she was surprised Beth even knew such words.

'There I've run out of ideas,' Beth said eventually. Then they both began to laugh. 'Oh, Dottie, you are good for me. But what about Mum? She'll be so upset.'

'She will, but your dad's there.'

'We're not going to stay with her. We've told her so in a letter. I can't think where she got the idea from.'

'Just hoping, that's what it is, just desperately hoping. Imagination can play cruel tricks when you're lonely. We'll have to feel sorry for her.'

Beth was still trembling with distress, so Dottie took matters into her own hands and got out Caroline's medicinal brandy from the back of the top cupboard. 'Here! Have a drop of this. The doctor gave me it that time when I cut my hand bad and nearly fainted.'

So Beth did, and was just finishing the last drop when her mum came home.

Caroline smelled the brandy as she wrapped her arms around this beloved daughter of hers. 'Darling! I am so sorry. So very sorry.' At the back of her mind Caroline was relieved that she and Peter had told the twins of Suzy's unexpected appearance. What if they hadn't been truthful? The twins would never have trusted them again. Caroline recollected their hurt, their astonishment when they'd heard she'd been in the Rectory, remembered Beth's explosive fury and Alex's bewilderment.

'Thank you, Dottie. I didn't realise Beth had heard.'

'I'll be off then, Doctor.' Dottie patted Beth's hand and left, wishing – oh, how she wished – she could put it all right. 'Gave her a brandy. Hope you don't mind.'

'Of course not. She needed something. Thank you.'

After she'd gone, Beth dropped into one of the rockers. 'What hurts is her saying that to the whole village. You know what it's like at the coffee morning. It's our private affairs being discussed. Why, *why* has she done this to us?'

'I don't know. Honestly I don't.'

'Poor Dad. Where is he?'

'I expect he's putting himself back together. He gave Valda a roasting and not half. I've never known him so lacking in compassion. It's not like him at all.'

The front door crashed back and in came Alex and Peter. Alex stood in the kitchen doorway, looking at Beth. They didn't need to speak because they each knew exactly what the other was thinking.

'Mum. I've decided.'

'Decided what, Alex?'

'Suzy Palmer has done her best to ruin things for Beth and me. She couldn't have been more cruel saying things like that to people in the village. To confirm our parentage to the world was monstrous. Therefore, as far as we are concerned, this is finito. That right, Beth?' He knew there was no need for her to confirm his decision, but he needed to hear her declaration out loud so there'd be no mistakes in the future.

'I agree.'

'Good. Then we'll put it behind us. We don't want anything at all to do with her, ever. What she's done is not what a real mother would do. She obviously doesn't truly care about us. She just wants her own way, at whatever cost to us and you. Mum, let's go out for lunch.'

'We don't normally on Sundays. I've got everything sorted, actually.'

'Not cooked, though.'

'No, not cooked yet.'

'I'll go and ask Dad.' Alex went to the study and found his dad seated at his desk, his head in his hands. House rules made Alex hesitate before speaking, but Peter, recognising Alex's footsteps, said, 'Yes, Alex, what is it?'

'Lunch? Shall we go out? We all need cheering up. Beth and I could pay for it with the money Granny sent us, like a special treat. Please, we'd like to. Please, Dad. We just need to get away from the house.'

Peter straightened up. 'Good thinking. Let's go.'

Chapter 6

Every member of the embroidery group arrived early on the Monday following the commotion outside the church, not wishing to miss a single moment of their opportunity to gossip about it. Barbara the weekender wasn't there but they had a new member. Much to their surprise, it was Mercedes Barclay, which was a little inconvenient as they'd been hoping to have an in-depth gossip about her, and Ford too.

'Have you got room for another one?' she said. 'I do embroidery, not nearly as well as you all, I expect, but I do try. I've got a sample with me if you'd like to see.' She rooted in her over-large bag and brought out a piece of work neatly wrapped in a snow-white linen tea-towel.

They crowded round to see, all hoping that they wouldn't have to pretend to like it. It was about ten square inches in size, and every single bit of it was embroidered in exquisite colours with gold threadwork woven throughout. It was quite like a section of a peacock's tail, incredibly detailed, almost blinding the eye with the richness of the colours. 'Intense' and 'splendid' were the words that sprang to mind.

There were gasps all round.

'Who taught you to do this?' asked Evie.

'I taught myself. Took a lot of goes till I got the hang of it, then it came to me one day. I love colours. I never wear black nor grey. Have I made it too vivid? Maybe it's all too gaudy? Is it?'

Sheila Bissett was instantly jealous of Mercedes' skill. At one time she'd have been sarcastic about it and deliberately hurt Mercedes, but since the death of her baby grandson Sheila had mellowed. 'Why, it's wonderful,' she said warmly. 'Absolutely wonderful. Isn't it, Evie?'

'It most certainly is. We shall be proud to have you join us. Is that what you would like to do?'

'Oh, yes please.'

'Have you ever exhibited?'

Mercedes almost froze at the prospect. 'No, of course not.'

'Well, there's an exhibition coming up in two months' time in Culworth. We're exhibiting a panel we've done for the church. Could we enter this as a sample from a Turnham Malpas embroidery group member?'

Mercedes blushed bright red. 'Do you honestly think it's good enough? Really?'

Evie waxed so enthusiastic that Mercedes was convinced.

Dottie said, 'You know, we have a flag to do on that ship, perhaps Mercedes could do it? It's got to be all vivid colours and very intense, no nice duck-egg blue background like I specialise in. This kind of work would be just right, don't you think?'

Mercedes was taken aback by their very genuine approval. She hadn't felt so happy since she'd arrived in Turnham Malpas.

Once they'd settled to work, naturally the main topic of conversation was the arrival of Suzy Meadows at the coffee morning.

'Frankly,' said Sheila. 'I don't know how she had the cheek. She did right to leave as soon as they were born. The hussy!'

'She said that the twins were going to stay with her for a few days. I find it hard to believe,' said Evie, who'd been helping behind the counter serving the cakes, and had heard every word.

'So do I. Those poor children. Well, they're not children, are they? They're almost grown up. Was there really any need to broadcast a fact which we all know already but never mention?' said Bel.

'Well, you can't, can you? As it happened, what he did turned out for the best anyway. Though he shouldn't have, now should he?'

'No, but heck, he was gorgeous at the time. Come to think of it he still is. He's got no business wearing a dog-collar.' Sheila looked rather yearningly out of the window.

Mercedes was thoroughly confused by all the innuendoes and no names. 'I don't wish to be nosy, but who are we talking about?'

Bel whispered into her ear the names of the main players and Mercedes' eyes grew wider at each sentence. 'No! Has she long blonde hair and big blue eyes and a round face and a lovely fair skin?'

Four pairs of wide eyes stared at her, awaiting further revelation.

'She was leaving the Rectory when Ford went to call. He thought she was the Rector's wife, till the Rector explained.'

Stunned silence greeted this remark. Needles were idly poised over the tapestry, mouths hung open.

'She'd called at the Rectory? Is he sure?' asked Sheila.

'Well, that's how he described the person who was just leaving.'

Sheila dropped the needle she was threading and bent to pick it up. Her voice floated up from somewhere near the floor. 'She'd better not turn up again in this village, or I shall have something to say.'

'Dottie, did you know she'd called at the Rectory?' Evie asked.

'No. Nothing was said when I was there this morning.'

Sheila, emerging from under the table, said, 'Well, Peter certainly had something to say Sunday morning. I've never heard him speak like that, ever. No matter how angry he is he's always a *gentle* man, but he wasn't yesterday. It's a wonder Valda didn't go into complete meltdown.'

Someone muttered, 'It'd have been better if she had, the old cow.'

Bel had been working at the Royal Oak that morning and was bursting to know what he'd said. 'What did he say then?'

'He came bursting out of church,' said Dottie, 'halfway through stripping off his paraphernalia, and caught Valda saying it all over again for those who hadn't heard. But then I saw Beth running home and I ran after her, so I don't know.'

'*I* heard.' Sheila put her errant needle down on the table, and, with the length of tapestry wool she'd been trying to thread clinging to the front of her jumper, she repeated almost word for word what Peter had said: 'I have never in all my years as a priest been so devastatingly angry. Whatever Suzy Meadows-that-was said about my children going to stay with her it is absolutely untrue. The children, my *beloved* children, are not going to stay with her and have already told her so in a letter. It is not your fault that the tale you have told is untrue but it *is* your fault, Valda, that you are deliberately causing my wife and my children considerable pain with your tittle-tattle, knowing full well it's very likely they'll be within hearing. You should be ashamed of yourself. Nothing short of a public apology will satisfy me.'

'And did she, Sheila?'

'Oh yes. Even Valda couldn't refuse once she'd looked into Peter's face and seen his pain. And quite right, too. He turned his back on us all and went back into the church. Caroline was absolutely stricken, she went home. Alex looked as though he was carved from stone and couldn't move. The rest of us were shattered. We've kept their secret all these years and wham! It was all out in the open, just like that.' She plucked the length of wool from her jumper and threaded her needle with shaking fingers. 'I still feel funny even now just thinking about it.'

They broke for tea at this point. As they'd moved their chairs to the tea table, the sound of Zack striding up and down the churchyard with his super-mower reminded them of Ford Barclay.

Dottie said to Mercedes, 'Didn't we have a lovely day at the races with you and Ford? It really was so kind of him to take us all, and it was all so posh. I wonder if we thanked him enough, because we did enjoy it.'

'Ford loves giving people treats, he really does. He's worked twenty-four/seven for years and now he's retired he can indulge himself in giving friends a good time.'

'Well, that's nice to know because it was smashing. Are you beginning to settle in, then?'

Mercedes paused for a moment and then said, 'I am now. This afternoon, thanks to you all.'

'You've got a lovely house,' Sheila remarked.

'Mmm.'

'Where did you live before? Not round here because your accent's different.'

Mercedes hesitated, then mumbled, 'Birmingham.'

Bel remarked, 'I've a second cousin who lives in Birmingham.'

Mercedes hurriedly said, 'It's strange for us living here, all trees and country.'

'Well, yes, but we all love it. You know everyone, you see.'

'Will you be coming to our wedding anniversary party? You'll all be invited.'

'We'd heard. Well, yes, I expect we all will. Got all your plans made?' Bel was puzzled that she couldn't seem to remember where they'd lived before. It was odd.

Mercedes positively blossomed. A lovely smile came over her face as she said, 'Oh, yes. That Jimbo is brilliant, you know. It'll spoil it if I tell you everything that's going to happen, but he's got musicians—'

'You mean a pop band?'

'No, no. One in keeping with the Elizabethan banquet. And

there will be dancers and a play and lots of lovely food and drink. I tell you, Ford has really gone to town on it, but we couldn't have done it without Jimbo. He's lovely isn't he?'

Bel agreed. 'Mind you, he has a temper. I remember once—'

'I say,' interrupted Sheila, who didn't want to listen to yet another of Bel's stories about working for Jimbo, 'What's happening with the youth club? There's rumours going round that Ford has decided to spend some money on it instead of the lunch club for the Senior Citizens. Not that I go, so it doesn't bother me.'

Mercedes launched enthusiastically into the latest news. 'Ah, well, they've planned some splendid trips out. I can't remember everything, but first there's a midnight walk on Brocken High Barrow next week.'

Dottie was amazed. 'Brocken High Barrow, at midnight? What are they thinking of? They'll be up to all sorts of things they shouldn't, up there in the dark.'

'Well, anyway, after that they're off on a weekend camping before the weather gets too bad with a hike along the South Coast Path.'

Someone muttered, 'Rather them than me.'

'They're all very excited about that. Oh, and then there's a trip to a bowling alley with another youth club before Christmas. And there's talk of a narrowboat holiday in the summer, a boat for twelve. Ford's so excited about that he's even thinking of going with them. Then, before Christmas, they're planning a ghost-hunting expedition in some castle or other, take your own candle.'

Bel was astounded. 'Have they gone completely mad? When I went to a youth club we got all excited about a table-tennis match against the Scouts in the church hall with the vicar and his wife standing guard just in case, though in case of what we never knew. Fat chance with a load of boring scouts with bare knees and woggles. None of this gallivanting about.'

Dottie asked if Peter knew what was going on. 'After all, it is a church thingy.'

Evie suggested that maybe Kate and Venetia had cleared it with Peter already.

'Well,' said Sheila. 'I am amazed. It's not quite the thing, is it? Too much temptation. You know what that lot in Penny Fawcett are like. They're on a par with that pub of theirs in the High Street, the Jug and Bottle – all drunk and no class whatsoever. Imagine *twelve* of 'em on a boat. Can't expect 'em to behave proper when it's a mixed group. The mind boggles. Glad I'm not in charge; I'd never sleep a wink.'

Evie was far more trusting than the others. 'Mrs Fitch wouldn't allow anything untoward, I'm sure. She is a teacher after all.'

'There was a piece in the paper the other day about these teenagers who'd gone swimming naked in a lake and—'

Sheila nodded briskly. 'I read that. It was disgusting. But look at that time when we had the pyjama party and those two were found upstairs in the bedroom at Glebe House, knowing nothing about the house being on fire at all. A lot of *them* were from Penny Fawcett.

Mercedes was laughing. 'Did you say at Glebe House? Really? A pyjama party? Which bedroom were they in?' Her eyes were alight with fun.

'It wasn't funny at the time, believe me, Mercedes. They could have died 'cept they got the fire out in quick time.'

Bel, sensing that there would be a big argument if they weren't careful, said softly, 'I'm sure Kate Fitch won't allow things to get out of hand. After all, some of them will have been at the primary school when they were younger. They know she has standards.'

'Yes,' said Sheila, tapping a well-manicured nail on the table, 'but what about Venetia? You can't say *she's* got standards. We all know what she was.'

Evie glanced at her watch and said, 'Shall we get on?'

At that precise moment Zack walked in for his usual Monday afternoon treat of a cup of tea. 'Hello, Merc! Surprised to find you here embroidering. Heard that wonderful mower of mine? I shall always be in debt to your hubby for that mower. Transformed my life, it has. Has Ford got any good tips this week? Last week's turned up trumps. Fifty-four pounds and fifty pence I won. Gone towards me and the wife going to America to see our daughter.'

Mercedes rooted about in her bag and took out a square of paper. 'Here you are. Polar Knight. Three-thirty at Doncaster on Saturday.'

No one in the embroidery group said a word. They finished their cups of tea as though not a thing had been said about betting, nor about Doncaster, nor the three-thirty, nor a horse called Polar Knight. They popped their cups and saucers back on the tray, and left Zack looking at his square of paper and sipping his own, very welcome cup of tea.

Polar Knight won at Doncaster, and every member of the embroidery group had put a bet on him. They couldn't wait for Zack to call in for his cup of tea the following Monday until they remembered he'd said it would be the last time he'd be cutting the grass until the spring. Drat!

Peter sensed the challenge in Beth's voice when she announced she was going with the youth club on the midnight walk on Friday to Brocken High Barrow. He winked at Caroline and, taking the hint, she didn't protest.

'Alex going, Beth?' Peter asked.

'No, and don't suggest it to him. He'll only interfere and tell me what to do, or, more likely, what not to do, and I'm not having it. Pass the sauce, please.'

Caroline passed Beth the tartare sauce. 'Here you are. You sound very definite.'

'No, but I am sixteen going on seventeen and so I'm going.'

'I see.'

'I mean it about Alex. Anyway, it's not his kind of thing. Too daring for him!'

'It'll be cold this time of year,' Caroline remarked.

'I'm tough, didn't you know? I don't care if it throws down with rain. I'm going. I'm fed up with being good little Beth, daughter of the Rector and the Doctor. I'm stepping out of line for once.'

'That's fine, darling. Quite right,' Peter said mildly. He poured himself a glass of wine. 'More wine, Caroline?'

'Yes, please. I'll be glad to see the end of this bottle; it's not to my taste.'

'I'll try it.' Beth passed her glass to Peter. 'Might as well help to finish it if Mum's not keen.'

'Are you sure about wine?'

'Some of them at the youth club buy wine and cider and stuff at the off-licence in Culworth, but I think it's better to drink at home. Still ... that is an idea. Something else I could try that I've never tried before.'

'What's brought this on?'

'It's boring, boring, boring being a Rector's daughter, always expected to be goody-goody, and I'm absolutely sick of it.'

Peter said he could see her point. 'I understand. It's people automatically assuming that you're well behaved and sensible, always doing your prep and helping with the junior church and going to visit Muriel.'

Beth, her fork full of food, hesitated and then came out with, 'That's another thing. I'm stopping doing that. It's ridiculous. She doesn't even know who I am. Well, sometimes she does, but usually not. It's a complete waste of time.'

'No, Beth, it's—'

'It is, Mum. An utter, utter waste of time. I've been going round there once a week for years—'

'One actually.'

'Well, nearly two, and I'm fed up with it. Then I take her to the Store for something to do. She doesn't know what she wants and Ralph doesn't give her a list, so we stand about for hours and I feel a fool. So I shall tell Ralph I'm not going any more. He might even be quite glad. He hates people seeing how bad she is. And it won't get better.'

Caroline began to challenge her about this but Peter forestalled her.

'If that's how you feel, then by all means go round and tell Ralph you don't want to do it any more, but please, do it gently. I can see your point. You've been more than diligent going round there every week but there is a limit and I don't suppose Muriel will notice. She is far worse than even just a few weeks ago.'

'Thanks, Dad. As soon as I've finished I'm going round there. And I might not even do my prep. See what effect that has at school. They can tut-tut as much as they like. Well I shall give them a surprise, and it's about time, too.'

The rest of their meal was eaten in silence, and Beth went round to Ralph and Muriel's the moment she'd finished her last mouthful of pudding.

She used to be able to open the door and call out, 'It's me, Beth, from the Rectory.' But now the door had to be kept firmly locked in case Muriel mistakenly decided to go out and subsequently went missing, which she had done several times.

Ralph opened the door and greeted her with pleasure. 'Why, Beth! How lovely. Do come in, dear. Muriel's in the sitting room, or she was.'

Beth's first thought was how weary Ralph appeared to be. Another sleepless night, she guessed.

'Hello, Muriel, it's—'

'Beth! How lovely to see you! How kind. Come and tell me all about school and what you've been up to.' She patted the seat next to her on the sofa and smiled cheerfully.

Beth felt dreadful. After her rebellion at home, now she was faced with this surprising recognition. What should she do? She'd never intended seeing Muriel tonight. What she wanted to do was to tell Ralph she wasn't coming any more and then quietly disappear, but no such luck.

'Did you win your netball match?'

'Yes, we did, thank you. They were a good team and it was a struggle, but in the end we won. Thank you. How have you been, Muriel?'

'Very well, thank you, dear.' She called out rather imperiously, 'Ralph, could we have a cup of tea?'

'Yes, Muriel. In a minute.'

Short of something to talk about, Beth told her about the midnight hike with the youth club. 'So we shall be leaving at ten-thirty in a minibus from outside the church.'

'Ralph! What have you done with my cup of tea? Where is it?'

'In a moment, dear.'

'Beth! I want a cup of tea. Where is it? Ralph never gets things done in time. Where is he? Has he gone out?'

'No, he's in the kitchen.'

'I want Ralph. Ralph?'

'I'll go and make the tea.'

Muriel began to get up. 'No, I'll make it.'

'No, Muriel, you sit there. You've had a busy day; you must be tired. I'll do it and send Ralph in to you.'

'I have been very busy. There's so much to do in the house. Must keep it tidy. The vacuuming is so exhausting.'

'Of course.'

Beth went into the kitchen and offered to make the tea. 'You sit with Muriel, Ralph. I'll make the tea.'

'Thank you, Beth.'

Ralph never made comments about Muriel's incapacity. He always treated her as though everything in her head was perfectly normal when it manifestly wasn't.

Beth carried the tray in. Muriel inspected it and found fault in a harsh voice that was completely different from her normal tone. 'You've not put a cloth on, Muriel. I never have a tray without a cloth on it.'

'Very well, I'll go and get it.' But she didn't, and Muriel instantly forgot then decided to pester for her tea.

'It's not brewed yet; it won't be a moment.'

Beth heard Ralph smother a sigh. She looked at him and said very softly, 'You need more help, Ralph. You can't manage single-handed.'

'She's not going in a home, Beth. I couldn't cope with that.'

'Then get some help with meals and the cleaning and bathing her. Then you needn't put her in a home. But you can't keep ignoring facts ...'

Muriel snatched the cup of tea from Beth. 'About time, too.' Between them they almost had a spill.

'It's too hot yet, Muriel.'

But she was too late. Muriel sipped it and then snapped, 'It's too hot. Why is it too hot?'

'You go, Beth. I'll deal with her. Please, just go.'

From his voice Beth knew he was acutely embarrassed by Muriel's confusion. So was she, and completely devastated, too.

She rushed home and burst into tears.

Peter heard her from the study and went to see what the matter was. He sat down on a kitchen chair and Beth sat on his knee and put her arms round his neck.

'It's Muriel! She's worse than ever tonight. Poor Ralph. She doesn't know how bad she is. It's Ralph who's suffering. I feel awful.'

'Have you told him you don't want to go any more?'

'I didn't get a chance. He showed me straight into the sitting room and there she was. How does he live with it?'

'I honestly do not know, but he loves her, you see, so he does his best by her. Did she recognise you at all?'

'Yes, and then she didn't and called me Muriel of all things, and was such a pest, so demanding, so unlike her. It's terrible. I can't go again. Ralph almost died of embarrassment. Dad, it could happen to anyone, couldn't it?' She began crying again.

'Yes. Anyone.'

'It won't happen to Mum, will it? I couldn't bear it if it did. I love her so.'

'I know you do.'

'I'm never, never going to stay with Suzy. She gave me away and I can't forgive her for that, but then I wouldn't have Mum for my mum, would I? And I wouldn't have it any other way. I never think she's not my mum, you know. Never. She is, you see.'

'Yes. I'm glad she is.'

'She must have been so brave when she found out about ... well ... about you and Suzy. So filled with love and needing a baby and so pleased she could adopt yours. At least we weren't anybody's. I've never really thought about it like that before. Were you embarrassed? About what happened?'

Peter studied her question and eventually said, 'Not embarrassed, no. Deeply ashamed of myself.'

'But you gave Mum what she longed for – two children to love.'

Peter felt incredibly confused. 'Not quite as straightforward as that.'

'Oh! Right. Can you love two people at the same time, then?'

'I'm not sure I should be discussing this with you.'

'I am sixteen and I need to know, and it is about me ... and Alex.'

Peter nodded. 'The most I can say is that I have deeply loved your mother since the very first time I met her. Nothing and nobody could come between us whatever happens, whoever happens, and what occurred with Suzy Meadows was something quite separate from that and I still don't know why it came about, but it did, and the guilt I felt has lain like a stone wrapped around my heart ever since. There, that's all I can say about it.'

'But you're glad you have us?'

'I haven't a vocabulary big enough to tell you how glad I am and always have been.'

'So it feels like a betrayal of Mum?'

'Yes.'

'She must love you dreadfully.'

Peter didn't answer for a moment. 'She must. And you see, there's no feeling in the world like it when you hold your child in your arms for the first time, adopted or biological. Nothing matches it. So I suppose that helps.'

Beth wrapped her arms around his shoulders and pressed her cheek to his. 'And I can tell you this: you are my dad and my mum is my mum and there'll never be any change to that. No change at all. Whatever anyone says or does.'

'Tell your mum that, will you? She's been broken-hearted by Suzy Meadows turning up so unexpectedly.'

'I'll do it right now.'

Caroline, still feeling threatened by Suzy presenting herself at the Rectory – after all, what was to stop her from arriving again and again? – was comforted by Beth's passionate declaration that she loved Caroline and had no need for Suzy whatsoever. The two of them clung together in such a meaningful embrace that they both cried and had to share a tissue that Beth found in her pocket.

'So don't ever worry, Mum, ever again. I'm yours and, like it or not, you're stuck with me.'

'That's the best thing I've heard in years, darling. I love you so.'

A final kiss and a cup of tea in front of the Aga, each in a rocking chair, talking about the meaning of life, brought healing to Caroline, and Suzy faded into the back of her mind. How she loved this girl for having said what she did. The love between them seemed to have increased tenfold.

Chapter 7

There were ten members of the youth club, plus Venetia and Kate, waiting for the minibus for the midnight walk on Brocken High Barrow. Ford, as they'd all been instructed to call him, came along to see them off. Five came from Penny Fawcett, two from Little Derehams and three from Turnham Malpas. Beth was in a defiant mood once more. She'd begged Alex not to go.

'Just because we're twins it doesn't mean we're inseparable and need to do everything together like we've always done,' she said.

'I'd like to go on the bowling trip.'

'Well, you do that and I'll not go then. Right?'

Alex hesitated. 'I'd much rather I came. You know what that lot from Penny Fawcett are like.'

'They're not bad. Well, Graham's fine, Ben's a nerd, thick as it's possible to be but harmless, Jake's a bit of all right—'

'Exactly. He's always hanging round you. Every word you say he treats as gospel.'

'You're being ridiculous, absolutely ridiculous. Tom's fine, like you, well behaved and totally boring with it—'

'That's a bit mean. I'm not totally boring, am I?'

'You can be if you think someone's not behaving as they should. Remember that time when George got you annoyed and you lost your temper! God, that was so funny! Your face went puce and you looked a nerd, just like Ben.'

'Thanks, Beth, thanks very much. I wasn't having him taunting you, and if he does it again I shall probably thump him.'

'I'm perfectly well able to take care of myself. I do not need you hovering, right?'

'Look, I haven't forgotten what happened in Africa—'

'Shut up! Shut up! I don't want to hear.' Beth clapped both hands over her ears. He mustn't remind her. He mustn't.

Alex prised her hands from her ears and said, '*That's* what I'm talking about. That Jake has so much testosterone. Sex is his total obsession, and you know that.'

'Shut up! This is the new Beth, not the goody-goody Beth I used to be. I'm taking charge and doing exactly as I like, so there. What you get up to is your affair and I shan't tell the parents, so don't you let on about me, OK?'

'I don't agree.'

'Well, I do, and that's that.' She stormed off to her own bedroom, slammed the door and burst into tears.

So now she stood waiting with the others, glad she'd put on her thickest anorak and that her mother had persuaded her to wear thick socks with her Wellingtons. Mothers had some uses, she supposed.

Beth had a wonderful time. The screaming wind bowled them along faster than they wanted but it was so exhilarating, with the dark, dark sky, the clouds racing across quicker than she could ever remember, and the feel of her cheeks getting colder and colder. How glad she was of Jake's arm around her waist keeping her upright. But at the end of the walk, as they were striding back along the Barrow towards the minibus, Beth's defiance fell away and she began to feel distinctly odd. 'Jake,' she said, 'that lemonade you gave me – what kind was it? I feel really weird.'

'Just ordinary lemonade, from home,' he replied casually. 'Here, let me help you; you don't want to get blown over the edge.' He put his arm round her shoulders and hugged her close. 'Let's hang back, they won't go without us.'

'I don't want to hang back. I'm cold and tired and I want to go home.'

But Jake had other ideas. Beth was by far the most attractive girl in the whole group. He'd always thought so since she was about fourteen and just back from Africa. As far as he was concerned, tonight was the right moment, in the dark. He held her back and made to kiss her.

'Jake! What the heck ... Stop it! I'm not interested.'

'But I am. Don't tease.'

'I'm not. I'm just walking along.' She gave him an almighty push and he almost lost his footing, so she grabbed him back and before she knew it he was kissing her, like she'd never been kissed before. It sent thrills up and down her spine and she wished ...

'Come on you two, or you'll be left behind.' It was Venetia.

'We're coming,' Jake said sulkily.

'You OK, Beth?'

'Apart from feeling very sleepy. What time is it?'

'One-thirty. Time we set off home.'

There was a throb in Beth's voice which Venetia recognised. She knew all about exciting throbs in people's voices and she made a note to mention it to Kate. That Jake! He'd even tried it on with *her* one night when they'd all been to the cinema in Culworth, but a good slapped face did the trick. But Beth! Peter would kill yours truly if anything happened.

Which wasn't exactly what Beth was thinking. She rather had the idea that she wouldn't tell her dad a thing about it. This was her life, her privacy, her doing as she wanted and not as the entire village and her parents expected of her.

But, shock of shocks, Jake came round to the Rectory the next morning.

Caroline answered the door and greeted him enthusiastically. 'Hello! It's Jake, isn't it? Do come in. Alex isn't up yet.'

'Oh, right. Is Beth up?'

Slightly taken aback, Caroline said she thought she'd heard her in the shower a while ago. 'I've been in the garden, you see, so I don't know what's happening. Go into the sitting room. I'll let Beth know you're here.'

So Jake sat on the sofa and looked around. This wasn't the sitting room of a member of the clergy living on his stipend, no, not at all. Then he remembered that Beth's mother was a doctor still in practice. He guessed Beth was very carefully brought up and he'd have to watch his step, but by her response last night, maybe ...

Beth walked in, and that thrilling kissing of his came vividly to mind and thrilled her all over again.

'Hi, Jake.'

'I thought we might go out this morning.'

'Out? Where?'

'Well, I don't know.'

'I've no money for going into Culworth. I've bust the lot on some DVDs.' She couldn't believe he'd turned up here. But that same thrill ran up and down her spine, making her wish for more.

'What about the coffee morning in the village hall?'

The idea of everyone seeing her there with him ... 'I haven't had my breakfast yet and I never go anywhere without it. Come in the kitchen and we can talk while I eat.'

Jake thought this a daft idea but better than nothing. He hadn't enough money to pay for two bus tickets and entertainment in Culworth so there was no alternative.

'OK then. Lead the way.' He made certain to sit as close as possible, not opposite but at right angles and well up to her corner of the table. She looked stunning this morning, as fresh as a daisy and young and just as untouched. Her platinum-blonde hair, fair skin and round cheeks, and those gorgeous blue eyes ...

'I'll carry on with my gardening, OK?' Caroline said as she breezed in, but Beth was too preoccupied with making sure she appeared her best to give an answer. 'See you in a while.' Caroline found herself rather nonplussed about the unexpected arrival of Jake. Still, she surmised, it might be the first of many such callers.

Beth was relieved she had showered and hadn't come down as she often did on a Saturday, in her pyjamas, with just her face washed and her hair roughly gathered in a ponytail to keep it out of the way. What did you say to someone you wished was kissing you and not sitting beside you sipping a cup of tea poured from your very own teapot in the shape of Winnie the Pooh? It was no good, she'd have to leave her childish things behind, but she did love this silly teapot of hers.

'You got much prep to do this weekend?'

Beth nodded. 'Well, yes, I have, rather a lot. I went on strike last night and didn't do a thing. This first year in the sixth form is hard work. Did you find it hard?'

'Upper Sixth is worse but I don't bother very much, just enough to keep the teachers quiet.'

'Where do you want to go after school?'

'I'm taking a gap year. Going to America or somewhere, and then to university.'

'To do what?'

Jake obviously had no intention of revealing what he was going to do because he changed the subject abruptly. 'When you've finished this banquet you're consuming, shall we go for a walk?'

'What about down behind Hipkin Gardens?'

'OK. That'll be fine.'

'Jake. How did you get here from Penny Fawcett?'

'Bike.'

'That's about four miles?'

'I came over the fields. It's quicker that way.'

'I see.' He must be very interested in me, she thought, because that's a rough ride.

'I'll clean my teeth then ...' She neatly cleared her dishes away into the dishwasher, smiled briefly and disappeared.

Jake remembered he hadn't cleaned his before he set out. He listened for footsteps and heard nothing, so he rushed to the kitchen sink and filled his mouth with water time after time, forcing it between his teeth to rid them of any stray bits of chocolate cake, which was all he could find in the cupboard at home. For the first time ever he wished his mother was a better housekeeper. He envied Beth her substantial breakfast. No wonder she was all curves. And God she was! Beautiful curves, and he wanted to touch her ...

There were footsteps in the kitchen and in walked Alex, just as Jake was sitting down again.

'Hi, Jake. What are you doing here?'

'Going a walk with Beth.'

'Oh! I see. Excuse me while I eat my breakfast, will you.' He weighed her Winnie the Pooh teapot in his hand. 'None left. Thought not. I'll have milk instead.'

Alex never spoke again. All he did was sit down and delve into his breakfast: a huge bowl of cereal, topped with a sliced banana, three slices of toast and marmalade, and two glasses of milk, followed by the remains of a big pot of yoghurt he found in the fridge. Jake sat, fascinated by the amount of food Alex had consumed. Well, he was a big chap, a lot taller than himself, so perhaps he needed it.

Where on earth was Beth? How long did it take to clean your teeth?

Alex still hadn't spoken.

Eventually Jake heard her coming down the stairs.

Alex did speak at last. 'Where might you be going with Beth?'

'Just for a walk.'

'Where?'

'Behind Hipkin Gardens, Beth said.'

Alex made a performance out of checking his watch. 'Right.'

Beth overheard their conversation. Head high, she marched down the hall, her teeth gritted and her temper rising. 'Come along, Jake. We've plenty of time. Lunch isn't till one.'

Through the open kitchen door Alex saw she was wearing her newest outfit and he was full of misgivings.

But Beth hadn't a care in the world. She was delighted that Jake was so good-looking. She hoped someone would see her. But then she guessed that perhaps they'd rush straight round to the Rectory and tell her dad. Well, if they did, so what? He appeared to approve of her breaking out of the mould of being a goody-goody child from the Rectory.

As they reached the entrance to the woods behind Hipkin Gardens, Jake gently took hold of her hand and squeezed it, and she loved the warm, confident feel of his fingers gripping hers and the closeness it brought. She remembered the kisses he'd given her, and hoped for more. Her heart thumped with excitement.

Soon they reached a clearing where there were lots of tree trunks that had never been taken away after they'd been felled, and Beth sat down on one in the hope Jake would kiss her again.

Jake obediently perched on the same tree trunk and said, as someone would who believed in being upfront, 'That brother of yours ...'

Scathingly Beth said, 'Take no notice of *him*.'

'Does he always make a note of where and why you're going out and who with?'

Beth lied. 'No-o-o. He doesn't bother about me very much. We each do our own thing.'

'He's timing us.'

'No, you're wrong. He's probably got somewhere to go and was just checking he wasn't going to be late.'

'Can't be Culworth; he's missed the bus.'

'He has a bike. Anyway, I haven't come out to discuss Alex's whys and wherefores.'

'It's just that at school he's good fun, a real mate.'

'Yes, well.' Beth looked into his face, a face so close she only had to lean forward less than half a metre and they would have been nose to nose. She looked directly into his eyes, those brown eyes with a kind of tigerish glint. He was altogether too tempting, was Jake. But even in her new mood of not caring one jot what people thought of her, she didn't quite dare ...

Jake grinned at her. 'Go on, then.'

'Go on what?'

'Kiss me like you want to. I can see it in your face.'

'No, you can't!'

'Yes, I can.'

So she did. Just a peck. But she knew there was more to it than that. She'd seen Mum and Dad kissing, lingeringly and meaningfully, and that was exactly what she wanted to do with Jake, like in films. Desperately wanted it to be just how she'd imagined it. She'd try it.

But then so did Jake and they were kissing as never before, more seriously than when they'd kissed on the midnight walk.

His arms went round her and hers round him, and it was delicious. This was living, this was! He was running his hands up and down her spine, caressing her and then his hands were feeling her rather than caressing. Beth drew back. Something about his urgency alarmed her.

'Come on. What's the matter?'

'Nothing.'

'You've never kissed properly before, have you? Tongues and such?'

She lied again. 'Of course I have.'

'All right, then, you have, but I know you haven't.'

'You're well experienced, are you?' There was a sceptical note in her voice which annoyed him.

'What? Me? Of course. Eighteen next month and not kissed anyone before? Come off it.'

Somehow Beth really began to feel alarmed. There was a slight threat coming from him now, and she wasn't having that. She sat admiring her new shoes, pretending to check the straps were tight enough, knocking a fallen leaf off the right heel, anything to give her time to assess this hugely attractive male who fascinated her so very much. 'Let's walk on further.'

'OK.' Jake got to his feet and offered her a hand to help her up.

Once they were on the move she began to feel better about him. She showed him a few birds she recognised, they stood on the little footbridge over the stream, admired the changing colour of the overhanging leaves, but when Jake suggested they crossed Shepherd's Hill and went into Sykes Wood she refused.

'Absolutely not. People from Turnham Malpas don't go into those woods.'

'Nobody? That's ridiculous.'

Indignantly Beth said, 'It isn't. Those woods are haunted.'

'Haunted?' Jake laughed at her.

'Yes. I'm not going in. The trees are so close together you can't see ahead of yourself, and there are strange noises. Witches met there a few years ago, and one of them got burned to death.'

'In Sykes Wood?'

'Not burned in the wood itself, but she did get burned to death during one of their meetings or séances, or whatever they call them.'

'Well, I live in Penny Fawcett and I haven't heard a word about all that. I'm going in. Come on. Cross the road.'

He stood temptingly in the middle of Shepherd's Hill waiting for her, smiling temptingly and crooking his finger to entice her. She felt like a little kid. She mustn't look foolish, not when she was striking out as an adult. Perhaps he was right. It *was* ridiculous to talk about witches and haunting in broad daylight. So she crossed Shepherd's Hill and, taking hold of his hand, climbed the stile and went into the woods.

'There you are, you see. It's perfectly all right.'

Beth didn't answer. Already she could feel the pressure of not being able to see ahead because of the density of the trees. The path was so narrow they couldn't walk side by side, so Jake went ahead and Beth followed obediently.

It was cold and sunny that morning, but in Sykes Wood it seemed as though the sun had gone in. She wished she hadn't worn her new jacket, which wasn't meant for outdoors in early October. She stumbled over a tree root but Jake was walking so fast he didn't notice. Then he was so far ahead he'd disappeared. Beth hurried round the bend in the path and he wasn't there. Where had he gone? Why had he left her? Was it the wood playing tricks? Then he sprang out from behind a tree shouting, 'Boo!'

Beth screamed in panic. Jake took her in his arms, pressed her back against a tree trunk and began to kiss her fears away, or so he said. But immediately her mind felt as if it were splitting apart, and the memory of that nightmare in Africa burst into life. The horror of how close she'd come to being raped came flooding back ... Beth pushed every ounce of energy she had into her arms and, placing her hands on Jake's chest, she forced him away, fighting him, thrashing him, beating him with every ounce of her strength, screaming, screaming, screaming as loud as she could.

Then her power went to her legs and she was fleeing, down the path, over the stile, into Shepherd's Hill, turning right and going hell for leather towards the village and safety.

Passing the school, she drew breath and tried to compose herself, but the urgent need to get home made her begin running again. She'd no door key. She'd have to ring the bell. Jake's bike was still propped against the house wall, and the panic came back. She hammered on the door and Alex was there, pulling her in over the step.

Gasping for breath, her mouth dry with fear, Beth struggled to say, 'Mum! Where's Mum?'

And she was in her arms.

Safe.

Held tight.

Kissed.

Loved.

'Darling! Come into the kitchen right away. Put the kettle on, Alex, and make a cup of tea for us all.'

Peter came in from the back garden. 'It's no good, Alex, you'll have to give me a hand. Your mother wants this lilac out and the roots are enormous ... what's the matter?'

Beth extricated herself from Caroline's arms. Not catching anyone's eye, certainly not Alex's, she gasped, 'Sykes Wood. It's haunted just like everyone says it is. I really got myself frightened. Jake wanted to go in and persuaded me ... it was all right ... but it isn't.'

'Where's Jake now?'

Beth looked at Peter. 'He must be following me home. His bike's still here.' She gasped for breath again and flopped down on to a chair. 'I'm so thirsty.'

Caroline caught Alex looking at her, and her heart quaked. It occurred to her that a word with Jake might be a very good idea, so she said, 'Peter, bring Jake's bike in, would you, please? You never know nowadays, it might get stolen. Tea for you?'

Peter nodded. After the tea, which they drank sitting round the kitchen table, Saturday morning became more normal, except that Jake's bike was still in the hall.

Beth knew instinctively they must never know about Jake kissing her, and more so that she enjoyed it until ... To them she'd blamed her panic on the stories of ghosts and witches in

Sykes Wood, and that was how it would stay. She wouldn't tell them or else they'd never let her out again by herself, and she wasn't having that. But his kisses were so exciting; she liked them until he got that urgent feeling about him. Would it always be like this for the rest of her life? That frightening memory spilling out of the deep enclaves of her mind? The vivid memory of that rebel soldier out there in the heat of Africa, threatening to rape her ... Oh, God! Thank you for Alex, who had killed him with the butt of the soldier's rifle ... No, she would never lose the fear.

'I'll start my prep, OK?'

Caroline gently trailed her hand along the back of Beth's shoulders. 'Feeling all right now? I've felt funny like that in Sykes Wood. No one likes it, and you won't be the last. Off you go. When I've cleared up I'm going to the coffee morning. I've a few people to see.'

Jake's bike was still there when they went to church on Sunday morning. In the afternoon Peter put it in the estate car and took it to Penny Fawcett for him, but he was out so Peter didn't get the opportunity to have a word.

On Wednesday morning Peter received a very disquieting letter from the headmaster of Alex's school. He read it twice before it sank in. Alex had beaten someone up in the changing rooms and was refusing to say why. Could Peter go to school to see the head? He would be free around 10 a.m. on Friday, if that was convenient.

He looked again at the beginning of the letter and saw it was Jake Harding whom Alex had beaten up. Alex never did anything without a very good reason and it struck Peter that maybe Beth's story about being frightened of witches in Sykes Wood and Jake not coming back for his bike might be connected. The phone rang and Peter had to pull himself together.

'Yes. Ah! Oh dear. I didn't know. Certainly. You say the

operation's today? In that case I'll call to see him tomorrow. He'll be home by then? Good. Thank you for letting me know.'

Back to his letter. And what was worse, he recollected that Alex had appeared to be in pain on Monday evening when he came home from school, and had said he was just a bit stiff after rugby, that was all. What was the matter with his children. They'd never given him a single cause for serious anxiety in all their lives and now this. Both of them.

Caroline came home at half past one and he sat down to lunch with her as soon as she came in. He'd wait till she'd eaten because she looked drained.

'Go on then, Peter, tell me the worst,' she said eventually.

'Old Ben Burton's having a gall stone operation today. I've promised to go and see him tomorrow.'

'Thank you for that snippet. But that's not it, is it?'

She was too perceptive by half, was Caroline. 'No.'

'Well?'

'It's a letter I've had from the head at Prince Henry's.'

'Oh no. Not Alex not doing his prep like Beth?'

'Alex beat up a fellow pupil in the changing rooms.'

Caroline was stunned. 'What? Alex? Who has he beaten up?' Her thoughts suddenly came together. 'Not Jake?'

Peter nodded. 'What makes you think that?'

'Mother's instinct. There must be some mistake, though.'

'Apparently not. I'm seeing the head on Friday.'

'Oh, God. As bad as that, is it?'

Peter nodded again.

'Suddenly we've got two crazy teenagers. We've never realised how lucky we've been all these years, have we, Peter? What's triggered all this? First it's Beth in rebellion and now Alex behaving completely out of character. Suzy Meadows coming has completely upset them both, as well as the two of us. You'll have to talk it through with him. Get at the truth before Friday. Or shall I?'

'In this instance I think maybe it's man's talk.'

'Right. But you tell me every word afterwards. I don't envy you.'

Alex categorically refused to explain. 'We had a push and a shove, that's all.'

'The head would not write a letter about such a minor incident.'

Alex sighed with impatience. 'We had a tiff and before we knew it we were fighting. He came off worse, but then I am much bigger than him so it's hardly surprising. Can I go now?'

'No. You're not seven, you're almost seventeen and know the difference between truth and lies, and I'm still waiting.'

Alex slumped down into the sofa even further and remained silent, not daring to look at his dad because he knew that piercing look of his would demolish his own determination.

'I'm very disappointed in you, Alex. I now have no case to offer to the head when I go on Friday. No defence of any kind. You leave me powerless. Off you go.'

Alex got to the door, put his hand on the knob and then turned back. 'If I tell you the absolute truth it is just between you and me. If you can't promise that then I won't tell you. Mum and Beth must not know. They'd be devastated.'

'I don't understand why, but very well.'

'Beth and I have always known you and Mum tell each other everything, but this time that rule has to be ignored, Dad. You've ignored that rule once before in your life, you know ... when we were conceived and now ... and now you've to do it again.'

Peter, totally humbled by Alex's forthright statement, knew he had no alternative but to agree, and braced himself for what was to come.

Alex folded his arms to hide the fact that his hands were trembling. 'I was in the showers after rugby, drying off, when

I overheard a conversation going on and I recognised Jake Harding's voice. It was the sniggering kind of conversation boys have and I realised he was saying that he'd "had" Beth while they were in the woods. That she was a virgin and he'd well, you know ... then he started talking dirty about her and I just saw red. So I beat him up there and then without saying a word. Dressed and left for lunch. There was quite a lot of blood about, and I'm not telling you what Jake was saying about her.' He got up from the sofa and made to leave.

'Just a minute. You're not saying that was the real reason for all her panic?'

Alex shook his head. 'No, I'm not. I asked her after she'd calmed down and I absolutely know she was telling me the truth. She said she panicked when he began kissing her because she remembered Africa and that soldier, and she just fled. He won't be saying it again about her if I'm around, because I shall beat him twice as hard.'

'Whilst I admire your defence of her, please remember, Alex, that beating someone up is perhaps not the answer.'

'I'm not daft, Dad. I do know the rules, but it gave me an awful lot of satisfaction.' He grinned that charming grin of his, and Peter had to smile. Then he remembered his meeting with the headmaster on Friday and wondered what on earth he would say in explanation of Alex's uncharacteristic behaviour. So much for Beth striking out into adult life. Damn his decision to take them all with him to Africa.

Chapter 8

The usual customers were sitting on their favourite settle in the bar of the Royal Oak when the main door opened and in came Ford with, very surprisingly, Muriel clinging to his arm. They were all so surprised that silence fell in the bar. Ford took her to the counter where Georgie was waiting to serve.

'An orange juice for this lady. She's thirsty, she says, so make it a nice big one, and a home-brew for me. Just a half, please.'

He took their drinks to the table where Jimmy and the others were sitting.

They all said, 'Good evening, Muriel,' but Muriel didn't reply as she was greedily drinking her orange as though she hadn't had a drink for years.

With half the glass of orange already consumed, Muriel looked up and spotted Don. 'That was nice. Hello, Don. How are you? That fall you had from the roof, you seem to have got over it.'

Rather surprised she remembered him, Don said, 'Yes, I have, thank you, Muriel. It's all the good care I had at the time. And how are you?'

'Oh! I'm very well.' She leaned across to speak confidentially to him. 'Who's that man I'm with?'

'That's Ford. He's just come to live in the village at Glebe House.'

'Oh! He's married to Liz?'

'No, Liz doesn't live there any more.'

'Oh! Doesn't she? I thought I hadn't seen her for a while. I'm going on holiday, you know.'

'Oh! Right,' said Vera. 'Where to?'

'I can't remember, but I am. Sun, that's what I want, some sun.' Then she drifted away in her head and was no longer with them.

Ford said softly, 'I found her wandering down Jacks Lane, not knowing where to go next. I'd no idea where she lived and she didn't seem to know, so I thought I'd bring her in here with me.'

'We'd better take her back. Ralph will be going berserk.' Dottie stood up. 'Come on, Muriel, we'll go and find Ralph.'

Ford swung Muriel's chair away from the table so she could get out more easily, and he realised then how little she weighed. Poor old thing. Such a lovely, distinguished face, almost aristocratic. It was such a shame.

Dottie took her arm and led her towards the door.

'Where are we going?'

'We're going back home, to your house. Ralph will be wondering where you are.'

'Ralph? I don't belong to Ralph.'

'Yes, you do, Muriel. Come along.'

The passive way in which Muriel agreed to go with her, holding her hand with childlike confidence, broke Dottie's kind heart. She remembered what a wonderful lady Muriel had always been, how thoughtful and generous in her behaviour, and how thrilled they'd all been when Ralph came back to the village and he and Muriel had married.

When they got to the door it was standing wide open. Dottie helped Muriel in over the step and took her into what she thought must be the sitting room, but it was obviously Ralph's study, because he was sitting at a desk, his head resting on his forearms, apparently fast asleep. So she turned Muriel around, found the sitting room, and seated her in front of the stove, which was sending out heat as though it were the depths of winter. 'You sit there and I'll make a cup of tea,' she said. 'Here,

I'll put the TV on; you watch that till I come back with the tray.'

First of all Dottie went to the front door and locked it firmly with bolts and keys so she couldn't escape again. Ralph was still asleep so she decided to leave him. The poor old chap, he's completely exhausted with looking after her, she thought.

They sat comfortably enough in front of the TV drinking tea. Suddenly Muriel said, 'Thank you, Dottie. I don't understand where Ralph is; he must have gone to the Store. My mother loved drinking tea sitting staring into the fire. She was very unkind to me, you know. Thought I shouldn't have a life of my own. She kept me at home to look after her when she was old, and she wouldn't let me go out with the others when I was young. Always said no, did my mother. To everything. Ralph dear,' she shouted, 'where are you? Has he gone shopping?'

'I expect he has. He won't be long.'

So they sat in silence a while longer watching TV. Dottie knew now that things were seriously wrong and that poor old Ralph had been keeping it all under wraps. Everyone in the village was aware of Muriel's illness, but she didn't think anyone had really seen just how bad it was.

Well, Muriel needed taking to bed. It was already half past ten and there was still no sign of Ralph waking up. What on earth should she do? What Muriel needed was a strong sleeping tablet to knock her out. No harm in that. At least Ralph would get some sleep. He couldn't look after her twenty-four/seven without sleep, now could he?

Dr Harris! She'd ring Dr Harris. She'd know what to do. She was only next door.

So Caroline, staying up to finish reading a book she couldn't put down, went instead to help with Muriel. She and Dottie tried to persuade her to take a sleeping tablet, but she refused point-blank, and finally they had to abandon the whole idea and get Muriel into bed without one.

Within a few minutes of lying down Muriel drifted off to sleep, and the two of them went to see Ralph.

He woke when Caroline tapped him on the shoulder. 'Steady, Ralph, careful,' she said. 'Don't get up straight away. Just listen to what I have to say. We've put Muriel to bed for you. She seems to be very settled and is asleep already. So there's no need to worry. Would you like Dottie to make you a drink before you go to bed?'

Ralph was acutely embarrassed by the situation. He simply didn't know what to say. 'I've been asleep a long time, have I? Muriel! Did she get out? Has she been missing? Is she all right? I'd no idea ...' He stood up, dazed and alarmed.

'Look, Ralph. Muriel managed to open the front door and go out. Dottie brought her home and then after a while she rang me because she was worried. And so am I. I'm very worried. Now go to bed and in the morning I shall come round and we'll have a talk ... about things.'

'Hot chocolate, Sir Ralph? And perhaps a biscuit or two?'

Ralph nodded.

'Go and sit by the fire in the sitting room and I'll bring it in.'

So they sat with him while he talked a little, but always along the lines that there was nothing the matter with Muriel except she did get a little forgetful occasionally. Caroline didn't press him. It was better left until morning.

Outside the house, after they'd waited to hear Ralph locking the door with every available security lock, they stood talking quietly.

'I'll give you a lift home, Dottie. It's a long way to walk at this time of night.'

'No, please don't. It'll do me good to have time to think for a bit. It's blooming well upset me, this has. He just won't accept she's ... kind of gone off the boil, will he?'

'Once he does accept it that will be the end as far as he is concerned, so he won't, but he obviously can't go on like this. Thank you, Dottie, for looking after her. If she was able to think straight she'd thank you, too. Goodnight, then. Are you sure I can't give you a lift?'

'Absolutely. God, I hope I never get like that.'

'She doesn't know she is unwell – well, perhaps only occasionally – so that's a blessing. Goodnight, Dottie, and thanks again for what you've done.'

By midnight the village was completely quiet. Not a light shone and nothing moved, neither car nor cat, except for an owl that swooped over the rooftops, briefly alighting on a thatched roof then diving away towards the fields again. Every other bird was asleep in its own secret spot. Even the badgers in Sykes Wood had given up their foraging for the moment. No smoke twirled from the chimney pots and there was no sound of a human voice, no squeak of a mouse nor scamper of a rat, not even a fox silently gliding by on the lookout for a foolish, unwary chicken. Quite simply, there was only the sound of silence, just as it should be in the autumn, in a village in the middle of the night when there was a hint of frost in the air.

But at about three in the morning, in the cottage with the heavily bolted doors, flames began leaping and crackling.

Chapter 9

It was Beth, sleeping on the first floor at the back of the Rectory, who was awakened first by the smell of smoke and the strange sounds of the crackling flames. She leapt out of bed the moment she recognised what had caused her to wake, and dashed to the window. All she could see was the weird, unaccustomed flashing lights in next door but one's back garden, but she knew instantly what it was and screamed, 'Dad! Fire! Fire! Get up. Now! It's Ralph's!'

Both Peter and Caroline jumped out of bed, forcing themselves to respond. They both rushed to the landing window and saw the colour of the flames lighting Ralph's back garden. 'Oh, God! Caroline, get Alex up! I'll ring the fire brigade! Quick! Quick, Beth! Out, right away! Through the front door.'

Guessing how long it would take the fire engine to reach the village Peter knew that they all had to act immediately. He dispatched Alex to get the church key from under the seat in the porch and get into the church to ring the single bell. 'For at least five minutes, Alex,' he said urgently.

Then he raced to Ralph's and hammered on the front door. But there was no response, so he shot through their own house and went through the back door and then into Ralph's back garden to bang and bang on the back door in the hope of rousing them both. The fire had obviously started in the kitchen and was already flaring up both windows and the glass panel in the back door.

The church bell began ringing, sending out a huge clamour over the village. No one could fail to hear it.

But more pressing for Peter was the sight of Muriel standing in the kitchen, apparently unaware of what was happening. Suddenly a great spurt of flame caught her night-gown and in a moment she was engulfed. Muriel didn't have time to scream.

Someone was screaming but he didn't know who.

Caroline stood behind him holding the garden hosepipe with water already gushing out.

He smashed a window with the end of it and poured water into the kitchen. But the flames ignored it and roared higher and higher as though they had a source of fire which the hosepipe was too feeble to put out.

Without considering logically what he was about to do, Peter turned the hose on himself and drenched himself and then smashed the panel of glass in the door, reached in to prise open the bolts and stepped in.

There was still someone screaming above the sound of the whip and crackle of the flames.

Caroline turned the hose on Muriel, which enabled Peter to grab hold of her and carry her outside. He laid her reverently on the path, saying, 'I'll go in and get Ralph. Do what you can.'

Caroline was distraught. She doused Muriel with the hosepipe again to put out the last of her burning night-gown and then trembled when she saw the extent of the burning of her skin. 'Muriel! Muriel!' Beneath the shreds of nightgown the flesh was dreadfully burned.

'Muriel! Muriel!' she cried. But there was no response, no movement. She was breathing but it was rasping and cruelly torturous, and Caroline wept, 'Muriel! It's Caroline!'

The kitchen still burned and she daren't go in. It was too hot, too dangerous, too frightening. Where was Peter?

She stood up and quickly studied the upstairs windows. Flames were already up there, greedily licking everything in sight.

'Peter! Peter!'

Muriel's rasping breath suddenly stopped. Caroline knelt

beside her. Her pulse had gone. Dear, dear Muriel. There was nothing to be done.

The church bell kept tolling.

'Peter! Peter!'

A window here and there cracked with the heat, and smoke began pouring out. Beth appeared and fell to her knees in horror when she saw Muriel. 'Do something, Mum! Do something!' Beth fidgeted with the remains of Muriel's nightgown, trying to make her respectable.

'Oh, Beth darling, it's too late for Muriel. It's your dad! He's inside looking for Ralph.'

As she spoke, torrents of water came pouring over the thatched roof, and drenched them. Water! Thank God ...

'It must be one of the neighbours wetting the roof to save the thatch. But where's your dad. Where is he?' Before Caroline could stop her, Beth shot inside the kitchen, dodging the flames as best she could. Caroline, paralysed by fear, hesitated briefly and then rushed inside to catch up with her.

'Peter! Peter!'

The church bell kept tolling.

Through the smoke now enveloping the hall, Caroline could see Peter at the top of the stairs, struggling with something, a bulk that was fighting to escape. Coughing with the effects of the smoke, Caroline climbed up the stairs to help. It was Ralph, refusing to leave the house without Muriel.

'Muriel! Muriel! My darling!'

'She's outside, Ralph. Let go of the banister. Come on, Ralph, come on.'

Caroline grabbed a leg and forced Ralph's hand from the banister, and Peter was able to rush down the stairs, dragging Ralph with him, causing a thump-thump as he hauled him down each stair.

'Out! Out!' he shouted hoarsely. Between them they forced Ralph out into the back garden. His eyes were streaming from the smoke, and he couldn't see. He coughed and coughed and coughed, and so did Peter and Caroline, fighting for breath, gasping for it, begging for it.

The church bell kept tolling.

Ralph lay on the path. For a man his age it was all too much, as indeed it was for Peter and Caroline, but they were younger and fitter, and so began recovering more quickly.

The fire raged more powerfully every minute and still the fire engine hadn't arrived.

Then Caroline shrieked, 'Oh, God! Where's Beth? She went in.'

Peter forced himself off the path and, dousing himself momentarily with the hosepipe, he rushed in again.

The church bell kept tolling but here was Alex, panting with exertion. 'Zack's ringing the bell. Where's Beth? Where's Dad?'

'Inside. Dad's gone in to get her. No Alex! *No*!'

But he went, doing as his dad did and dousing himself with water before he plunged in.

Ralph, energised once more, carefully tried to rise, but the coughing got the better of him and he had to lie down again.

'Stay there, Ralph, there's a good chap.' She didn't tell him about Muriel and he hadn't noticed as his eyes were still streaming from the smoke. He seemed grateful to be told to lie still. 'I'll get you a blanket and a cushion from our house. Won't be a moment.'

And indeed she was back in a moment with two blankets, one to cover Muriel right the way over, and the other, plus a cushion, for Ralph. Then, with all three of her beloved family in the burning house, Caroline fled inside. The smoke was thicker than ever but she persevered, found her way into the hall and shouted upstairs. They were still intact as far as she could tell, so Caroline began climbing the stairs, then she heard Alex's voice: 'She's here, Dad, she's here!'

And through the smoke she could just see the outline of Alex's tall figure carrying something and the something was Beth. Down the stairs he came with Peter right behind him and they all went out into the back garden.

Everyone coughed and coughed, and they were just recovering when the sound of a fire engine siren broke into their consciousness. It was the most wonderful sound they'd ever heard. After it came the sound of an ambulance. They heard a cheer go up and relief flooded them as they clung to each other, wet through and shocked.

The smoke was still spiralling above the roof of Ralph's house and the thatch was smoking and blazing.

'Ralph! Oh, God! Ralph.' Caroline's cry brought all four of them back to earth. Ralph was kneeling beside Muriel. He'd pulled the blanket back from her face and for the first time ever they saw Ralph weeping. Time after time he said, 'Muriel! Muriel!' Calling for her, because he didn't know what else to do about losing her.

Caroline pulled the blanket up to her chin so he couldn't see how badly burned she was.

His voice, incredibly sore with smoke inhalation, was husky and painful, but he said, 'Say something for her, Peter. Say something.' Kneeling beside Muriel, Ralph put his hands together in prayer and waited.

Peter knelt the other side of Muriel and said, 'Into thy hands O Lord we commend the spirit of Muriel, our beloved friend. Safe in the arms of Jesus for ever and ever. Loved by all. In your infinite mercy, Lord. Amen.'

Beth snapped a flower off a sweet pink dahlia and laid it reverently on the blanket covering Muriel, and then flung herself into her mother's arms and wept.

Peter and Alex got Ralph to his feet, put the blanket around his shoulders and led him down the path, round on to their own garden path and then into the house, to find the firemen banging on their door.

'Out, please. Out immediately.'

Peter opened the front door feeling ten years older than he had ten minutes ago.

'Your thatch has caught alight, sir. Come on, out. Out!'

So there was to be no refuge in their own home. But outside they found almost all the village there, the firemen still striving to put out the flames, their own roof now well alight, Grandmama Charter-Plackett serving tea, aided by other neighbours, and a general air of caring and helpfulness despite the hour.

Caroline went to speak to the ambulance driver. 'We have a fatality in the back garden. I'm Doctor Harris. I work in the Culworth West practice and I can certify her as dead.'

'I see. Any idea how this started?'

'None.' In Ralph's presence she wasn't prepared to declare that Muriel had become senile and it could be her fault. Time enough for that. 'This gentleman needs hospital treatment.'

'No, no, I don't. I have to stay with Muriel. Who will look after her? She needs me.'

'Muriel's going, too, Ralph.' Very gently, Caroline steered him towards the ambulance, and he and Muriel were taken away.

'Here's a cup of tea, Caroline. You look as though you need it.'

It was Grandmama. This redoubtable lady had exhaustion written deep in her heavily lined face. 'It'll help, believe me. What's happened to Muriel?'

Caroline shook her head. 'It was too late for Muriel, I'm afraid. There was nothing I could do. Peter put the flames out but ...' All at once the two of them were holding each other, tears flowing. It appeared to be a night when old feuds counted for nothing.

Everyone rallied round. Jimbo had been in the Store and

brought out packets of biscuits, which Fran was handing round to everyone. Offers of a bed for the night were made. The firemen were staying on duty in case the fire erupted again, thatched houses being notorious for staying alight when they looked to be safe.

Anxious eyes were watching the roof of the Rectory. Fortunately, whoever had sprayed water from a garden hose on to the thatch had very possibly saved it from destruction. Ralph's house, though not a shell, was badly damaged by the flames, smoke and water, and would be uninhabitable for many weeks.

Peter dressed and went straight to the hospital to be with Ralph, leaving Caroline and the twins sleeping for what was left of the night in Grandmama's cottage.

Beth and Alex lay on the sofas in her sitting room. They couldn't settle and so they lay quietly talking.

'My throat feels sore. Does yours?' muttered Beth.

'Mmm. A bit. You can see why smoke kills people, can't you? You can't see, you can't breathe, your eyes are streaming, you don't know where you are ...'

'Firemen must be so brave going in to rescue people. If we lived in Culworth they'd have been there in five minutes.'

'Yes, but they are equipped for it, aren't they?'

'Yes, of course they are. Alex?'

'Mmm.'

'Do you think Muriel did it?'

'Possibly. Making a cup of tea in the night and Ralph didn't know.'

'Exactly. She didn't have an electric kettle. She always used the gas ring and a whistling kettle. But then ...' She sat up. 'I remember the frying pan was on the ring and there was a smell of bacon.'

'Poor Muriel. Ralph must be devastated.'

'I know I sound uncaring, but perhaps it's for the best.'

Alex turned over. His feet, hanging over the end of his sofa and sticking out from the end of the duvet, were icy. 'She was much worse than people realised, but I don't expect Ralph feels it's for the best right now.'

'No, but he was at the end of his tether and she was so bossy with him. She wasn't like herself at all – demanding, you know, ordering him about. The real Muriel was gentle and considerate.'

'Well, it's Ralph we have to think about now, Beth. He's the one suffering.'

'Poor Ralph. Always a gentleman in the real sense of the word.'

Alex looked at his watch. 'It's almost five. Do you think we might get some sleep? Please?'

'I'm not going to school tomorrow ... today that is. If your house on fire isn't a good excuse for not turning up I don't know what is.'

'It's not really been on fire.'

'The thatch probably still is. Can you see from the window?'

'I'm not even looking.'

'Please, Alex, just open the curtain a bit. You're nearest.'

Sighing loudly, Alex did as he was asked. 'No, it isn't. The firemen are standing about drinking tea and there isn't a flame or cloud of smoke to be seen.'

'All Mum's memories in the loft will be soaked, I bet. Hope those red shorts I had when I was three will be OK. I loved those shorts.'

'They'll dry out.'

'Will the water have got into the bedrooms, do you think?'

'Beth! Shut up!'

'You're mean, you are.'

'No, just tired.'

'Sorry. I'm dying for a drink.'

But Alex didn't reply so Beth resettled herself and lay worrying about Ralph and wishing she hadn't decided she'd never go and sit with Muriel again. Still, at least she hadn't told them, so that was a good thing. Then Jake came to mind and she lay thinking about him and wishing it was Jake on the other sofa and not Alex. God, he was so handsome, Jake that was, not Alex. Although if he wasn't her brother she probably would think Alex handsome, she supposed, because he was so like dad and *he* was the handsomest of men, really gorgeous. No wonder Mum had fallen for him and no wonder Suzy Meadows had fallen for him, too. Beth thought about that for the first time ever and quickly wished she hadn't. Dad doing *that*! With *her*! She could just about manage thinking about Mum and Dad because it felt right, them still loving each other as they did, but Dad and Suzy? How did he manage the guilt? Because he must have felt guilty, with his principles, then when he found out abut the two of them being expected. She thought about herself as a baby and then somehow slid away to sleep.

And none of those asleep in Grandmama's cottage woke until half past nine, which made school definitely out of the question. So they spent the rest of the day exchanging fire news with everyone, sorting out the rectory attic and opening windows to get rid of the smell of smoke, and answering questions from the police. Beth said she thought that Muriel must have had the frying pan on and forgotten about it. Nothing quite like burning fat for producing a spectacular fire.

Three days later the village received the most terrible shock when they learned that Ralph too had died. The news passed round the village faster than light and their distress about Muriel was multiplied tenfold. Muriel's funeral had been planned for the Friday. Zack had used the newfangled digger to dig the grave for two coffins, and he'd cut the grass again for the very, very last time before the winter to make the graveyard fit for an important funeral. Jimbo had prepared the refreshments for the mourners and they were to be eaten in the Old Barn as they were expecting lots of people. Ralph was well known from the diplomatic service, and from being a magistrate and a churchwarden, so they'd all want to support him.

The entire village was determined to be at the church in good time, guessing, quite rightly, that there wouldn't be sufficient room for everyone who wanted to be there. Fortunately, Peter had the forethought to organise loudspeakers in the churchyard, which many people thought was more than a little over the top. But it proved very necessary, for anyone arriving as early as ten minutes before the service was due to start found themselves, no matter who they were, standing outside. Orders of service were distributed and then the two coffins came in.

First Muriel's, as that would have been what Ralph would have wanted, and then Ralph's. There simply hadn't been time to inform everyone that Ralph had died only two days before the date of Muriel's funeral, so a large number of people were in shock. Most people said it must have been a heart attack he died of, but the villagers knew better. They all declared very firmly that Ralph had died of a broken heart.

It had been a difficult decision to make but Peter decided that being buried together on the same day was what they would have wanted, and as no relatives appeared there was no one he could ask if he was doing the right thing, so it was arranged with the best of intentions. The two of them, inseparable in life, were now to be inseparable in death. Years ago Ralph had bought a plot close to the little wicket gate which had given access to the Big House from the church for the Templeton family for generations, so they would be buried close to the gate where they had kissed as teenagers for the first time, not knowing that they would one day both return to the village and get married.

Peter had officiated at funerals for more times than he wished to count, but this double funeral felt to be the most difficult. They wouldn't have wanted to live without each other. Muriel was no longer enjoying her life and in a lot of ways her going was a blessing. But Ralph ... that did hurt. And what does one say?

He chose the hymns they both loved, and with Gilbert Johns choosing the incidental music in collaboration with their new and inspirational organist, Tamsin Goodenough, he just knew there wouldn't be a dry eye in the church by the end of the service.

Tamsin gave a wonderfully impressive rendering of 'Abide With Me' and everyone both inside and outside the church found it difficult to keep singing. That two such well-loved and respected village people should be laid to rest together touched everyone's hearts. The singing was tremulous, but full of feeling and sung with great heart.

Then everyone settled down to hear Peter's address. He spoke of their popularity, of their wisdom, of their mutual love of the village and its life, of their laughter and generosity, and the uprightness of their way of life: 'Together in death as in life, we thank you Lord for their lives. God bless us all.'

Then came a surprise. Some people who'd known Ralph all their lives stood up in turn, without being asked, to say something about the two of them, recalling episodes of their lives and the admiration in which they had both been held by everyone who'd been privileged to know them.

Tamsin played a wonderfully tender but triumphant piece to accompany the two coffins going out into the churchyard for committal. It had been thought that they might be laid to rest in one of the Templeton tombs in church but apparently, the word went round, Ralph had bought the plot so that he and Muriel would be sleeping for ever under the giant trees which had sheltered the graves for centuries, the trees which Muriel so loved.

Chapter 10

Of all the people who'd attended the funeral service, the one who had escaped notice was Suzy Meadows. It was Alex who first realised she was there in the Old Barn where the post-funeral refreshments were being served. She tapped his arm, and he turned and found himself looking straight at her. For a split second he didn't recognise her. Then she spoke and he did. Good manners made him reply, 'Yes, it's terribly sad.' Then, like a fool, he added, 'My dad's been very upset about it all. I'm glad for his sake it's over. How did you know?'

'Of course he'll be upset. He'd a lot of respect for Ralph. I had a phone call from Hetty at the school; we've kept in touch since Michael left. He'd have been sad, too. He always—'

Thinking he'd be caught listening to her reminiscing, which he didn't want, Alex interrupted. 'I'll get you a cup of tea, shall I? Sandwich?'

'Yes, please. I don't think I could fight my way through the crowd. You're so like your father, you know. Handsome, too, just like him, and so very considerate.' She smiled up at him and Alex flushed. This wasn't what he wanted and if Beth saw them talking ... he fled towards the sandwiches.

When he got back to her, Suzy was talking to Grandmama Charter-Plackett. Sensing that Alex was embarrassed, Grandmama took charge.

'Come with me, Suzy, there's a table here. I'm no good at balancing cup and plate and talking and eating, too. Come along.' She swiftly turned her back on Suzy for a split second and winked at Alex. Grateful for her understanding, he departed rapidly to get his own cup of tea.

But he'd been seen by Beth. 'I'd no idea she was here. Had you?'

'No.'

'Cheek. That's what. I bet she said she'd come because of Ralph and Muriel and not for any other reason. She's a liar. I'm not speaking to her.'

'Do as you choose. As you told me not long ago, we're not joined at the hip.' He turned away from Beth and surveyed the crowd.

'You don't seem bothered.'

'About what?'

'Me not speaking to her.'

'Like I said, it's your decision. We're not under any obligation to speak to her. I just wish she hadn't come.'

'Has Mum seen her?'

'I don't know. She's busy doing her wife-of-the-Rector bit, so possibly she hasn't.'

Beth spotted Caroline standing at Peter's side, doing just as Alex had said, and she wandered off to catch up with her. She took her chance and whispered, knowing it wasn't a good idea but dreading her Mum coming across Suzy without any warning.

'Mum, did you know she's here? Suzy Meadows. Have you seen her?'

Already tense after the funeral and having to deal with all these strangers who'd come to pay their respects, when all she wanted was to go home to grieve, Caroline reached the end of her tether when she heard that. 'No, I haven't, and I don't want to. I shall avoid her at all costs.' But Caroline was not going to be allowed to ignore Suzy for there she was, standing beside her and Beth, waiting to speak.

The steady look Caroline gave Suzy was unfathomable. She

was both troubled and angry, endeavouring to be polite because these were not the right circumstances for arguing out loud, but above all defenceless. She wanted to hide behind Peter and leave him to deal with her, but he was speaking intently to someone who'd known Ralph in his diplomatic service days. So she spoke her mind. 'I wish you hadn't come. Appearing like this, uninvited and unwanted. You're making a nuisance of yourself, causing us all a lot of pain, especially the children, and it simply isn't fair. Just leave me and my family alone.'

Caroline very pointedly turned her back on Suzy then, and promptly spilt tea in her saucer and down her skirt. Beth used her napkin to dry her up, and squeezed her mum's arm to reassure her, but Suzy was determined this moment was not to be lost, and she'd take whatever was coming to her.

'Beth! I'm not causing you pain, am I? Just coming and bumping into you like this? I've only come to pay my respects to Ralph and Muriel, you know. You don't mind, do you?'

Beth forced herself to speak, knowing she was causing pain to this person who'd given birth to her, but knowing too that not hurting her own mum took precedence. She took deep breaths to control her emotions and said, 'Please ... I'm ... not ... don't want ... to get to know you. I wish you wouldn't ... try. Alex told you in his letter we weren't interested. Can you not take no for an answer?'

Then she spoilt it all by bursting helplessly into tears.

Grandmama Charter-Plackett appeared in full sail. 'Suzy, come with me. Come on, leave the child alone.'

Suzy snapped loudly, 'She isn't a child. She's a young woman, with a right to get to know me, and why not? Come along, Beth, sit over here and talk to me. Let's dry your tears. There's no need for tears, you know, not with me.' Suzy took out a handkerchief and tried to dry Beth's cheeks, but she snatched herself away. Then Suzy tried to pull her to the table she'd just vacated, but Peter intervened.

'Suzy! This must stop immediately! Beth, do you wish to sit and talk?'

Beth shook her head emphatically.

'Then please, Suzy, leave her be. You stay here with your mother, Beth. Come, Suzy, we'll talk.'

He marched purposefully towards the table Suzy had vacated and sat down. Alex appeared from nowhere and sat down with his dad. Keeping his feelings well under control, he continued drinking his cup of tea as though nothing serious were afoot.

Suzy, delighted she'd got the attention of both male members of the family, willingly sat with them. Beth and Caroline walked away, arms around each other's waists, the picture of filial love.

'Well?' This was Peter asking for an explanation.

'It's not much to ask for a chance to get to know my twins. That's all it is. I know what's making the two of them refuse me.'

'You do?' Peter sceptically raised his eyebrows.

'Yes. Caroline is putting every possible stumbling block in my way. She's been viciously against me having contact with my twins ever since the beginning.'

Alex sprung to his mother's defence. 'That is absolutely not the case. Mum has never tried to influence how we think about you. Never. We have not heard from you for over sixteen years. That letter you sent each of us was the very first communication we've had from you. How's that for caring? Just because you have a great gap in your life now does not justify opening up old wounds. Beth and I have talked long and hard about this situation, and neither of us wishes to get to know you better. We know how hard it must be for you, but it's also hard for the two of us. We are perfectly happy to be with our dad and our mum, and that's how we want it to stay. Trying to tear us apart makes us even more determined.'

'But that is ridiculous—'

'No, it isn't, it's what we want.'

'But it isn't what *I* want.'

'No, you want *us*, but we don't want to be four people. Alex and Beth who belong at the Rectory ... and ... Alex and Beth who belong to you. Will you not understand? Please?' He gazed steadily at her, his eyes frank and honest, his face passionate, and sounding more like his father than she'd thought possible.

Suzy laid a gentle hand on his forearm. 'I'd be content with just a teeny-weeny bit of you.'

Alex got to his feet. Leaning his hands on the table, he bent over her and said, 'Not even a teeny-weeny bit, because then you'd want more. I've listened to boys at school who have divorced parents. They say they belong in two houses all at the same time, and neither of them feel like *home*, and when they wake up each morning they have to remember which house they're actually in. It makes them two people all wrapped in one, and the opportunity for playing one set of parents off against the other is just too tempting, and they blatantly admit to doing it. Beth and I are *not* putting up with that.'

'You don't know what Beth wants, not deep down.'

'I most certainly do and I'm not having her upset any more. This is our final word. *Our ... final ... word!* In the unlikely event of us changing our minds we'll be in touch. Until then, just bloody well stay away!'

'Alex!'

But Alex had rushed away, deeply angry and seriously distressed by what he'd said, and he went to sit out in Turnham House Park by himself under the trees until he'd calmed down, leaving Peter with a distraught and horrified Suzy.

'How could he? How could he speak to me like that?' Out came her handkerchief.

'Because he feels passionately about what he said, and you've to *let them go*. You don't listen because it's simply not what you *want* to hear. I'm sick and tired of this whole business. The children have told you that at this moment they don't want to get to know you, and as far as Caroline and I are concerned that's how it is. It's their decision, not *ours*. Do as he says and bloody well stay away.'

He heard her sharp intake of breath when he swore, but he didn't care.

'Peter! Please!'

'Has the message not gone home, then? Are you still going to keep persuading them to build a relationship with you? Despite Alex's anger? Despite Beth's tears?'

'It's so lonely, you see, with my three girls away from home. They hardly ever come to see me. And Beth and Alex are the children of the man I love. Had you forgotten that? What love did I ever get from Patrick? None at all. From Michael? Huh! I should have known not to marry a dyed-in-the-wool bachelor. But you ... I have loved you ever since that day we made love, every hour of every day.'

Peter was devastated. A declaration of love from her was not what he wanted after the week he'd had. He didn't want confrontation and protests and promises of undying love, not today. What he wanted was Caroline's common sense, Caroline's uncomplicated love and understanding, not the over-the-top emotional desire of this apparently obsessed woman. What he'd done that day long ago was to answer her need as well as his own; that the twins had been the result was both shocking and wonderful, but for certain he wanted an end to this.

He stood up, took her arm and, to the astonishment of everyone present, he marched her out of the Old Barn and into the open air. 'Your car? Where is it?'

She was sobbing now. 'Outside the Rectory. I got a lift from the church.'

'Get in my car. Here we are. Get in.'

Peter drove out of the grounds of Turnham House and down towards the Rectory in absolute silence.

He pulled up behind her car and went round to open the

passenger door for her to get out. She looked up at him with those bright blue eyes of hers, those eyes his Beth had inherited, and for a nanosecond his resolution wavered.

Standing as close as she could, she whispered, 'I shall always love you.' Then she reached up to stroke his cheek.

He jerked his head away. 'You'll never have me, Suzy, so you'd better create a life of your own, and at the same time ask yourself why your girls don't see much of you. Perhaps you've been obsessive with them, like you're being with Beth and Alex. Think on these things.'

He made the sign of the cross on her forehead, saying as he did so, 'God bless you, Suzy. Goodbye.'

Before she'd unlocked her car door, he'd already got back into his own car. Because of his distress, he revved the engine far too much and drove round the Green like a man possessed, praying as he did so that he was seeing the end to her obsession.

Chapter 11

Monday afternoon meant the Turnham Malpas embroidery group was in session, and Zack, though it was autumn now, had decided not to give up calling in for his cup of tea just as he did in the summer when he was grass-cutting. In fact, he made a special point of visiting, because Merc still came every Monday with one of Ford's tips for him. But what Ford didn't know was that everyone in the group also bet on his tips and they were having a rare old time winning every week. Some of them were saving up their winnings and even putting on much bigger bets than they'd ever done in their lives.

Dottie put £100 on one week – stupidly reckless, she knew, but she did it all the same – and what was more, she won! Four consecutive weeks they'd been betting and every time winning. It stood to reason it couldn't go on, but somehow they pushed that threat to one side and their confidence grew.

Merc found it hilarious and despite her telling them Ford couldn't be right every single time, ad infinitum, they persisted. This Monday he had selected Paddy Myboy. They all carefully made a note of the name, the racecourse and the time of the race, and then and only then did they continue with their embroidery. Merc had just finished her special project of doing the flag on the ship and they gathered round to study the effect.

Evie was delighted. 'Well, I must say, Merc, it's fabulous. Just what that bit of the tapestry needs to give it a lift.' Joking, Dottie declared she wasn't impressed with that remark as it made her duck-egg blue background sound like a waste of time.

Evie hastened to reassure her that that was not the case at all, that it was the immaculate simplicity of her beautifully worked background that gave the flag the best possible setting. Dottie puzzled over this and then decided it was meant as a compliment and settled to her work happily enough, thinking as she stitched that she might spend this week's winnings on a weekend away. And why not?

Naturally the main subject of conversation was the joint funeral service for Muriel and Ralph.

'It was a beautiful service. I thought the Rector got it just right. Poetic, it was, and very moving. But,' said Dottie, 'without them, things won't feel the same, will they? No lord of the manor, no more—'

'But Ralph hasn't been lord of the manor since he was about fourteen when his mother sold up after his dad died in the Second World War.' This remark came from Bel, who could behave uncommonly like a socialist on occasion.

'We know that but he still always had our interests at heart. One trip down to the council and he got his own way, like a real gentleman.' Sylvia snipped her wool with her special embroidery scissors and added, 'Which he was.' She looked up, expecting a protest from Bel, but Bel merely commented, 'You couldn't deny that. Lovely man, he was. So sad him joining her so soon. Still, he'd have been no good without her. They really loved each other, didn't they?'

'Question is,' said Merc with more practical matters in mind, 'who inherits?'

In their deep sadness at the deaths, none of them had got as far as thinking on those lines. This weighty question foxed them all.

'Well, they were childless,' Barbara the weekender ventured. 'And he was an only child and so was she, so that rules out immediate descendants. It'll have to be a cousin or something, twice removed or whatever. Wish we had a family tree, then we could perhaps work it out.'

'How do you know all that?'

'I specialise in genealogy,' said Barbara, rather self-importantly.

'What's that when it's at home?' asked Dottie.

'Tracing family trees. I did it for a friend once and she wished I hadn't 'cos I found out that her father *and* her mother were illegitimate *and* one of her great-grandmothers. She was furious, but I didn't make it up. It was all facts. It was on their birth certificates. "Born out of wedlock! My mother? I think not!" she said. Didn't speak to me for months after. But I was only telling her the truth.'

'Hey!' said Sheila. 'That happened with Ralph's family, you know. I think it was his grandfather who had a son born with his wife and one with a parlour maid from the village the very same night, right in the middle of a massive thunderstorm. The oak on the Green had a whole branch come down and they all said it was the wrath of the gods. Beattie Prior, she was; married, too. Her baby was the grandfather of Arthur Prior, who owns Wallop Down Farm.' This amazing statement brought a complete halt to their sewing.

Sylvia, thrilled by being reminded of this old story, burbled excitedly, 'My Willie knows all about that. Maybe Arthur Prior might inherit. Not the estate obviously and not the title, but I bet there'll be an awful lot of money somewhere laid about. Think how the price of his cottage will have gone up since he bought it, and that's just for a start. Mind you, Arthur is knocking on so I expect his eldest son will benefit most. Won't go far, though, will it?'

Sheila giggled. 'Not with all those daughters he has, and only one boy. I say! Perhaps the boy, Sebastian, will get all the money. You never know, do you? Like a kind of grandchild in a way? 'Cept, of course, we've forgotten his cottage is in ruins with the fire, so there'll be no counting on the money for that.'

Evie didn't like this kind of tittle-tattle and did her best to stop it. 'There's no point in us speculating. There might be a nephew in some distant place like Canada or Peru or somewhere who'll inherit the money. There must be other Templetons somewhere. Now, about this next bit after the ship—'

'There will be,' said Sylvia, 'because I remember Willie saying that the Sir whatever-his-name-was at the time that had a baby with Beattie Prior had two other boys after with his wife, so there must be someone somewhere. They might even come to live in the village.'

'About the next section, I've been thinking—'

But Sheila asked Merc what the youth club was doing this week, so Evie had to wait her turn.

'This week? Which red should I use for this bit, Evie?'

'Scarlet.'

'Right.' Merc threaded her needle and looked up at Sheila. 'It's the ghost hunt week – bring your own candle.' She didn't know why but that phrase, bring your own candle, fired her imagination. It spoke to her of long stone passages and archways, of patches of light and then incredible darkness, and the heart-twitching screech of owls in the depth of the night.

Bel nodded. 'I thought so. They've been in the Store buying candles as if there was going to be a power cut. They'll have a great time. The twins are going and Fran Charter-Plackett and loads from Penny Fawcett.'

Sheila raised her eyebrows in surprise. 'Just the kind of thing they'll enjoy, I bet. I don't think it's quite what they should be doing.'

'But,' said Evie, 'the twins will keep up good standards. With parents like they've got they can't do any other.'

Rather darkly Sheila remarked that she wasn't too sure about that. Immediately everyone pricked up their ears and needles were idly poised above the tapestry … waiting …

'Not sure? What do you mean?' asked Barbara, scenting a story she could tell her neighbours when she got back home.

'I was in my car going down Shepherd's Hill with a message

about the flower festival and I saw Beth and that Jake from Penny Fawcett popping into Sykes Wood. He's that handsome boy, the one who's always after the girls. Then, on my way back, she came racing out of the wood up the hill heading for home and she looked almighty scared. I saw her in my rear-view mirror.'

Dottie, her head down, employed her needle rather rapidly, desperately hoping no one would ask her anything about it. What was Beth thinking of? Still, let's face it, she was almost seventeen and lots of girls weren't even virgins by then ... but Beth! That Jake was a fast one. She'd heard tales about him, but my word he was good-looking. By the time she'd come out of her shock they were discussing the ghost evening as though it were the most depraved happening anyone could imagine. She noticed that Merc stayed silent, then suddenly she burst out, 'Don't anyone go blaming my Ford for it. He didn't choose where they went. Oh no! Pay for it, yes, though Mr Fitch pays for the transport ... Oh! By the way, I have your invitations to the banquet in my bag. When we have our tea, remind me and I'll get them out.'

This closed the speculation about the ghost evening, and as there were one or two sly hints that a cup of tea would be welcome, Evie gave in and made the tea and the invitations were revealed.

Merc fished about in her over-large bag. 'You've got yours first. The others are going out by post today.'

If the invitations had been to a banquet at Buckingham Palace they could not have been more glorious. Fabulous, they were, gilt-edged and very stiff card with a kind of silvery white marbled effect. Big, too, and instantly the wedding anniversary celebrations became the event of the year.

'Oh my God! We've to dress up! I shan't know what to wear!' Dottie quaked at the prospect of thinking up fancy dress.

'Not fancy dress, Dottie, *Elizabethan* dress,' said Merc. 'We want it all to look genuine.'

Sylvia began to laugh. 'Wasn't that when the men wore tights? I can't see my Willie in tights.'

The vision this prospect conjured up sent them into hysterics.

'Nor Jimbo!'

'The Rector will look stunning!' said Dottie, and they all agreed.

'What about your Ron, Sheila?' This came from Bel, with a grin. She remembered how rotund Ron had become now he'd very little gardening to do in the house in Little Derehams.

Sheila had had the very same thought and was angry beyond belief at this snide remark. 'He most likely won't go. He's not really into dressing up.'

Inside herself Sheila was bitterly disappointed. Of course he wouldn't go, except she longed to attend more than anything in the whole world. She simply couldn't miss it, not the social event of the year. But knowing Ron, he'd dig his heels in and there'd be endless rows. The invitation, propped up against an ornament on the mantelpiece, would look so impressive, but if they wouldn't be going, what was the point?

They'd exhausted the subject of the banquet by the time their cups of tea were finished, and it was then that Dottie had her inspiration. Somehow the invitation had opened up her mind to new horizons.

'Why don't we use our winnings to go away for a girls' weekend?'

'A girls' weekend!'

'Why not? If the young ones can have a night ghost-hunting, why can't we go away for a weekend? We're not exactly decrepit, are we? And we're not senile.'

'No, we're not!'

'The men'll think it funny us having money to go away.'

Dottie grinned. 'So, like me, you haven't let on we bet each week, then?'

Sheila agreed she hadn't. Bel declared she hadn't told her Gary, nor her brother Dicky. Barbara confessed she hadn't told her hubby. Evie said she hadn't mentioned a word to Tom. Vera declared she definitely hadn't told Don. Sylvia hadn't spilt the beans to her Willie. And Dottie said she'd not told nobody.

Merc spoke up. 'If you don't mind, I shan't be going because we're going to visit an old aunt of mine – on her last legs, poor thing, ready to die any minute, but you have my word that I have not said a word to anyone about the betting you've been doing, so your secret is safe with me. *Enjoy*, as they say.'

'We can afford it, can't we? And if we win this week as well . . .' Barbara giggled.

'We very well could,' said Sylvia.

Caught up in the excitement, Barbara declared, 'I tell you what: I could book it on my computer. I've done it for our holidays more than once.'

'London, eh?' Dottie suggested. 'We might as well do it right.'

'London! I second that,' agreed Sheila, trying hard to sound very cosmopolitan, as though she frequently popped up to London for her shopping.

'Oh!' said Evie, feeling slightly shocked by the prospect.

But they all agreed that London it was, and no husbands allowed. With the discussion it entailed they were half an hour late packing up, and Barbara drove home that same afternoon with a list of their telephone numbers in her bag and a ceiling price for accommodation above which she must not go. She rang each of them that night. She had found a bed and breakfast package with theatre tickets thrown in for less than two hundred pounds this coming weekend. It was a special autumn offer, you see, and the hotel even had its own casino! It sounded perfect. They all agreed. Next thing was to tell their husbands. Only Dottie felt no obligation to anyone at all.

★

The departure of the embroidery group for London took place at 10.45 a.m. on Friday. They all squeezed into Ford's 4x4 with much excitement, and much in the way of misgivings on the part of the husbands left behind.

Nobody in the 4x4 had any qualms about their adventure. After all, they had a posh afternoon tea to look forward to, as well as a leisurely stroll around the shops on the way to the theatre and *The Sound of Music*, which they were all longing to see. It might not be Julie Andrews playing Maria but they knew it would be good, and full of memories with perhaps a few tears. Then they were planning to hit the hotel casino! Saturday morning they were going to the Portobello Road market, which Dottie was particularly thrilled about as she considered herself A1 at finding bargains, then sightseeing in Westminster Abbey and St Paul's, followed by a meal in a steak house and the cinema. Afterwards, the more daring were off to the casino again, if they'd had success the night before. They didn't intend going to bed on Friday until 1 a.m. at the earliest. They had to be up early for their Saturday sightseeing but they didn't care. They felt abandoned, released and *free*! Turnham Malpas had been left far behind.

The embroidery group agreed on the train on the way to London that they were going to have the most wonderful weekend of their lives. The nervous ones like Evie were egged on by the more carefree ones like Barbara and Dottie to actually allow themselves to *enjoy* everything instead of worrying about the time and the traffic and the milling crowds, and with encouragement they all did truly revel in the excitement of the weekend. The casino was not altogether as successful as everything else because losses were enormous compared to what they'd won on the gee-gees (with Ford's assistance). The first night was reasonable but by the second night their heads, dizzy with all the excitement, didn't allow them to concentrate properly. Dottie lost £40, which was a lot to her, and Sheila lost £55, which made her look over her shoulder once or twice, fearing Ron might miraculously materialise beside her.

The worst moment of the weekend was when Evie and Bel got separated from the others in the Portobello Road market. They'd all been together one moment and the next the pair of them were nowhere to be seen. They'd never thought to specify a meeting point in case they got lost – after all, they weren't children – and there was an anxious twenty minutes of standing on tiptoe, peering through the crowds, until they heard Evie's voice calling and there they both were!

Evie was as white as a ghost and trembling. Bel was trying hard to look calm when she very definitely wasn't, because there were beads of sweat on her top lip. There was a unanimous vote to find somewhere for lunch to calm everyone's nerves.

But even the worry of that incident didn't mar their enjoyment of the entire weekend, and they went home on the train still buoyed up with delight at their adventure and promising to do something same-but-different in the immediate future.

Chapter 12

The embroidery group had decided that their girls' weekend away would be well worth repeating, but the same could not be said of the youth club after their ghost hunt in the castle. They'd all been so scared that a re-run was out of the question.

They'd set off enthusiastically enough, though. Beth sat next to Jake on the minibus, and allowed him to hold her hand after a few minutes re-establishing their relationship after her fright. On Jake's insistence they chose to sit on the back row, as far away from Alex as they possibly could; he was in the seat immediately behind the driver, sitting with a friend of his from school. Beth briefly felt disloyal to Alex, but the feeling didn't last long when she remembered her frequently repeated saying that they weren't joined at the hip.

'Beth?'

'Yes?'

'Last time ... I'm sorry. I didn't mean to cause any trouble.'

Beth stared out of the window. She wasn't going to tell him the real reason for her panic. It was bad enough Alex knowing, and her mum and dad. They chatted about school and friends and films they'd seen, and before they knew it they'd arrived at the castle. It seemed to arise out of a dark mist, with turrets and battlements and softly-lit windows that were merely slits in the vast stone walls.

Venetia had matches and so did Kate, but they didn't need their candles until they were well inside the castle, as the drawbridge over the moat was lit by lamps.

In the great hall they were given a hot drink, which was spiced and Christmassy and very welcome. A lively castle servant gave a talk, telling them the history of the castle and the ghosts which were regularly sighted by the family and the staff. One ghost was a small child whose skeleton had been discovered during some repairs. Another apparition was an eighteenth-century man, a family member who had died in India; he'd always loved the castle and had suddenly appeared shortly after his death sitting in his favourite chair in the library, reading.

Almost all of them shuddered, and shuddered even more when they heard about the strange bright light which appeared from time to time on the landing, followed by Lady Emily, who, from time to time, flung herself over the banisters to her death on the floor of the great hall, as she'd done on the news of the death of her fiancé at Trafalgar on Nelson's flagship. Her screams as she fell were often heard, even if her ghost couldn't be seen.

By the time the talk had finished everyone was apprehensive. On the instruction of the castle servant, who'd worked at the castle man and boy, their candles were lit and the tour began.

Kate, ever the sceptic, said as they were setting off, 'Don't let yourselves get too alarmed. It's just *fun*. Right?'

They were taken first to the nursery at the top of the stairs. By the light of their candles they could make out a huge rocking horse in the window, toys laid out on a table, a puzzle half-finished, a Noah's ark with the animals lined up to go in, as though a child had only just left the room. A small fire glowed in the fireplace. They stood in silence ... then the rocking horse began gently moving. Beth clutched Jake's hand; he slipped an arm around her shoulders. Not one of them had been close to it but there it was, rocking silently back and forth. Then the fire went out and the only light came from their candles. In the complete silence that ensued the voices of young children enjoying a nursery tea could be heard, not loudly but enough to be able to catch a few words.

As the voices died away the castle servant said, 'Three children were having nursery tea up here in 1902 when a terrible fire broke out. A nursemaid had locked them in, and they couldn't escape. Sometimes her ghost, full of guilt, wanders about up here, but not tonight.

Melanie from Penny Fawcett dared to ask, 'Those children's voices we heard just now, were they the children who died ... kind of?'

The servant seemed very surprised. 'Voices? You heard children's voices?'

They all nodded.

'I heard nothing. My word, you must all be very special, very sensitive. I've never heard them.' He cleared his throat nervously and added, 'Let's go down, shall we?'

Those at the front of the group, including Jake, Beth and Venetia, were able to lead the way down the stairs to the first floor, when they felt an icy cold draught. Venetia trembled, Beth grabbed Jake's hand even more tightly, and then they felt something swish past them with a rustle and a rush, nothing they could see but definitely something. Their candles fluttered and then they all heard terrible screams, which seemed to go right down to the floor of the great hall.

By this time everyone was scared to death and Kate had difficulty in calming nerves. 'Gently, everyone, steady now. We don't want an accident.'

But then the candles blew out altogether, and they were standing in utter darkness. Two girls began to cry. Jake put both arms round Beth as she shivered with fright, and Kate said, 'We'll light our candles again. Stand still while I light mine then I can see yours.'

Melanie said, 'I'v-ve n-never seen darkness as bad as this before.'

Jake replied, 'Well, we've got street lighting, haven't we? Beth here is brave as brave because she's used to complete darkness at night, aren't you, Beth?'

Wanting to keep her image intact, Beth said, 'Nothing to be afraid of.' She swallowed hard, and someone else said, 'Let's get downstairs right now. Light my candle, Kate, please.'

'Light my candle,' whispered Jake in Beth's ear. So she did, and he squeezed her arm, kissed her cheek and held her tighter still as they went down the stone staircase. The darkness and the fear made Beth grateful for his reassuring arm around her, and she was glad, so very very glad it was Jake holding her.

Alex caught up with them. 'All right, Beth?'

'Of course I am,' she replied tartly. 'A few ghosts don't bother me.' But she clasped Jake's forearm, and kept him holding her. The ghosts *did* bother her and she would have been happy to go out to the minibus immediately, but there were more rooms to visit, more ghosts to look for, and now Fran had joined her and Jake.

'I don't like this, do you, Beth?'

'It is a bit creepy.'

'Bit creepy! It's terrifying.'

As they reached the bottom of the stairs, Jake, determined not to be impressed by this ghost business, pretended he felt a tremulous wisp of something brush across his face as he passed through a doorway. He took flight, dragging Beth with him and closely followed by Fran, who'd panicked when she saw Jake's apparently stricken face in the light of his candle.

The three of them were outside the giant castle door and running for the minibus before anyone could stop them.

Kate followed to persuade them to finish the tour, but the two girls vehemently refused to go back in and sat shaking and afraid in the minibus waiting to go home. Their nerves slowly calmed and eventually they began reassuring each other.

The sight of Beth's face, bleak and afraid, made Jake confess his joke.

'That,' said Beth, 'is the nastiest thing you could have done. You knew I was already scared to death. Alex wouldn't have done that to me.'

'Not goody-goody Alex, oh no! So thoughtful, your Alex, so protective! It was all pretend, didn't you realise? All made up by that servant.'

Fran was furious. 'But he didn't hear the children's voices having tea, did he? We all did, so why didn't he?'

Beth came to her aid. 'Yes ... but the draught we felt ...'

'What about the screams that floated all the way down the stairs. They were real enough.'

'Whatever ... it was all for entertainment. God! What a fantastic scheme!' Just for fun Jake rubbed his face briskly with his hand as though brushing cobwebs away again. Beth grabbed his hand and began beating him with her fists, but it turned into a game and then became serious and Jake was kissing her like he'd never kissed her before ... Beth subjected herself to his embraces because they were at that very moment what she wanted most in all the world, so her mock fury melted into need of him and she adored his passion ... and like that old advert, his kisses reached places never reached before. Beth, enraptured by Jake's burning desire for her, longed for him. If seeing and hearing ghosts meant his need for her manifested itself like this then ...

Fran didn't know where to look, so she got out of the minibus and sat on the bottom step of the stairs leading to the main door of the castle to wait for the others.

Then she began to worry. It didn't seem right, not that kind of frantic kissing, and she wished Beth wasn't liking it. But she was. Fran hovered between staying where she was and taking no responsibility, and getting back in the minibus and embarrassing them into stopping. Mind made up she got back in and shouted, 'They're all coming back!' That did the trick. Jake released Beth, who straightened her clothes and got out a comb and put her hair to rights.

The moment Jake knew she'd told a great big fib he shouted, 'Just shut your mouth. What business is it of yours?'

'Beth's a friend of mine.'

'So?'

'And it's not on.'

'So?'

'Well, it isn't. You shouldn't.'

But then the others did come back. Kate instantly noted Beth's flushed cheeks, the air of excitement about her and her laughing eyes.

Everyone was entirely convinced that each incident was absolutely real.

'He says we were lucky tonight,' said one. 'Sometimes people come and see hardly anything at all.'

'Well, we did. I wonder if the Scouts would like to go? That'd get their woggles all of a jamboree, wouldn't it?'

They all fell about in helpless, giggling heaps.

'We saw that man who died in India sitting there in the chair holding a book. Two hundred and fifty years later. In his dressing gown in the library.'

'I'm never going there again.'

'W-worse still, he got up and disappeared through a bookcase.'

'Then the old servant showed us that it was a real door he'd gone through, a bookcase but a door as well. So he remembered after two hundred and fifty years of being dead. I feel terrible. I'll never forget this night. *Never*!'

'Who suggested we came here?' asked Alex.

Venetia admitted it was her idea. 'But I'm never, ever coming ever again. It's all been too much.'

But it hadn't been too much for Beth. As she lay in bed that night she realised that the ghostly appearances must have been man-made because it was all too coincidental that they'd seen every possible ghost all on the same night. In any case, she had far too much to think about how frightened she'd been.

Now she knew all about kissing. Mum and Dad definitely knew what it was all about, she could see that now. Beth recalled the feel of Jake's arms around her, and his kissing ... it was truly divine. She could take a permanent fancy to kissing. It was fantastic. All that closeness and his body against hers and his arms round her and her arms round him ... Life would never be the same again. How had she managed all these years without being kissed like that?

Chapter 13

The arrival of the glossy invitations to the Elizabethan banquet from Ford and Mercedes was greeted with sheer delight by the majority of villagers. Plans were made for their outfits, comparisons were made with others. The telephone lines buzzed with conversations about it. Isn't it wonderful? Can't wait! Four weeks to go! Wonderful!

But there was one household where the husband refused point-blank to have anything at all to do with it.

'The man must be mad, Kate! Stark raving. There's no way I'm going dressed like … a … a … Sir Walter Raleigh, in doublet and hose. What does he think we are? Children? Not right in the head? I am not … *we're* not going. Send a refusal immediately.'

Then Craddock Fitch stormed off to London and the airport, glad to leave the whole matter behind him. He'd not liked Ford right from the first time he met him, the ridiculous man. The puffed-up, boastful twit. The idiotic upstart. Thinking he was the village benefactor buying the mower and then the digger for the graves! Huh! Well, he'd soon find himself demoted by the real benefactor. Craddock Fitch would show *him*!

Mistaking Kate for his daughter indeed. He couldn't think of anything more designed to anger him. Ford nearly got punched on the nose about that, and then he trumped it by assuming that Craddock Fitch was retired, living in rented accommodation and couldn't afford to help him with his charitable flirtations. As for his wife, Mercedes, she had no taste, no education, no finesse. He patted his own stomach, proud of its taut muscles. Compared to the pair of *them*, he was a prime example of a vital, healthy man. Ask his wife, *she* knew how vital he was!

His driver heard him snorting and muttering in the back and knew this was not the morning for idle chatter. The financial markets he'd carefully read up on before turning the ignition would have to wait. He pushed his own copy of the *Financial Times* under the front passenger seat and concentrated on driving. His passenger continued to grumble, and the grumbling grew louder when they were caught up in a massive traffic jam and appeared to be running the risk of missing the plane.

Mrs Kate Fitch decided not to send a refusal immediately. Experience had taught her that sometimes, with only the smallest amount of persuasion from her, Craddock could quite happily change his mind once he'd calmed down. Instead she went off to the village school quietly smiling with joy, for the school was where she loved to be.

She hadn't bargained for Maggie being eager for a chat about the banquet.

'Isn't it marvellous? Never thought I'd get an invite but there it is on my mantelpiece as large as life. I've no doubt you got one too?'

'Of course. However, I've things to do ...'

But there was no escape.

'There's two fancy dress shops in Culworth and as soon as I've finished dinners I'm off on the lunchtime bus to reserve my costume. I wouldn't leave it too long if I were you. They'll all be gone, you'll see! Must press on. You will keep me talking, Mrs Fitch. Mr Fitch will look good in tights with his lean figure. You must feed him just right for him to be so good, especially at his age.'

'Got to get on.'

'So 'ave I. Someone said Ron Bissett's not going under any circumstances. Sheila'll be disappointed and not half. They say there's entertainment, too, not just the food. It'll have to finish at midnight with it being Sunday the next day. Have you ever tried mead?'

'I should warn you that it is extremely potent. Be very, very careful. Too much mead and you're anybody's. Not a care in the world.' Kate winked wickedly.

Maggie was shocked. Standing in the middle of the school kitchen, propping up her mop, she wondered if Kate was serious. She'd confirm it, straight after school started, with Jimbo. He always knew everything, Jimbo did. He'd know about mead.

'Are you and Harriet going to the banquet?' Maggie asked him two hours later in the Store.

Jimbo nodded.

Maggie leaned confidentially against the till counter and asked, 'You're serving mead at the banquet, they say. Have you tried it?'

Jimbo nodded again.

'I'm told it's very potent.'

He nodded vigorously.

'Two glasses enough?'

Another nod.

'Enough to make you drunk?'

He nodded once more.

'You lost your voice or something?'

One shake of his head.

'Well, answer me, then. This is getting ridiculous.'

'Just having fun. You must be the twentieth person who's come in here since yesterday asking that very same question. I can tell you that we shall all be lucky to sleep in our own beds afterwards.'

'Sleep in our own beds? Do you mean we'll never get 'ome?'

'We'll get home all right, but it might not actually be *our* home. We'll be so drunk we shan't know the difference which bed we're in.'

'Oh my God!' The possibility intrigued Maggie. 'Jimmy's? Oh, definitely not. I don't think he'll change his sheets that often, do you? And if there's one thing I can't abide …' Her nose wrinkled at the thought of unwashed sheets. 'Or it could be Paddy Cleary's. He might be small but he's got some powerful thighs with all that digging he does. Or even Barry Jones. You should see him stripped off sawing wood. Tanned, he is, as if he's been on a cruise, but what Pat might have to say …'

'Go away! You're making me blush.'

'*You* blush? That's a laugh.'

Purely for devilment Jimbo said, 'My mother's going,' simply because she'd just walked in.

'Well, if it's her bed I end up in I'll definitely realise where I am. There'll be hell to pay.' Maggie used a couple of very unkind epithets about her which Grandmama heard.

'Well, really!' said Grandmama. 'Just what are you saying? That my bed linen isn't clean?'

'I do apologise! We were only joking and I'd no idea you were here. It was Jimbo who set me off, talking about the mead at the banquet.'

'Heaven alone knows what you might be saying once you've had some, then. And you should know better, Jimbo.'

'Just improving my customer relations.'

'I must say you've a funny way of doing it. I need one of your coffees. Am I too early?'

'You most certainly are not. It's just freshly brewed. This is the second pot today so far. Never been busier. This banquet is bringing me more business than ever.'

'Where's Tom?'

'Taken Evie to the coast. She's not been well.'

'Not her old trouble, I hope?'

'No. Just a heavy cold. She needs some sea air.'

'Have a coffee with me, Maggie, go on.'

'Very well, I will. Show there's no ill feeling.'

Grandmama raised an eyebrow, feeling that if there was any ill will it should be on her part. They squeezed together on the seats provided and Grandmama opened up their conversation. 'You're not one of the embroidery group, are you, Maggie?'

'No, but I wish I was. Where the heck did they get the money from to go to London? They had a smashing time, you know. Theatre, cinema, sightseeing, casino, posh afternoon tea. Do you happen to know how it came about? The men were grumbling like mad about it in the pub while they were away. What puzzled them same as me was where did the money come from? There's none of 'em earning much.'

'Well, I happen to know.' Grandmama tapped the side of her nose and winked.

Maggie gave her a sharp glance. 'You do?'

'Oh yes.'

'Well?'

Grandmama leaned closer to Maggie's ear and whispered, 'Betting on horses.'

'No! Really?'

'Definitely.'

'So they must be winning a lot, then. My hubby liked a bet on the Derby and the Grand National, that kind of thing, but 'e never won anything big, just a few pounds here and a few pounds there.'

'No prizes for guessing where they get their tips from.'

Maggie hesitated for a moment and then suggested, 'Not Ford?'

'Exactly. You've hit the nail on the head.'

'Well, I never. The cheeky monkeys never even told their husbands.'

There appeared to be a few customers conspicuously lurking close to the greeting cards, which happened to be displayed near the coffee machine, and they were obviously listening in. The result was that the word went round the Store in a flash.

At that very moment, so opportune it was unbelievable, Ford walked in with a parcel for the post. Instead of the usual hubbub he was accustomed to in the Store, silence fell. Ford looked around and called out, 'Good morning' loudly and headed straight for the Post Office.

Jimbo leapt into the Post Office 'cage'. 'Inland?'

'Yes. How much?'

'Three pounds and eight pence.'

'Right. I want my *Racing Post* while I'm here.'

'Absolutely. I've saved it for you. There's your change.'

Was this indeed divine intervention? All seven customers in the Store converged on Ford and stood patiently waiting for Jimbo to present him with his paper.

'Morning, Ford. What's your tip for today, then? We've been hearing all about your kindness.' This from Don who, well set up at finding out where Vera had got the money for her trip to London, couldn't let this moment pass by.

Ford grinned. 'I only give Zack a tip, no one else. Has he been talking?'

They were all a little nonplussed by this remark. Only Zack? What did that mean?

Don asked, 'And then some. How about my Vera, Evie and that Barbara and them others?'

It was obvious that Ford knew nothing about the increase in his influence in the betting department. 'I don't know about them. I thought it was just Zack. Of course! The embroidery group!' He paused for a moment while they all waited, scarcely breathing in their anticipation. 'Look, I'm not really in the business of giving out tips, not now, just a favour to my friend Zack. But just this once ...'

There was a lot of gleeful hand-rubbing, shuffling about

in handbags and pockets to find paper and pens, and grins all round.

Ford, loving the idea of an audience, took a while to open his paper. He pretended to study form, with much rustling and head-scratching, then proclaimed, 'It must be clearly understood that a run of luck is possible, but horses don't always run to form, as I well know to my cost, so sometimes you'll lose, sometimes you'll win and there's to be no comeback.' He looked sternly round the group, catching the eye of everyone so there could be no mistaking his meaning. 'For this weekend, I suggest – *suggest*, mind – Flybynight, two-thirty, Ayr, Saturday.'

He folded his newspaper, stuck it under his arm, and marched out. Coming back in again, he said, 'It'll be word of mouth, nothing written down. No evidence. Right?'

'Right!' they all promised.

He shouldn't have agreed, he knew that. It could cause endless bother. But he loved the thrill of it. He'd put bets on all his life and didn't suppose he'd made a fortune at it. No doubt all he'd done was break even at best. He didn't bet these days, not since making his fortune in scrap metal, but he missed the rush of adrenalin, the excitement, the disappointment, the triumphs. Merc would kill him.

Crossing the Green, Ford paused to admire the geese busily grazing. He loved the stocks, the huge oak tree they were all so superstitious about, the ancient cottages. Then he glanced across at Glebe House and wondered if indeed they would have been better buying a cottage, as Merc had wanted, because there was one thing for certain: their house would never be full of comings and goings. A cottage would have been big enough. All his fault, too, not Merc's. It coloured your thoughts, year in year out. Now with no business to keep him occupied twenty-four seven he only had the race meetings to fill his life, though he did love going.

Still, the replies to the banquet invites would be coming in soon and he guessed there wouldn't be a single refusal. That was going to be the social event of the year! He'd show 'em what life was about, and not half. They all needed waking up. He strode up his garden path with a spring in his step.

But the first reply to the banquet invitation was from Craddock Fitch, on his business headed paper. It was a curt refusal. Ford and Merc were devastated.

'He's refused on purpose, not even had the courtesy to claim they'd be away. I'm so disappointed.' Merc flung his reply down on the breakfast table and buttered her single piece of toast with enough butter for two slices, piled the marmalade on top and bit into it as though breaking a long fast.

Ford couldn't bear for her to be so bitterly let down. His mission in life, due to his inability to give her children, was to give her everything else she might want, whatever it was. Well, he wasn't putting up with it. He'd go round this minute and ask why?

'I'm going for a walk,' he announced. 'Shouldn't stay indoors when the sun's shining.'

Ford raced upstairs, cleaned his teeth, checked his appearance in the bathroom mirror and set off. He didn't wear his old gardening boots, couldn't prance about in that historic old house in them, so he crept out, hoping Merc wouldn't notice he was wearing his gleaming tan leather shoes, which he wore to race meetings.

It was a long walk up the drive so he had to pause for a moment behind a tree to catch his breath. The view of the Big House was breathtaking. It was quality and not half. Living there you'd feel ... well, you'd feel special and no mistake. Really special. Slightly intimidated, Ford marched up to the front door and into the magnificent Tudor hall.

Yes, Mr Fitch was in, the receptionist said. Would he please take a seat for a moment while she checked if he was available.

So the beggar was in. Now what did he say? He hadn't planned what to say he'd been so angry.

The receptionist returned quickly. 'Do come this way, please. Mr Fitch is free.'

He followed her into a large office.

Hand outstretched in greeting, Ford said, 'Good morning, Mr Fitch. Kind of you to make time to see me.'

Craddock Fitch sat back in his chair, waved a vague hand towards a chair for Ford to use and waited.

But Ford didn't speak.

So Mr Fitch said, 'How can I help you?'

'Mercedes and I are so excited about the banquet and we want everyone to come and enjoy themselves. Jimbo is performing miracles, he's making it very special, and it would have given us great delight if the two of you, your wife and yourself, would come. Merc's so disappointed you're not coming, and, like you, I expect, I don't like to disappoint my wife.'

'Can't come.'

'There'll be excellent food, good wine, entertainment, music in keeping with the period, not pop or rock or whatever, no awkwardness because we all know each other. Please will you come?'

'No.'

'Can you tell me why ever not?'

'It is not the kind of entertainment I enjoy. In fact, I can't think of anything more painful. Having to tolerate a whole evening of it would be just ... well, too much.'

'What kind of entertainment would you like, then?'

Mr Fitch shrugged.

In a flash Ford grasped the essence of the man. Mr Fitch couldn't find the banquet beneath him intellectually, because he wasn't superior in any way to Ford Barclay. No, not he. He really hadn't got an excuse. It was pique that was making him refuse. Damn the man. He stood up, his eyes glazed with temper, leaned his hands on the edge of the enormous desk and said, 'I see. Don't think you can pull the wool over my eyes. You were damn well not *born* a moneyed person. You might have made pots of the stuff, but deep down you're an ordinary bloke just like me. There's nothing upper-class about you. Pretending the banquet's beneath you! Huh! You and I can look each other in the eye as equals. Dragged ourselves up by our bootlaces we have, left education behind on the shelf and concentrated on making money. I've met too many guys with inherited money at race meetings not to know the difference in their accent, compared to yours. Accent might not count for much nowadays but it still tells an awful lot about a chap. It's all there too in their bearing, in their style. Hang your Savile Row bespoke suits. I,' he forcefully tapped his own chest, 'have got *your* measure, believe me.'

All anger gone, he could see clearly now, and when he studied Mr Fitch's face he honestly thought the fellow was about to have a heart attack. He was too kind-hearted not to feel dreadful about it.

'Here! Let me get you a glass of water. Don't get up.' He rang the bell on the desk. The receptionist came in almost before the sound had died away.

'Glass of water and quick.'

One look at Mr Fitch and she disappeared through a discreet little door and came back with the glass of water.

'Here we are, Mr Fitch, sip it gently. I'll get some ice.'

Ford froze with fright. The man's colour was kind of puce and grey all at the same time, he was breathing in great gasps, and sweating, there were beads of sweat all over his face. What if he died?

The receptionist loosened his shirt collar, pressed his head against the back of his perfectly splendid leather chair and held the bag of ice to his forehead.

'Breathe gently, Mr Fitch, try to breathe gently. That's better. Steady. That's it. Slo-o-ow. Good. Good.'

'Is he going to be all right?'

'I think you'd better leave.'

But Mr Fitch, despite his distress, signalled to Ford to sit down again. So he did, feeling guilty and useless and appalling all at the same time.

Gradually the strange colour receded from his face and his breathing became more normal. The receptionist removed the ice bag and Mr Fitch spoke, but not with his usual crisp delivery. 'Get me a whisky, if you please.'

'I most certainly shall not, Mr Fitch, not when you're in this state. An ambulance would be more appropriate. I'll ring for one immediately.'

'I didn't bloody well pay for you to go on a first aid course for you to tell me whether or not I can have a drink. Get me a whisky and one for Ford.' When she didn't move to do as she was told he roared, 'Now!'

The receptionist hesitated, then she caught sight of Mr Fitch's glare. 'Why pay for a first aid course for me and then completely ignore my advice?' she said as she returned with the two whiskies.

'Because the Health and Safety said I needed a qualified first-aider on the premises and I chose you, so away with the ice bag and leave Mr Barclay and me to talk.'

Neither man spoke at first, just quietly sipped their whiskies. Then Mr Fitch said, 'Not a word about just now. Don't want my wife to know; she's not to be worried. In fact, my wife *mustn't* know, ever. Right?'

Ford nodded. He daren't speak and he needed his whisky just as much as Mr Fitch did.

After he had drained his glass Mr Fitch began to speak. 'The chap who helped me start my business, when it was just me and him with a stolen wheelbarrow and one shovel between us, was the only one who dared to speak to me like you've just done. Kept my feet on the ground all the years he worked for me, even told me when he met Kate the first time that I'd better hurry up and marry her because she'd keep me cut down to size. He reckoned nothing to people who thought too much of themselves, you see.' Mr Fitch sighed.

'Right.'

Mr Fitch sat up and leaned his elbows on his desk. 'We'll come if you'll allow me to take back my refusal.'

'Of course. I'll put you and your wife on our acceptance list, then?'

Mr Fitch nodded. 'Good. I shall be delighted to come.'

Ford stood up, reached across the desk and shook hands. 'Thanks.'

'I needed that.'

Ford didn't know if Mr Fitch meant the whisky or the straight talking.

Chapter 14

'You see, Mum, it's not fair, is it? All of us can go to the banquet, but I want Jake to go, too. He'd love it, and I'd enjoy it so much more.'

'Well, darling, unfortunately only people living in Turnham Malpas and Ford's own family can go. Invitation only, as it says.'

'I know that. But could I just sneak him in?'

'How old are you? Six? No, of course you're sixteen, therefore you know you mustn't.'

'They wouldn't notice just one more.' Beth pouted, but to no avail.

'About Jake.' Caroline sat down on Beth's bed and took hold of her hand. Beth looked so lovely, so young, so vulnerable sitting up in bed in her Shaun the Sheep pyjamas that were far too small now. Caroline's heart almost broke. If only she didn't have to say this. But she had to.

Beth got in first. 'I know what you're going to say.'

'Tell me, then.'

'You're going to say that I have to be very careful about Jake, that's he's not my type, that's he's sex-mad and I've to watch out and not let things go too far.'

'Exactly, my very words. I know this sounds an old-fashioned thing to be saying nowadays *but* ... my old headmistress always said that it was the woman who kept a relationship in balance.'

'OK! And no sex before marriage, I expect.'

'What she said was that the woman drove the relationship. If you dressed like a tart men treated you like one, because that was the message you were giving out. If you conducted yourself with dignity and never deliberately egged the man on to go too far, then you would be in control. Let's face it, girls do dress far too sexily—'

'Oh come on, Mum. Honestly!'

'They do, Beth, and then they wonder when men want to go the whole way. I'm saying this because I don't want anything to prevent you from reaching your absolute potential in life. A husband and babies before you're twenty-five do that very thing.'

Beth couldn't bear this kind of talk any longer. 'Look, Mum, I—'

'Young men like Jake have great difficulty in controlling what they want most of all. Let's face it, Jake is up to the brim with testosterone right now and wanting to have sex more than anything in the world.'

'I want it, too.'

'Exactly. So that makes two of you. That's why it's up to you to keep the matter under control.'

To keep her face hidden from her mother, Beth put her arms round her mother's neck. 'But he is gorgeous, you have to admit. He's just so tempting, so good-looking, and sometimes I can hardly bear for wanting him to kiss me ... He can kiss blissfully, can Jake, you know. All the girls say so.'

'I do not want Beth Harris to be another notch on his bed-post.'

'Tell me this one thing if you feel you can ... Did Dad and you get together ... you know, before you were married? Don't answer me if you feel it's too private.'

There was a long silence, so long Beth began to wonder if she'd committed some terrible offence by asking and she desperately wished she hadn't.

'Your dad and I met in my surgery,' Caroline said eventually.

'I'd only been a fully-fledged GP for about two weeks and had an awful lot to learn. But my first patient that morning was your dad, wearing his clerical collar so I knew exactly who and what he was. I thought my heart had stopped beating and my lungs had burst. I could barely speak, and neither could he. You know that wonderful charisma he has even now, it was all there even though he was ill. He wasn't looking his best, believe me. He had an appalling cold, his eyes were red and watery, his nose was even redder and he had a fearful cough and a box of tissues under his arm because his nose wouldn't stop running.'

'Oh help!'

'I listened to his chest, between his sneezes, wrote out a prescription to bring his temperature down, told him to go home to bed and stay there, and if there was no improvement in three days he'd to ring for a visit. You've no idea how much I longed for him not to improve!'

'*Did* he ring for a visit?' Beth asked, having wonderful visions of her mum ministering to him in bed.

'No, but a bouquet of flowers arrived at the end of the week, with a thank you card saying that when he was definitely one hundred per cent he would ring me and we'd have a drink together. So that was the start of it all. Four months later we were married. It was the most wonderful four months of my life up to that date, and the same for your dad, too. That's what I want for you. That's why I'm asking you to be careful.'

'I see. Does Alex know all this?'

'No, but he can. I don't mind.'

'Don't worry about me, will you? I'll be all right. But he is absolutely spectacular. You can see that, can't you?'

'Oh yes, I can, very definitely. Invite him for supper this weekend, Friday or Saturday. Now see here,' Caroline stood up, 'it's late and it's school tomorrow and you should be asleep. Goodnight, Beth. Thank you for listening to me.'

'Thank you for telling me. Alex won't like Jake coming.'

'He's too well-mannered to cause a fuss when Jake's here.'

'OK, then I'll ask him. I can see what you mean about knowing when it's the right person. I wish I'd known Dad when he first met you. I'm not a tart, Mum, you know. I wouldn't sleep around.'

'I'm sure you wouldn't. Night-night.'

Caroline laughed as she heard Beth chuntering to herself as she left her bedroom. It sounded as though she were saying, 'Much chance I have to go off the rails with Alex standing guard over me.'

So Jake came for supper on the Friday night. He was immaculately dressed, carrying flowers for Caroline and an old school textbook he'd promised to lend Alex. He'd had a lift from someone so the bike had been left at home.

'Good evening, Doctor Harris, these flowers are for you. Thank you so much for inviting me. This is for Alex; I've been trying to remember to lend him it all this term.'

When Caroline, out of natural curiosity, turned it over to see the title, Jake said, 'Physics. I just hope he understands it better than I did when it was compulsory for me.' He gave Caroline an amused conspiratorial look and she saw immediately what it was Beth found exciting about him. He wasn't tall for his age, not like Alex, but he had a certain style which impressed her, and a cheeky grin which was very appealing. On the other hand, she couldn't forgive the fact that he had deserved a beating from Alex for something undefined.

'Please, Jake, go into the sitting room. Supper's almost ready, Beth's just finishing the white sauce; we won't be a moment.'

Beth was hiding in the kitchen, not quite able to cope with him being up for inspection.

She glanced up as she heard Caroline's footsteps. 'Well? What do you think?'

'Now I've had a proper look at him, he's certainly got plenty of charm.'

'Ooh! Good. You like him, then?'

'We'll see.'

'Will Dad?'

'I've no idea.' Knowing full well that Beth had no idea that Peter had been up to Prince Henry's to see the Head about the fight in the changing rooms, she couldn't honestly answer that question favourably. She called Peter from his study and Alex from his bedroom, and went into the sitting room to announce to Jake that the supper was all ready and she hoped he didn't mind eating in the kitchen.

'We always eat in the kitchen,' he said. 'We haven't got a dining room.'

Meeting Alex wasn't easy for Jake. After all, he'd said all those stupidly inaccurate things about Beth and got beaten up for it, and seeing him not at school but in Beth's home in front of her and Alex's father, whose clerical collar frightened the life out of him, he wasn't entirely sure how to behave. But he was relieved to find Peter in mufti, which did make things a little easier for him. 'Good evening ... sir.'

Peter, lost in thought, shook his hand. Then, standing behind his chair, he bowed his head and said Grace. They all chimed in with the Amen and so did Jake who was blushing furiously, never having said Grace in a house before. School, yes; someone's home, no.

Beth sat down next to him, just as embarrassed and uncomfortable as he was. Jake wasn't accustomed to tureens and serving dishes, but my word, the food was fantastic. Just right for a chap his age, and especially now he appeared to be having a growth spurt. The lamb chops were unbelievably tender – he and the Rector and Alex had two each – the new potatoes were minted and supremely tasty, and the broccoli, coated in Beth's exquisite white sauce, and the fresh peas were just delicious. Silence was the order of the day as they all dug in to this superb food, the like of which Jake had never had at home, ever.

'This meal is terrific, Doctor Harris. Thank you so much.'

Beth was tempted to tell him she'd made the white sauce but decided to be grown up about it. After all, if Mum could see what it was she liked about Jake then she could take all the glory there was for the white sauce.

Conversation, once the main course had been eaten, began to flow and Jake found himself feeling rather more comfortable. The pudding, a wonderful sticky toffee sponge, hit the right spot, too, and he became quite chatty once he'd scraped the last remnants from his dish. 'This wine's good, sir.'

'I didn't think to ask if you are allowed to drink wine.'

This question rather floored Jake. Allowed to have it? My God! oh! Sorry for that God. 'Of course, sir. We drink like fish at home.'

'I didn't want to upset your parents, Jake. I should have asked.'

Jake's reply came out in an embarrassed rush. 'That's all right, sir, my mother doesn't mind, and as for the idiot she's shacked up with at the moment, well, he doesn't care one jot about me. Glad he doesn't; the less I have to do with him the better. The day he interferes with what I do is the day I leave home.'

Jake put his wine glass down on the table and looked up at Beth. When he saw the shock on her face he could have died. What a stupid blasted thing to have said, in front of the Rector, too. Jake began to push his chair away from the table in preparation for leaving the premises pronto.

'I'm sorry about that, Jake, it must make life hard for you. Do you see your own father at all?'

Jake found it hard to reply. The Rector was too considerate, too thoughtful, and Jake wasn't used to that. 'About every six weeks,' he managed. 'He works abroad a lot so it's not easy. I'd prefer to live with him, but as he's away on business so much

… He can't help it … it's his job. He'd have me too if things were different.'

'I'm sure he would.'

To improve their opinion of him Jake said, 'It's him I get my brains from. Dad read maths at Cambridge; that's where I'd like to go, but … when I won a scholarship to Prince Henry's he was so thrilled …' He shrugged desperately, finished the wine in his glass and sat looking down at his hands, at a loss to know what to do next, feeling childish and unutterably foolish.

Caroline recognised his embarrassment so she suggested that Alex, Beth and Jake took their coffee into the sitting room and watched TV. 'Or talk or whatever. Take the coffee tray with you; Dad and I have enough.'

Alex took the initiative and stood up. 'Come on, you two.'

Left alone, Peter got up and closed the kitchen door, and when he sat down again he said, 'The poor chap. What a mess. I really upset the applecart, didn't I?'

'You didn't do it in purpose. Beth thinks he's gorgeous.'

'Does she know his history?'

'I don't think so.'

'So it's not sympathy for his plight?'

'No.'

'Right.'

They all spent an hilarious evening playing cards, which wasn't what Beth had planned; an evening with just the two of them listening to music in her room would have been more to her liking, but somehow the card games, with Alex being in a brilliant mood and Jake much happier and winning most of the games they played, turned out far better than she had expected. Then Peter asked Jake how he was going to get home.

'Don't worry, sir, I'll walk over the fields. It won't take long. Thanks all the same.'

'I think not. I'll drive you home. Coming, Beth?'

So, the three of them, Beth and Jake in the back holding

hands, and Peter driving, set off for Penny Fawcett. It rather felt to be a perfect ending to a perfect evening, and Beth went straight up to bed when she got back, to enjoy going over all that had happened.

They agreed that he'd come over to Turnham Malpas on Saturday morning and go to the weekly coffee morning, and then they'd catch the bus into Culworth. Beth decided it would seem odd going with Jake and not Alex, but as she acknowledged, there came a time when twins had to go their separate ways, and this was the time. It was called growing up and not before time at nearly seventeen. She really had been very backward where boys were concerned, but now she would make up for it. Then she remembered Jake's embarrassment when he'd burst out about his home life and then realised that perhaps he shouldn't have said what he did. She felt deeply sorry for him and determined to make it up to him as best she could. He really was absolutely terrific.

Across the valley, under the eaves of the house called Forge Cottage in Penny Fawcett, Jake lay in bed thinking about Beth. He honestly didn't know what to think about her. Her brother had beaten him up, without a word of explanation, though Jake knew full well why, and her father was in the Church and Church wasn't his thing, definitely not; he'd only been in one for his granddad's funeral and a cousin's wedding.

What had he to offer her? Nothing. Well, apart from his charm and his brilliant brain and his marvellous social skills and his sex appeal ...

There was one thing for certain: he'd have to watch his step. The Rector's eyes were enough to put the fear of God in anyone, not that he was all that bothered about God, but his eyes could be unnerving, kind of all-seeing right through to your guts. It wouldn't be the Rector who gave you a beating; he'd look so ashamed of you that hell would be the easier option. He debated about giving her up. There were easier girls than her, much easier girls, without the Harrises' standards. That'd be best: just forget her.

He turned over and instantly Beth filled his mind. He recalled how beautiful she was. Her perfectly splendid light blonde hair, those stunning blue eyes, her fantastically clear skin, the sweet, clean smell of her, her curves . . . Oh yes, her curves. Jake craved her.

No, he couldn't give her up, but he could have someone else for fun. She wouldn't need to know. He could keep Beth for serious and just accept a higher standard of behaviour from himself. He might even go to church; there might actually be something in it for him, and he could sit next to her in her pew. Then just before he fell asleep Jake remembered that girl who'd gone with them on the ghost trip. She looked up for it, and had kept catching his eye. She lived just down the road. Very handy, that. Yes. She wouldn't need much persuading. Now, what was her name?

Chapter 15

Jimbo stood in the middle of the Old Barn, thrilled to the core by the look of the whole place. He glanced down at his buckled shoes and thought, yes, this is all absolutely right. My doublet and hose, my velvet cap, the gleaming cutlery, the huge jugs filled to the brim with mead, the musicians tuning up in the minstrels' gallery ... thank goodness he'd had the sense to make sure of a gallery; it was so entirely fitting for an entertainment of this kind. He was barely able to stand upright he was so exhausted by all the organization, but at the same time so energised that he couldn't wait for everyone to arrive. He heard the jingle of the Morris dancers' bells at the main doors, and he sniffed the air to relish again the glorious aroma of the pig roasting on the spit outside.

He punched the air with vigour. Yes! Jimbo Charter-Plackett had done it again. This, for sure, was going to be the most fantastic night. What fun!

He spun round as someone called his name. It was Merc, dressed as Queen Elizabeth, with Ford as the Earl of Leicester. He'd picked up a lot of gossip in the village about Merc and Ford's costumes but even he had no idea how splendid they would be. If they'd been featuring in an international film they couldn't have been bettered. There were rumours that the pair of them had been up to London to a top-notch theatrical costumier, and my word, it must be true.

Ford wore a rich chestnut-brown tunic with a fur collar. His velvet hat had a rim of matching fur, but surely not real beaver as it used to be? His hose also matched the colour perfectly and his shoes were enhanced by silver buckles. No expense had been spared. As for Mercedes, well ... for a brief moment it was as though Queen Elizabeth herself had walked in. Her dyed hair was hidden by a spectacular auburn wig, around her neck hung lavish necklaces, her ringed fingers glowed with semi-precious stones, and her gown was a soft sage-green velvet that toned in a stunning way with Ford's outfit.

Jimbo swept off his velvet cap, pointed his right foot and bowed low. 'Your Majesty! We are greatly honoured by your presence. My lord, welcome.' He'd practised it to perfection at home in the long bedroom mirror, because he knew how thrilled Merc would be. The musicians began to play, a positive stream of wenches quietly took their places in readiness, and the Queen, at the sound of her first honoured guests arriving, strode majestically to the doors in readiness to greet them.

As always with any event in Turnham Malpas, everyone arrived in good time. No one could bear to be late in case they missed anything.

At the top table the Queen and the Earl of Leicester took centre stage with Peter and Caroline, Craddock Fitch and Kate. Then all the guests on the lower tables were allowed to be seated. There was a fanfare of trumpets and Jimbo announced the reason for the gathering, namely the fact that Her Majesty had graced this humble home with her presence and that wine and mead would flow, superb food would be served and the musicians and actors would entertain.

Maggie, Sylvia, Willie, Jimmy, Dicky and Georgie were all sitting together at the end of one of the long tables, feeling very impressed with the authenticity of it all. They drank the mead, then a second tankard was offered and they accepted that, too. The food was brought on, beginning with steaming vegetable soup brought to the tables in enormous tureens and served to the guests by the wenches. A delicate fish course came next which brought appreciative comments from every guest. A welcome lull allowed them to enjoy some very special music wafting down from the minstrels' gallery, then the serving wenches entered the hall with military precision, weighed down with the vast dishes and bowls holding the pork and the beef, the three different kinds of potatoes, dishes heaped with vegetables and steaming flagons of gravy. Then a pudding, an old-fashioned English pudding covered with brandy-soaked cherries and sourced from an ancient recipe book Craddock had once found at the Big House. Delicious!

'Fancy Mr Fitch helping like that,' said Dicky. 'I thought he wasn't coming.'

'He wasn't till Ford gave him a telling-off,' Georgie declared as she began on her second tankard of mead. 'Dicky, I thought you said this mead was potent. It's nothing of the kind. It's delicious.'

Jimmy winked at Dicky. 'That's right – you get it down, Georgie. It's bringing colour to your cheeks.'

'Stop encouraging her. It is potent and it's too late when you realise it.' But Dicky had to laugh.

The tables were cleared of dishes and the wenches were just bringing on great jugs of coffee and bowls of cream and sugar when there was a hammering at the main doors, a loud hammering which couldn't be ignored. Everyone stopped what they were doing to see who dared make such a din.

Jimbo as Master of Ceremonies went to fling the doors open. With tiny microphones hidden on the intruders everyone could hear the noisy exchange of opinions.

'We are the players from the Cock and Hen Inn in London and we have come straight from there to entertain Her Majesty with song and dance and a play, and we demand entry.'

'Absolutely not! Her Majesty the Queen is our honoured guest, and we already have entertainment for her.'

'*We* have come to entertain her! *We* insist on entering.'

'You may not. We have musicians, a fool, minstrels and dancers, and we do not need you. Go!' But they would not take no for an answer.

'Ask Her Gracious Majesty if we may perform!' they shouted from the doorway. 'Beg Her Majesty to allow us in,' they shouted louder still.

Eventually Jimbo approached the royal table, bowed low and asked if the players might be allowed entry. 'They are very insistent, Your Majesty.'

In appropriately regal tones Mercedes declared they were to be allowed to perform, whereupon the whole gathering was encouraged to roar their approval.

Then followed a hilarious half-hour of entertainment. One of the songs called 'The Chastity Belt' went down famously. It was bawdy but even the most prudish of the guests couldn't help but join in because it was such fun.

Sylvia said, 'If I didn't know different I'd think that singer with the beard was Gilbert Johns. It isn't, though, is it?'

Willie peered more closely as the singer, accompanied by a lutenist, performing a particularly lewd song came between the tables, and decided that, yes, indeed it was Gilbert Johns.

Sylvia was indignant. 'And him the church choirmaster. It's not right. That sanctimonious face he has on Sundays will never be the same again. I shall think of this song every time!'

Then she burst into giggles and so did Maggie. Then the people around them began to laugh uncontrollably and Maggie fell off the bench on to the floor, where she lay giggling helplessly, and they had to leave her there because they couldn't get her up.

Then the strolling players began seeking out guests to participate in the entertainment. They chose mostly young people who were eager to take part, and they were gathered together to sing the chorus while one of the actors performed a song.

Unsuspectingly, Peter commented to Caroline how quickly

the chosen guests picked up the words and the actions they had to perform. As he watched, there was something about one of them which he recognised ... it couldn't be, could it?

Caroline realised, too. 'Peter! It's Jake!'

'I've just noticed.'

'I told Beth he mustn't come. He's no business here.'

'How has she got him in?'

Caroline shook her head. 'I am very angry about this. I told Beth no, but she wanted him to, said how much more she'd enjoy herself if he was here.' Then she spotted Beth, but Beth had eyes for no one but Jake, and no wonder. He looked absolutely splendid, as though he'd stepped through the centuries straight from Elizabethan times, and when the strolling players picked him out to take a bigger part in the drama they were doing, Beth's face glowed with pride.

'I'm ignoring this until we get home.'

Maggie picked herself up from the floor and rather dazedly sat down again on the bench. 'I feel terrible.'

Georgie patted her arm. 'Never mind. It'll soon pass. Just sit tight.'

Finally the strolling players took their leave, but one of the women tried to take Jake with her, saying, with a lot of hip-waggling and daring glances, that he could share her caravan. Before they knew it there was a commotion, and the woman was brought before Mercedes.

'Wench! How dare you take away one of my gentlemen of the court? It is against my express wishes. Well? What have you to say for yourself?'

The wench flung herself to the floor and begged the Queen's pardon. 'Your Gracious Majesty, excuse a poor girl who has no man of her own. You must agree he is delicious.'

'Away with her to the gallows! Immediately!'

But the Earl of Leicester got to his feet, reeling slightly with the mead he'd consumed. 'Your most Gracious Majesty! I pray your indulgence. May I plead for her life? She is but a girl.'

'More than any girl, Lord Robert, if she fancies him for her bed. Stand forward, youth!'

There was nothing Jake could do but go forward. He was prodded into bowing low to the Queen. 'Your Majesty.'

'Have you a maiden of your own?'

Jake was dumbstruck and the first person to come into his head was Beth.

'Indeed I have, Your Majesty.'

'Bring her to me.'

Jake, bowing low, stepped away, took hold of Beth's hand, even though she resisted him, and pulled her reluctantly in front of the Queen.

'A comely maiden, indeed. See, my honoured guests, what a treasure she is. Do not fear, maiden, I mean you no harm. This youthful lad has no need of a trollop when he has this comely maiden to bed.' She turned to her guests. 'Shall I save the life of this trollop? Yea or nay?'

All the guests, fully into the spirit of the whole evening roared. 'Yea!'

Beth shrank back to her place, followed by Jake, who was laughing.

'Oh, Jake, don't laugh. Please, don't laugh. Dad's furious.'

'It was only fun.'

'He doesn't think so. I've never seen him so angry.'

Sounding far more confident than he really was, Jake told her he'd speak to Peter afterwards and make everything all right.

Immediately, so there was no gap in the entertainment, the Morris dancers came in, tambourines crashing, bells jingling, sticks clashing, and the whole of the barn was taken over again. More mead flowed, the crowd grew merrier, Beth calmed down and began to enjoy herself again, and before they knew it the clock was chiming midnight.

All the guests milled out through the huge main doors, laughing and joking, filled to the brim with food, their heads full of all the exciting things that had happened that night. Some, like Maggie, were unsteady on their feet due to the consumption of too much mead; others were wildly delighted by the whole evening and voluble in their praise.

'Best night we've ever had in Turnham Malpas.'

'Even Craddock Fitch can't compete with this.'

'It's made me really glad that Merc and Ford have come to live here!'

'I could come again next Saturday!'

This last comment was overheard by Jimbo, who, shattered though he was, took note and decided to go ahead with his idea to launch Elizabethan banquets for the general public. After all, it had been a wild success. He owed a lot to the Barclays, and he gave Merc a huge kiss as she and Ford thanked him for the wild success the evening had been.

Craddock Fitch complimented Ford and Mercedes openly and willingly, and Ford was delighted by his enthusiasm.

'I tell you what, Ford, do you play golf?' Craddock added.

'Of course. A golf club is a marvellous place for meeting the right kind of people when you're in business.'

'Exactly. I play golf, more for relaxation than anything, only a middling handicap, but would you enjoy a game with me?'

'I would.'

'Well, then, when I've had a chance to check my diary I'll give you a ring.'

'Wonderful. And thanks for coming.'

'Well, it was a very good night. Thanks for the invitation.'

Kate Fitch got a kiss on both cheeks as she added her thanks, but when she and Craddock walked across the park back to Turnham House she questioned his enthusiasm.

Aware she was far too curious about his motives, and even though he'd enjoyed himself far more than he had imagined he would, he feigned surprise at her question. 'Of course I enjoyed it. In fact, I've suggested he has a game of golf with me.'

Kate stopped, took hold of his arm and made him face her. 'Craddock, what are you up to?'

'Me? Nothing. Just being civil, a good neighbour, you know the kind of thing.'

'No, I do not. You *are* up to something.'

'Certainly not. Come on, let's get to bed. I need a good cuddle from the best wife in the world.' He put his arm round her waist and hugged her close.

In the darkness she couldn't see the half-smile on his lips.

In the Rectory things were not quite so harmonious. Peter was stupendously angry.

'But, Dad, please, it's only for the one night. I thought Jake could sleep in the guest bedroom, you see. He's gone into the back garden to wheel his bike round ready for leaving, but please, let him stay. It's a long way to go in the dark.'

It was becoming embarrassing for Beth now. She wished she'd asked her dad days ago and then there would not have been this fuss, but then he'd have known that Jake was planning to sneak in without an invitation, so that would have been hopeless.

'No, he may not. Absolutely not. He cannot have one scrap of respect for you doing what he did, not one scrap, and I'm deeply grieved over it all. Every person there knows who you are and—'

'So? I don't care what people think—'

'You not caring has nothing to do with it, and well you know it. What has made me so angry is the fact that you talked to your mum about it, she said he mustn't come as he hadn't been invited, and yet the two of you planned for him to sneak in. What has made me even angrier still is the episode of him getting involved with the strolling players and you being pointed out as his . . . well, to put it bluntly, his tart, in front of everybody.

That I am very angry about, Beth. You have a reputation to keep and tonight yours is in shreds.' He stabbed the air with his forefinger to emphasise his point.

'Dad! For goodness' sake, it was all make-believe. It wasn't *real.*'

'The whole evening was pretence but so well done it *felt* extraordinarily real. I am mortified about the whole matter. It is disgraceful and it'll be a while before I recover from it. Your mother feels exactly the same. I cannot imagine what people will be saying about you and Jake ... Is he ashamed of what he did? I guess not.'

Beth had never seen her father so angry. In fact, she didn't know he had it in him. She began to shake with fright over it all and to wish she'd never agreed to bring Jake to the banquet. She'd done it all for love, yet it didn't appear to have worked out as she'd wished.

There was a knock at the front door.

Peter flung it open. 'Jake! You're ready for off, I see. Excuse me from driving you home. I have an early start with it being Sunday, and I've drunk too much mead to be driving. You enjoyed yourself?'

'Enormously, thank you, sir. I'm sorry about what I did. It's not what you would have wanted for Beth, I realise that now. I owe both you and Doctor Harris an apology.' He glanced at Beth and saw she looked frightful.

'How right you are, Jake. I would have thought you would have treated her with rather more respect. Goodnight. You have a lamp on your bike, I hope?'

'Yes, thank you, sir. Goodnight. Goodnight, Beth.'

After he'd gone Beth decided on contrition. 'I'm deeply sorry Dad about what happened. It's all my fault. I should never have agreed to bring him. I just so much wanted him ... to be there, I mean, and it all went wrong. Please can I apologise to you, and to Mum for disobeying her.'

His temper spent, Peter accepted her apology. 'That young man needs watching, Beth. He hasn't had the upbringing that you've had ...'

Beth sneered, 'Oh, I see. He's working class so he's not allowed?'

Caroline stepped in. 'Stop! Before you say too much, just go to bed.'

Beth opened her mouth to add something else, but Caroline put her finger on Beth's lips to silence her. 'Do as I say! Now! Before it's too late.'

Jake had been very tempted to give Beth a kiss as he was leaving, but one look at Peter's face and he changed his mind. He could tell the Rector had weighed him up and found him wanting. Those all-seeing eyes of his! Oh well, there was always Janey from down the road. She was proving very accommodating, was Janey, and she hadn't a father who wore a dog collar. What's more, like his own 'uncle', her father didn't really care what she did, so that saved a lot of bother.

Then he wished he hadn't thought that, because the mysterious something that he had for Beth plagued him when he got to bed and he couldn't get to sleep. She'd looked so beautiful in her blue costume. It made her look like paintings of the Virgin Mary you saw in books, which in a way she was with her innocence, which her dad was only trying to protect. He'd make it up to Peter tomorrow by turning up at church. That would prove his good intentions where Beth was concerned.

At home in Glebe House the Queen and the Earl of Leicester were removing their costumes, delighted with the brilliant success of their evening.

'That mead! Heavens above, it's a wonder they weren't all laid out on the floor. Did you see Maggie? She must have been unconscious for nearly half an hour. It was all such splendid fun, wasn't it, though? I'm so glad we did it.'

'You acted your part wonderfully well, Merc. Very regal, I thought.'

'I felt so nervous, but it worked out OK, didn't it?'

'Absolutely terrific, and the Fitches enjoyed themselves, too. He's not nearly so stiff and starchy when you get to know him. Did you know he's asked me to play golf with him one day?'

'He has?'

'Yes. I'm really pleased. Everyone needs a friend.'

Merc's hand shook as she placed a necklace back in its box. Her instincts told her there was something ruthless about Craddock Fitch, and it worried her, but Ford didn't appear to feel that way. 'Mmm.'

'What do you think?' By now Ford was in his pyjamas and heading for the bathroom.

'We'll wait and see.'

'What does that mean?'

'Like I said. He'll probably forget all about it, anyway.'

'Oh, no. We are chums now, since I saw through him and told him so straight from the shoulder.'

'Just watch your step, Ford. I don't trust him an inch.'

'What is there not to trust? He's like me, pulled himself up out of the mire and doing rather nicely, thank you.'

'You won't listen, will you?'

'When have I ever slipped up about anything? Eh?'

Merc dropped her nightdress over her head and, as her face emerged, she said, 'There's always a first time and he's the very one to do it without batting an eyelid, because he has no conscience whatsoever. The only one he cares about is himself ... well, and Kate. He does care about her, I can see that.'

'Look, Merc, what on earth could he do that would harm us? We've left all that ducking and diving behind, haven't we? A new start, new house, new everything.' He gently kissed her cheek. 'Just enjoy yourself – that's what this new start is all about, enjoying ourselves, with plenty of money to do it.'

'You're right.'

But when Merc finally got into bed her heart was heavy and she dreamed about Ford locked up, dressed in an outfit with arrows all over it and her staring through bars at him, with tears streaming down her cheeks. She comforted herself by blaming it on the mead.

Chapter 16

Despite their late night, everyone at the Rectory was at morning service at 10 a.m. as usual, Peter having already conducted early Communion at 8 a.m. Beth felt very odd and it required a lot of self-control not to wobble about as she walked. It was the mead, she guessed. She'd drunk far too much of it.

How, how she'd longed for Jake to share breakfast with her at home, but her dad was still distant with her at breakfast, and that was very unusual for him, because he didn't harbour grievances overnight, so she knew things were decidedly touchy. But she realised why, because she'd been devastated, too, when Jake had grabbed her hand and dragged her in front of Merc and Ford. But she wouldn't let herself care. After all, the whole event was pretence, every single minute of it, so it simply didn't matter.

Just before the service started – in fact, only a minute before it all began – there was Jake standing in the aisle, looking at the three of them sitting in the Rectory pew. Beth's heart leapt with joy. She scarcely recognised him. On the school coach he wore his uniform, Prince Henry's being old-fashioned and not allowing the sixth-formers to wear casual clothes, and she was used to that, but this morning he wore a smart suit, a really smart tie and, when she looked down at his feet, highly polished shoes, too. He'd done all this for her sake. Her heart swelled with pride. He looked so good, so incredibly handsome.

'Good morning, Doctor Harris, may I join you?'

Caroline looked up and instantly knew he was trying to curry favour with Peter. She moved her feet so he could squeeze past her and sit next to Beth.

Jake took Beth's hand, raised it to his lips and kissed it, and Beth loved him for it. Alex made a point of showing his disgust by pretending to vomit, so she kicked his ankle. Why on earth had she been given a brother? God, he was awful.

Jake swiftly found his way through the service, finding the right places at the right moment, with no fumbling or hesitation, which made her prouder still, because she knew he never went to church, ever, and here he was behaving as a regular churchgoer should. He could sing, too – a light tenor, she judged – and she blushed bright red when he caught her admiring him singing.

At the point when the choir sang their anthem, the entire congregation was amazed to see Ford Barclay step forward, obviously about to sing the solo part. Gilbert Johns gathered the eyes of every member of his choir and they burst into song. Everyone knew Ford was a member of the choir but had no idea he was good enough to sing solo. But was he? More than one cringed at the prospect.

His glorious voice rose to the rafters in the manner of an Italian tenor, impressive, pitch-perfect. Ford gave everyone a wonderful experience and the rest of the choir rose to the occasion. A moment of silence greeted the conclusion of the anthem and then, spontaneously, the congregation burst into applause. A restrained murmur of delight ran through the church as the choir sat down and Ford returned to his place.

For Beth, apart from her appreciation of Ford's big moment, the entire service passed in a mist while she planned how to get Jake invited to lunch. But she needn't have bothered because her dad did it himself, much to her total astonishment. She began to suspect he was hatching some kind of plot to discredit Jake, but as the time wore on and they'd had coffee, sat talking in the sitting room and eaten lunch, which happened to be another of Mum's triumphs, Beth began to relax. So Dad wasn't being devious. But what was he doing?

There was an antiques fair in the village hall in Little Derehams that afternoon, and as a way of escaping parental supervision Jake suggested he and Beth went to see it. 'We could go on our bikes.'

Beth quickly agreed, went upstairs to change, hoping he wouldn't suggest detouring into Sykes Wood on the way. But he didn't. He was courteous, thoughtful and chatty.

In some stretches of the road to Little Derehams they cycled one behind the other as the road was so narrow, then as they cycled side by side when the road was wide enough Jake said, 'Considering your brother beat me up the other week he has been uncommonly friendly.'

Beth's brakes shuddered her bike to a stop. 'I beg your pardon?'

'Didn't you know?' Instantly he regretted mentioning the fight, because now she'd ask the hows and the whys, and before he knew it he'd be on the rack ...

'I did not. He's never said a word. What made him do it? When? That's not like him.'

Jake had to lie. 'I think it was because we went for that walk that Saturday.'

'That's ridiculous. I'm going home to challenge him about it. Right now.' She turned her bike round.

Jake put his hand on her handlebars. 'Don't do that. It'll spoil our afternoon together. I like your parents but being on our own is much more fun.' He leaned across and kissed her mouth, and kissed it again and then once more, and he felt her calm down. 'There, let's push on. He didn't mean anything by it, honestly, and I wasn't hurt.' He remembered his heavily bruised ribs and stiff jaw, and knew he'd lied again, but it was all in a good cause. To his relief Beth agreed, having loved his kisses and, like him, wanting to spend time together. They chained their bikes together outside the village hall and wandered in.

They dutifully paid their entrance fee and set off round the stalls. There were a few things they fancied but didn't buy, and then they bumped into Merc and Ford. There was no way of pretending not to have seen them, the hall was too small for that. Beth was horrified. They'd be bound to say something about Jake being at their party last night. But they never mentioned it, not a word, and Ford suggested that they all sat in the little café and had a drink and some cake.

'Would you like that, Beth?' Merc asked. 'I can imagine what it's like being short of money when you're still at school.'

'Thank you. That would be lovely, wouldn't it, Jake?'

Jake nodded.

So they sat down together and ate slices of lemon cake oozing with lemon curd. Jake and Ford had a second slice, and Ford ordered another pot of tea. They chatted away as though they were lifelong friends, which seemed odd with people their age, but the two of them made it so easy to talk.

'How did you get here?' Ford asked.

'Well, I've been to lunch at the Rectory and we've come on our bikes.'

'In that case, I'll put the bikes in our 4x4 and drive you back. It's a long way uphill for Beth and it's on our way. Finished?'

Before they left Jake helped Ford to load a 1930s solid oak bureau they'd bought into the back of the 4x4. 'Merc saw it and it reminded her of one her granny used to have. It's the genuine thing, you see. Needs a bit of cleaning up, but it'll be all right. Thanks, Jake.' Then he leaned towards him and said quietly, 'Didn't know Beth had a boyfriend.'

Beth overheard him and blushed furiously when Jake answered, 'We're just friends, you know, that's all. Her brother Alex goes to the same school as me.'

'Ah! Right.'

She'd thought they were more than just 'friends', that he was her friend not Alex's. She wanted to cry. Was that how he really saw her? As Alex's sister?

They stopped outside Glebe House for Jake to help Ford lift the bureau out and carry it into the house, then he and Beth lifted their bikes out and wheeled them along to the Rectory.

Jake stood holding his bike. 'I'll just come in and thank your mother for lunch and then I'll go,' he said.

'I see. Don't worry, I'll give her your thanks.' Her voice was tight and squeaky because she was so upset. But she was glad he was going home, and hated the thought of seeing him on the school coach the next morning. She'd probably not even acknowledge him, not after what he'd said to Ford. 'See you then.'

Jake took hold of her hand and squeezed it, 'Did you mind me coming to church? Was it all right?'

'Of course. After all, you are Alex's friend. I'll take my bike round the back. See you Monday.'

She felt shrivelled inside, smaller and insignificant. How could he? How *could* he? Not even a kiss. What had she done wrong? Expected too much, pushed things along too fast? She hadn't, though. Dad had warned him off and that had made him cool it. He, her dad, was to blame. Tears formed in her eyes, but she couldn't let them, because before she knew it Dad would be comforting her and she could not allow that, because she wouldn't be able to be cross with him then.

She stormed in through the back door ready for battle. Caroline was reading the Sunday paper.

'Where's Alex, Mum?'

'Doing his prep.'

'Huh! Typical. Dad?'

'In the study.'

Beth crossed the hall, and though the study door was shut she burst in without knocking, which she knew from babyhood was not permitted. She'd always accepted it as a fact of life and never questioned it, but today ... life-long restrictions were for casting aside.

But she was brought up short. He was at his desk, looking at their old photographs, which were spread out on his desk, still not in those photo albums Mum had bought specially years ago and never got round to filling with the myriad photos she and Dad had taken of them over the years. He was holding one of her in those favourite red shorts of hers, taken when she was almost three. And there she was, a pretty little blonde, blue-eyed cherub, laughing with glee at something or other, then her dad looked at her, and his eyes began to fill with tears. 'Obviously I can't, but I wish, right now, that I could keep you like that for ever and ever.' He reached out a hand to her and she took it and squeezed it tight. Damn, she thought.

'I feel concern for you, Beth, about him. You can feel his sexuality almost taking him over sometimes and I do not want you to be the one ...'

'You mean you don't believe in sex outside marriage?'

'Not sex so freely indulged in as it is at the moment, generally speaking, among people of your age. I feel it can't be right, more especially for women than for men.'

'But men have to have women to do it with, haven't they? Well ... some don't, I suppose.'

'However, my darling, you be in charge, right? This day and every day. You do not allow anything to happen to you about which you have the smallest qualm, nothing shifty nor sneaky nor mean, because that is damaging to one's spirit. Real love has nothing of that in it. Real love is beautiful. Have I your promise on that?'

Beth nodded.

'Keep this picture of all that innocence in your mind.' He held up the cherub to remind her. 'Don't lose it to any Tom, Dick or Harry. OK?'

'OK.'

'I'm going for a walk. Want to come?'

'No, I've got prep to do. Dad, you're not saying sex can't be decent and respectable?'

'I'm talking about *loving*. That's something special and worthwhile, completely different from common-or-garden sex that people talk so glibly about.'

'Can I ask you something?'

'Of course.'

'Have you had a word with Jake, warning him off, kind of?'

Peter shook his head. 'Absolutely not.'

She knew he was speaking the truth, him being so keen on it.

'Thanks, Dad. Don't talk to Alex about this, will you? What you've said to me?'

'Strictly private. Help me collect this lot together.'

So she did. They were all put back as they usually were in a box file till that mythical moment when Mum had time.

'Must go and change. I admire you for working hard at school; it is the only way to achieve your objectives.'

'You don't know what my objectives are.'

'No, I don't. Do you know?'

'Oh, yes. I decided the other day, I'm going for a PhD in archaeology. All that mud and unearthing things buried for generations. Tramping along in trenches and finding just a little something someone used hundreds of years ago and being able to hold it and feel it and think about them and lift up a tiny corner of their century to throw some light on the way they lived their lives.'

'Right!' He placed a kiss on her cheek. 'I'm surprised by that. I'm beginning to think I don't know my daughter at all.'

Beth looked up at him, admiring his loving, handsome face and the sheer incandescent joy of him, and said, 'Oh, I think you do, dearest Papa, you truly do.' She shook her head. 'You truly do. Enjoy your walk.'

Caroline accompanied Peter on his walk, leaving Alex and Beth in the Rectory alone. Beth made a cup of tea just how Alex liked it and took it upstairs to the attic for him.

'It's me with tea and biscuits for the workaholic.'

She pushed the door open with her knee and walked in. He was sitting in his easy chair reading the physics book Jake had given him the other day. He put his bookmark in and closed it.

'Thanks. I need that. And biscuits, too. Thanks. Enjoy your ride? Buy anything?'

'Yes. No. Why did you beat him up?'

Startled by the unexpectedness of her question, Alex answered cautiously, well aware he was in treacherous territory.

'Felt like it.'

'Alex Harris does nothing without a very good reason.'

'OK. I overheard him boasting.'

'Boasting? About what?' Then her face drained of colour. 'Not me?'

Alex nodded. 'This tea's nice. Thanks.'

'I haven't known you all these years without knowing how you like your tea.'

'Mum and Dad gone out?'

'Yes, for a walk. I think you owe it to me to tell me why you beat him up. Really tell me.'

Choosing his words with the greatest care, Alex told her not the actual words, they were too foul, rather their implication. 'I know it's not true because you told me about why you ran home. I know it's hard to forget what happened in Africa ... but remember ... it ... *didn't actually happen*, only might have done, and that's the difference.' Alex swallowed hard, recalling smashing the soldier's skull with the butt of the man's own rifle. 'Jake exaggerated what happened in Sykes Wood to boost his own ego and make himself appear special – men can be like that, you know. I couldn't stand letting him get away with it, that's all. Not when it was you.'

Beth sat silently for a while, thinking about Jake and wondering why he said what wasn't true. If he had real feelings for her he wouldn't have said what he did in the showers. She knew Alex wouldn't have spoken like that about a girlfriend of his. Her voice trembled when she next spoke. 'I find it so hard to believe he talked about me like that. There's a side to him I know nothing about, isn't there? Why didn't you tell me sooner?'

'No need to. I don't know him all that well. We simply go to the same school, that's all. Pass me another biscuit, please. How did you know?'

'Jake mentioned it and then immediately I could see he wished he hadn't. Now I know why. He's definitely gone off me. I thought Dad had said something but he hasn't and I believe him, so it must be my fault.'

'I doubt it by the look on his face when we were having coffee.'

Hope rose for Beth. 'Look on his face?'

'I caught him admiring you.'

'Oh! Wow!'

'Remember, when you sup with the devil, Beth, you need a long spoon.'

'Where on earth did you get that from?'

'Grandmama Charter-Plackett. She used it once and I thought it was rather a good thing to remember.'

'Right. Thanks for standing up for me, anyway.'

'Anytime. Here, take my cup.' He picked up the physics book and Beth thought about it being with Jake in Jake's room, in Jake's bag. His hands had held it, his fingers had touched it, his eyes had read it ... then she recalled he was not all pure gold, and, yes, she'd better be in charge. In fact, she rather gloried in Alex fighting him. No more than he deserved for the things he'd lied about doing in Sykes Wood. She'd have to alter her tactics where Master Jake was concerned. A dose of indifference might be effective. But it would be hard, so very hard. He had such ... kissability. He was just the most truly sublime man she'd ever met.

So it was Jake feeling rejected on Monday morning when Beth ignored him and didn't even offer to sit next to him on the coach when it arrived. Had she learned about Janey? He rather hoped not. He wouldn't want her hurt because of him. She couldn't have heard; he and Janey had been so discreet. He'd have to win Beth back for the simple reason that the beauty of her, both inside and out, would not leave his mind. He'd never met a girl who appealed to him as much as she did. Even her family, especially the Rector, somehow raised his aspirations, made him know for certain that there were better things in life than a careless mother with a string of men, than a father deeply lonely for his son, than the chaotic lifestyle he suffered: a place where life was ordered and uplifting, where respecting each other was valued. He'd deserved the hiding Alex gave him, for what he'd said about her was completely untrue and unforgivable, and he needed to make it up to her.

On the Wednesday of that week Caroline wasn't 'doctoring', as Dottie called it, so she had time to read the post when it came just after the twins had left for the school coach. Peter had gone out early to attend a retreat at the Abbey in Culworth, so once the breakfast was cleared up and Dottie had got cracking with her Wednesday chores, Caroline settled down in her rocking chair beside the Aga and found the first letter was for Beth in a handwriting she didn't recognise. For a brief moment her heart lurched. Not Suzy Palmer again, please God. But then she knew it wasn't and saw she had one, too, in the same handwriting.

Intensely curious, she quickly opened her envelope and found it was a very beautiful card from Jake, obviously chosen with great care, thanking her for the lovely lunch on Sunday and saying how much he had enjoyed their company, the conversation and the welcome. Signed, Sincerely yours, Jake Jonathan Harding.

Caroline had to laugh. He was certainly trying hard, was the boy. She closed the card and studied the picture on the front. It was a wonderful print of a painting by Turner called *Sunrise Between Two Headlands*. So the boy had taste, then. She wondered about him, about how much he truly valued Beth, or how little. It was difficult to assess. He certainly hadn't valued her when Alex had that fight with him. But on Sunday she'd noticed how intently he listened to Peter's sermon, and how at lunchtime she'd caught him listening to Beth with a lovely expression on his face. His home life sounded appalling but it didn't mean he was, and she mustn't pre-judge.

Three letters for Peter, two catalogues she hadn't asked for and then ... another letter for her, the address handwritten, and she knew immediately who it was from. Her heart thudded and there was an unaccustomed beating in her ears. She tore it open, ripping the letter out of the envelope, almost tearing it in half.

She unfolded it and read at the bottom 'Sincerely, Suzy Palmer'. Caroline groaned.

Dottie appeared at the kitchen door. 'All right, Doctor? I thought I heard you call out.'

Caroline swallowed hard, her throat dry, her eyes pricking with tears. 'I'm fine, thanks.'

Dottie said, 'Well, I don't think you are. You're as white as a sheet. I'm either putting the kettle on or getting the brandy out.'

The snappy reply she got shook her. 'No, thank you, I need nothing at all. Get on with your work, if you please.'

Dottie crept away, chastened but worried, too. The Doctor had never spoken to her in that tone before. Opening a letter, she was. Not from that dreadful Suzy, surely to goodness.

Dear Caroline,

Have you ever thought what a very lucky woman you are? Not only have you my children but also the only man I have ever loved. I know I have had two husbands and to outsiders it must appear that I have had two wonderful chances for happiness in my life. In fact, I know now I loved neither of them. I thought I did but in truth it is Peter who should have been my husband. How can you be so cruel as to withhold from me what he and I created in a moment of deeply intense passion?

You alone – Peter would never have done such a thing – have put pressure on our children in a very underhand manner to prevent them from getting to know me and, worse still, your love for Peter is keeping the two of us apart, two people who should be together.

This letter is to ask you to insist the children come to stay with me now and again, and to release Peter from his marriage vows and let him become my husband, which at the bottom of your heart you know is where he belongs.

Church of England priests can be divorced and still carry on with their ministry, and of course I would not be teaching and could assist him in every way possible in his work, which you as a doctor cannot possibly do with the same devotion.

Think hard, Caroline, about what I have written and search your heart as to whether or not you are doing the right thing. I think you will find I am right.

Sincerely,
Suzy Palmer

It was the words 'deeply intense passion' that burned into her heart. Those words destroyed the idea of a one-off happening that gave her, Caroline Elizabeth Harris, the children she could never have. Had she only forgiven Peter his treachery because she had got the children she longed for, the children she knew he longed for, too? The woman must have gone mad to accuse her of deliberately preventing the children from seeing her. Had she gone out of her way to encourage them not to go? She hesitated for a moment. Had she really? No. She'd deliberately left it to Peter, because it was his problem, not hers. And the twins had both been adamant about their decision.

Caroline unfolded the letter and read it once more. All the heartbreak flooded back and consumed her anew.

Dottie walked in. 'Shall I make our coffee? It's time.'

'Yes. Of course. I'll have mine in the sitting room if you don't mind.'

'I'll bring it in when it's ready.'

'Thank you.'

Dottie always loved the mornings when they had coffee together. Anyone would think that the differences in their levels of education and their ages would make easy conversation impossible, but that wasn't so. What worried Dottie was Caroline's distress. What worried Caroline was how on earth she would find the right words to tell Peter. Did she in fact *need* to tell him?

Chapter 17

Ford prepared for his game of golf with Craddock with meticulous care, determined to be properly dressed when he appeared at Mr Fitch's prestigious golf club. This was his confusion: one minute in his head he called him Mr Fitch, the next Craddock. Which should he use? He couldn't really call a golfing chum by his formal name, now could he?

The second niggle he had was the other two making up the foursome. According to Craddock, he wasn't much cop at golf. Ford grinned, thinking that neither was Ford Barclay. Craddock said the other two were businessmen he'd known for years, so maybe they weren't much cop, either. Oh, what the hell! A game of golf was nothing in the scheme of things. He'd asked around if anyone knew Mr Fitch's golf course but no one did, except to say it was ultra-posh.

He checked himself in the long mirror in their huge bedroom.

In a mad moment he'd once bought plus-fours but had decided not to go to such extremes. Instead he'd chosen a pair of quietly checked brown trousers, made to measure so the fit was excellent, until he saw himself sideways and knew his stomach was far too big. Bit late now to do something about that! His front view was better. He'd chosen a cream shirt, an Argyle-patterned cream tie with an identical matching sweater and a brown leather jacket to keep out the cold. Some golf courses had a hell of a wind blowing across them.

Ford went to ask Merc what she thought.

'Well?'

'You look splendid,' she said. 'Got money for the bar?'

Ford nodded.

'Handkerchiefs?'

He showed her two sparkling clean ones, neatly pressed by her fair hand.

'Clubs?'

'In the car.'

'Have a good time.' Merc turned her back to him and carried on polishing the stainless-steel doors of the kitchen cupboards.

'What's up, Merc?'

'Nothing.'

'There is.'

She turned round and leaned against the worktop. 'I'm bothered about this golf business. Just watch yourself. He's not beyond getting you tipsy on purpose to ...'

'Eh? What do you mean for heaven's sake?'

'Find out things you don't want him to know.'

Ford paused for a moment, rattling the change in his pocket. She had a point but ... it was all nonsense, just Merc being over-cautious.

He flung back his shoulders, drew in his stomach and said confidently, 'He isn't like that. I shall watch my intake, don't you worry. Bye, my love.'

'You're too trusting.' Merc carried on with her cleaning, knowing full well she was right. Ford *was* far too trusting, that's how it all got started in the first place; him trusting and finding out too late. Still, it had brought them more money than they had ever dreamed of in the end. But what about peace of mind? Which was of more value, money or contentment? She had a feeling it was contentment, but as she looked around her utterly splendid kitchen, thought about the garden, now not so stiff and starchy as it had been when they moved in, about their luxurious bedroom and the bathroom to die for, she decided that living in Glebe House was definitely a plus. She was getting accustomed to their lifestyle and, what was the best, becoming accepted by everyone in the village.

She actually had real friends here now, especially at the embroidery group, helped along by Ford's weekly racing tips. They all loved them and fingers crossed every week so far he'd been bang on the nail. She loved that, and what was a real plus her own embroidery had come on by leaps and bounds since Evie had taken her under her wing. Soon she'd have the blissful pleasure of going to the town hall in Culworth and seeing her jewel-like pieces of embroidery hanging in the exhibition with her name alongside them. She knew that the glorious colours and the gold and silver thread she made use of were a true expression of her soul, something which amazed her, as all her life she'd been limited by being comparatively uneducated by endlessly having to change schools. There seemed to be nothing in her grim childhood which had indicated that she might one day produce such fantastically vibrant work. Now, even longing for the children she and Ford had never had seemed not to figure so largely in her mind. Maybe the pictures she made were her children, was that it?

She wouldn't tell Ford that; he'd think she'd gone crackers. And in any case, they never talked about not having children because it caused Ford such pain. She glanced at the clock. Half past nine. Her mind flitted to the golf course. He'd have had a bet as he always did. He couldn't resist. But was he winning?

Ford began suffering the moment he met the other two golfers. First off, he'd overdone it on the outfit front. Craddock and both his business acquaintances were very expensively casual in classy baggy chinos, cashmere sweaters, scarves wrapped round their necks against the cold and shabby slip-on shoes, unlike Ford's smart brown and white lace-ups. Their clubs were top of the range, however, far superior to Ford's, and their accents were what he called true blue. Craddock winked at him when they met, and this made Ford feel more comfortable.

'This is Marcus Phillips, and this chap here, with the whisky in his hand already, is Nigel Farrow. This is the Ford Barclay I told you about, a friend of mine from the village where I live.'

Nigel Farrow toasted Ford with his whisky. 'What's your handicap, Ford? Mine's nine. Par for the course is seventy-four.'

Ford shook in his shoes. 'Twenty-one. I did say I wasn't much good.'

Marcus tried hard to smother the sneer on his lips. 'Mine's eight. Craddock's is eighteen. We'll play you two, four balls. Two hundred pounds between us? How about that?'

Ford nodded. He couldn't have answered to save his life. It struck him that running away might be the best bet. A hundred pounds to pay if he lost! Dear God! He prayed he'd win because he'd never bet so much on a game. Suddenly he sensed he was outclassed, in terms of clothes, money and golf.

And he was. Craddock, who'd admitted to not being very good at golf, proved to be above average, and the other two were nothing short of brilliant. It didn't appear to bother Craddock that they were being beaten hands down by the other two, but it bothered Ford, because he was beginning to feel ridiculous. The more uncomfortable he became the worse he played, and the others were starting to laugh and slap him on the back rather too heartily, saying, 'Hard lúck, old chap.'

Then a miracle occurred. Ford holed in one! He'd never done it before in his life and never would again, but today he did. He was breathless with the thrill of it. He'd done nothing special, just whacked the ball as hard as he could clean over the hazard of a small lake, straight between two trees ... a short hole, 175 yards and hey presto! the biggest stroke of luck he could possibly have hoped for. A million to one chance. He trembled with the shock of it. Nigel and Marcus were stunned but summoned up enough enthusiasm to give him loud praise. 'Drinks all round!' they shouted, almost visibly grinding their teeth at his success.

This silenced the laughter, and from that moment on Ford played the game of his life. Craddock, who'd never beaten the other two all the time they'd played together, was both elated and inspired, while Marcus and Nigel, angered by Ford's success, couldn't summon up their usual feisty play.

'Well, done, Ford. Excellent! Oh! Well played!' Craddock couldn't hide his delight.

Marcus and Nigel played grimly on, facing defeat by two men they both considered absolute incompetents. When the game was finished they handed over their £100 each and went for their showers. They all met up again in the bar. It appeared that the two of them had decided to be gracious in defeat.

'Well done, Ford, you certainly came up trumps. Where do you play?'

Quickly Ford declared he hadn't played for years. 'Just a one-off, that hole in one. Drinks on me.'

Something in the atmosphere changed during lunch, though. It was as if the other two had planned something together, and only they knew what it was all about.

The dining room was superb. Ford couldn't begin to imagine what the membership fees might be. It was busy, and it would need to be to keep this kind of standard up, with waiters rushing about attending to their smallest requirements, silver service, fresh flowers and crisp, snow-white table linen.

Ford remembered Merc's apprehension and twice managed to pour his drinks into a handy vase right by his place setting. His stomach rebelled by the time the dessert trolley came round. He waved it away with a casual hand. 'Diabetic, sorry. Pity, they do look marvellous.'

He never touched the sweet wine meant to go with the dessert, nor the liqueur the others had to finish their meal. Out of the blue Craddock mentioned Ford had retired from owning his own metal company, carefully refraining from using the term 'scrap metal', but the other two were on to it immediately. Ford tried to turn them from talking about scrap metal to racing, which he claimed was his major interest now, but he was wasting his time. The two of them were determined to keep on and on about scrap metal, the one subject Ford hoped he'd left behind when he came to Turnham Malpas.

Nigel Farrow finished his liqueur, and then, looking very determinedly at Ford, he said, 'Scrap metal! No wonder you've retired in your forties. Money, money, money in metal, especially if you know the trends.' He knocked some ash from his cigar and winked. 'I'm right, aren't I? Come on, out with it.'

Poker-faced, Ford replied briefly. 'There's money in most things if you study the trends.'

A cloud of smoke from Nigel's cigar drifted in his direction. Ford wafted it away impatiently. Merc was more astute than he'd realised; the two of them were obviously after his blood, just as she had warned. He noticed that Craddock Fitch was quietly smoking his cigar and looking anywhere but at him, dissociating himself from the concerted attack. Thank you kindly, Craddock. He'd remember this, he would, asking him out for a friendly game of golf with his business chums and encouraging them to winkle out of him all the underhand, borderline illegitimate deals he'd done. All the deliveries of roofing lead which, much too late, he'd realised were stolen goods, but which he never queried, the new copper piping he suspected had been lifted from building sites all over London, but had never rejected. All the secret brown envelopes he'd handed out to ne'er-do-wells driving battered old trucks and scraping a living from theft. God, what a fool he'd been not putting a stop to it. He'd have made an ample living just dealing with the honest ones, but somehow he'd been bullied into accepting stolen scrap and not daring to refuse. Foolishly, he'd imagined the law would never catch up with him. Then, sickened by the dodgy position he was in, he'd decided to sell out. It seemed to him to be the easiest way out rather than to allow the threats to get even more severe.

Marcus Phillips sneered at him now as he held the bottle of Cointreau in his hand, offering to fill his glass. 'Taste the fruits of your labours, Ford. I remember when we were building our new office block we lost a thousand pounds-worth of copper piping in one night. Took days to find replacement piping.' Marcus leaned confidentially across the table and, lowering his voice, said, 'It wasn't you was it, paying half its value, handing the cash over at midnight? Discreet paper parcels, no questions asked?'

Craddock began to feel uneasy. This persecution of Ford was not what he'd expected at all. Just a bit of teasing perhaps, but not this. He knew for a fact no such thing as an office block existed in Marcus's shady dealings. Mentioning one was all a sham to catch Ford out, and he felt ashamed. He hadn't asked the two blasted blighters to go for Ford's jugular, had he?

Ford briefly wondered if it was too early to leave. Would he look more guilty if he did not stick it out?

Nigel Farrow offered him a cigar. 'Very good quality, I do believe. Even if you don't smoke regularly, you'll enjoy one, believe me.'

'No, thanks, it's a foul habit.'

Nigel's eyebrows arched. 'Come now, we need to have a few vices, surely, and you must know all about vice, considering the circles you must have moved in … in the scrap metal trade. It's full of rogue traders. Isn't it?'

Ford, not yet too seriously alerted by the goading he was receiving, said. 'Of course, just like lots of businesses where cash in hand and no questions asked is common. I've met that kind of dishonesty. I remember a chap …' Ford clamped his mouth shut, then changed tack. 'The Inland Revenue loses millions every year because of it.' He managed a bleak smile.

Nigel laughed with delight and pointed a finger at him. 'Go on! Go on! *I remember once* … Tell us!'

Ford didn't reply.

'You see! You're as bad as everyone else. Tax-dodger sublime! No wonder you can retire before you're fifty. The whole of the scrap metal trade is swimming in money since China decided to turn capitalist and build and build. Is that where it all went? Eh?'

Finally Ford saw where it was all heading. He pushed his chair back and rose to his feet. 'I'm damned glad I beat you today: it was just what you deserved.'

Ford glanced at Craddock Fitch but he remained impassively detached, as though watching a play in a theatre. Ford's stomach rumbled with nerves. Was Craddock really at the root of all this? When he'd thought they were friends? Now what should he do? That hole in one and the triumph he felt came up from somewhere and gave him courage. He didn't care if he upset Craddock Fitch. He was saying it and damn the lot of 'em.

'I wouldn't dream of telling two bastards like you the intricacies of my business. There's straight and there's crooked and I was one of the former ... to the best of my ability. Think what you blasted well like. I'm as clean as a whistle.' He crossed his fingers behind his back. 'Thank you for the hundred pounds I won. I'm glad we beat you. I'll pay for the lunch and the drinks because I don't want to be beholden to two nasty, sly devils like you. I'm also bloody glad I got that hole in one. Thanks for the invitation, Craddock. I know you won't be inviting me again and I don't want you to. Good afternoon!'

He stormed off to pay the day's bill with his credit card. It was twice what he had expected but he didn't give a damn. He'd come so close to 'fessing up he was sweating from head to foot. His clothes clung to him and he felt disgusted by the way in which drink had almost been his downfall, because those two glasses of Cointreau he'd been bullied into drinking had finally taken him right to the edge. As for Craddock Fitch. Well, he hadn't enough vocabulary to describe how he felt about him.

Merc was right. Craddock had set him up good and proper, and he, Ford Barclay, would never forgive him for it. To catch him out had been Craddock's intention all along. If those two nasty beggars were the kind of friends Craddock had, then he didn't want to be one of them.

As he triggered his remote control Ford did wonder if he was fit to drive after all that drink. But he had no way out of it. Ford drove home very steadily, sweating anew each time he thought about the close shave he'd had. It worried him that he hadn't seen it coming. This rural life had slowed him up and it wouldn't do.

As he approached Glebe House he pulled himself together, straightened his tie, put a mint in his mouth, a smile on his face, and thrust the whole episode behind him. Well, almost. Thank God Craddock hadn't suggested they travel to the golf course together. He would probably have murdered the beggar on the way home and dropped him in a ditch. He'd concentrate on the hole in one, the wonderful food and the superb clubhouse when he told Merc how he'd got on.

Craddock Fitch went home delighted with his day. He'd done exactly what he'd intended, to persuade the other two to ply Ford with drink and flattery until he let spill something of how crooked he'd been. He'd always suspected him of not being entirely honest and that one short sentence had proved it, though Ford had been astute enough to turn the tables by telling the other two exactly what he thought of *them*. He grinned at Ford's discomfort but had to admire him for standing up for himself, even when it was all too late, and leaving the premises with dignity. For certain, Ford couldn't blame Mr Craddock Fitch. He'd not said a word, had he?

Even better was the satisfaction of beating Marcus and Nigel at golf. What a game! It was the first time he'd ever beaten them, and the pleasure of it was most satisfying. That hole in one had done wonders for Ford's golf and his own.

Wait till he told Kate. She'd laugh, and he loved to see her laugh.

But he didn't get the chance to love her laughter. She was furious with him.

'How *could* you? He and Merc may not be out of the top drawer, a state of affairs you admire greatly apparently, but they are kind people and fitting in well here in the village and *doing good*, with the youth club and such. I'm ashamed of you, I really am.'

Craddock could tell from the tremor in her voice that the anger was real.

'I never said a word.'

'Come off it! Don't play the innocent with me. You set it up with those two nasty beggars. I've only met them once and that was once too often.'

'We beat them at golf, though, so that was a plus. It'll be a long time before Ford forgets his hole in one.'

'Good for him. I shall congratulate him next time I see him. Mind you, he probably won't speak to me after this episode. I am ashamed of you, darling. I truly am. It was beneath you.' She got to her feet. 'I'm going for a bath and don't bother me when you come to bed. I shall be asleep.'

'Right. Right.'

'You can spend the silence thinking of ways to make it up to him. Goodnight.'

Blast Kate's passionate belief in honesty and integrity. She could afford it. She hadn't been dragged up as he had been, or needed to learn to fight her corner. But he preferred her that way, gentle and kind, forthright and beautiful, and a wonderful lover. At his age, what more could he ask? She was a gift he didn't deserve when he did things like he'd done today. He'd get into bed before her, scrubbed and smelling promising, and see what happened. He'd give her a full apology with a promise to grovel to Ford with another full apology for his own crass stupidity. But the fact was, Marcus had big contacts in the business world and Craddock had a nasty suspicion that he'd very likely use them to shop Ford. Craddock suggesting he shouldn't would only make Marcus laugh uncommonly like a drain, which was what he was: a sewer, both in his business and in his private life. For Kate's sake he'd drop the chap pronto.

Craddock fell asleep as soon as he got into bed. As for Kate, she slept in the guest bedroom, a very real indication to Craddock when he woke the next morning of how angry she was with him.

Chapter 18

Caroline hadn't slipped the letter from Suzy in between Peter's letters on purpose, but when he got back about half past nine from the Abbey retreat Peter found it in his study amongst his other post. The need to read it, even though it wasn't addressed to him, overcame him and he did just that. It broke his heart. In his adult life, when his eyes had filled with tears, he'd always wiped them away. Tonight the tears ran down his face unheeded, and a man weeping is so very painful to witness that he was glad to be alone. He read it three times and longed to tear it into shreds so tiny no one would ever be able to piece them together.

All the internal peace, the space for reflection the retreat had given him fled. He was more broken than he could bear. How could she describe what had happened as *intense passion*. In fact, it was over in moments. His beloved, darling Caro must have spent a terrible day and yet she'd greeted his return with love. Just as he decided to wipe his tears and ask her for a word there was a knock at the door and, thinking it was her, he said, 'Come in.'

'Dad, I wondered if you'd … why, Dad, whatever's the matter?' Alex quickly closed the door when he saw the letter in his hand. 'Not from … you know …'

'To your mother, not me.'

'Has Mum read it?'

'I assume so.'

'So that's why she's been so quiet since we came home. What does it say?'

'The usual, but now she not only wants the two of you, she wants me, too.'

Alex flung himself down on the sofa, bereft of speech. Half of him knew his dad would never leave them, but the other half did wonder if what he dreaded most of all, the break-up of his family, was about to happen.

It was Peter who broke the silence. 'What's Mum doing at the moment?'

'She's in the kitchen making bedtime hot chocolate for the four of us.'

'Do me a favour – take over and tell her I need a word.' He tapped his desk. 'In here.'

Unaware he'd seen the letter, Caroline was completely taken by surprise when Peter said, 'Close the door, darling, please. I've read your letter – I assume that was what you wanted me to do. Suzy must have gone completely mad. She needs to be sectioned. Every word of this letter is a lie and I'm not putting up with it any longer. Do you understand? I won't have it. She is making a whole life-changing tragedy out of nothing. She is not getting the children and definitely not getting *me*. Do you hear? I don't know how to go about stopping it but don't doubt that I shall. You're to take no notice of her, and if another letter comes, put it in a safe place for evidence and don't open it.'

Caroline didn't answer him. She simply went to sit down on the sofa, floored by his outburst.

'I'm so sorry, my darling, that a few brief moments of … over-heated blood are causing you such devastating trouble. So very sorry. But I shall put my mind to it and settle the matter once and for all.'

'How?'

Peter leaned his elbows on his thighs and studied his hands. 'I honestly don't know at the moment. I shall think about it long and hard.'

'I see.'

He looked up at her. 'Have you nothing more to say?'

'No. What can I say? A matter I thought was settled and forgiven has erupted into this. It's unbearable.'

Peter went to join her on the sofa.

Caroline leaned against him for comfort. 'I've been thinking about it all day. Whatever she does or says, you and I and the children are a complete family and I shall resolutely refuse to allow anything to break that up no matter what pain it causes me, no matter what I have to face.'

'We shan't break up. I have no more feeling for her than I have for any other human being. I hate what she has become. Unfortunately Alex knows we've had this letter. He walked in when I was reading it and guessed what it was.'

'You know I have never said a word against her to the children?'

'Of course I know that.' He took her hand in his and, turning it over, kissed the palm. 'You are the love of my life until my very last breath and beyond.'

'And you are mine.'

'We'll get over this, believe me. I thank God every day of my life for you.'

Caroline touched his cheek gently and kissed his lips. 'So long as we hang on to what we have for each other that's ... that's how we shall defeat her.'

Alex kicked the door. 'Chocolate and biscuits in there or the kitchen?'

Caroline answered, 'Kitchen! Thanks. Just coming.' She said to Peter, 'He's such a stalwart, is Alex, just like you.'

'So is Beth. We had a talk about Jake last Sunday. She has such a lot of common sense, you know, she's learned that from you. You're the loveliest mother any girl could wish for, remember that, and she loves you dearly and so does Alex. For their sakes I shall get all this sorted. I'll answer the letter on our behalf, right?'

They walked into the kitchen with their arms round each other, and Alex smiled, relieved that blasted letter hadn't upset them or alienated them from each other. Why his natural mother should be so ridiculous as to think the whole family could be broken up just to resolve her loneliness he could not understand. She obviously cared for them as little as she did the day she gave the two of them away. Thank God she had. Her kind of possessiveness he would not have been able to tolerate.

This was how it should be – the four of them at the kitchen table passing the biscuit tin round.

Chapter 19

Although Saturday was his day off, Peter claimed he had matters to attend to and would not be free to go anywhere at all with anyone.

Alex and Beth were overloaded with prep that weekend, so Caroline found she had a Saturday all to herself. Although Peter had said nothing about where he was going even to her, she knew for certain he was going to solve the Suzy question. The whole matter was driving her round the bend and added to that was the pain of worrying about the idea of Suzy and Peter together. Would there still be some spark left? No, of course not. She and Peter had the strongest of relationships and were united in their desire to be rid of Suzy. The thing was, should they want to be rid of her? Should they not perhaps keep some door open so if the children changed their minds ... would they? Perhaps they might as they became adults. Maybe it would be better all round to maintain an opening for the two of them, just in case.

Was she being too afraid? Under-estimating the strength of their love for her? Not being sufficiently aware of their needs, making it impossible for them to make the first move towards Suzy because of the hurt she as their adopted mother might feel if they did?

She'd go into Culworth and see the embroidery exhibition, take her mind off her problems. Grandmama had been and told her how fabulous it was, especially the work of the Turnham Malpas embroidery group. 'Though how such wonderful talent has emerged from such a motley collection of women, I simply do not know,' she added. That comment had rather shocked Caroline, because everyone in the group was dear to her heart.

When she got to the town hall Caroline was surprised to find a queue winding out of the entrance and down the street. A glance at her watch told her the doors had opened only ten minutes ago so she was glad to have arrived early. In the catalogue Caroline saw that the Turnham Malpas entries were in the upper gallery so she made her way there immediately.

Sitting on a chair directly opposite her entries was Mercedes, looking absorbed but also different from usual. She wore no make-up at all, not even lipstick, which made her look younger, not older as one might expect. It seemed to Caroline as though some crisis had broken her spirit.

But there was no wonder she was absorbed by her work. It was fabulous – jaw-droppingly fabulous. The exhibition drew work from all over the country, so the Turnham Malpas group should be proud of their contribution. The wall their exhibits occupied glowed, helped by the exuberant joy of Mercedes' work.

Caroline sat down next to her and stayed quietly in admiration. The sadness emanated from her in great waves of distress and Caroline was moved to take hold of her hand. Mercedes never spoke; she simply sat there, accepting Caroline's sympathy.

Eventually Caroline said, 'Your work is very beautiful. Very inspiring. You are so lucky to have talent like this.'

Mercedes smiled sadly and squeezed her hand. 'I don't know where it comes from. But it is, isn't it? Beautiful?'

'It certainly is. You must be proud.'

'I'm not. Grateful perhaps, but not proud.'

A small approving crowd had gathered around the Turnham Malpas collection.

'Listen to them, Mercedes, they're loving your work.'

The two of them silently listened to their comments and

Caroline couldn't help saying, 'What with your talent for embroidery and Ford's wonderful voice, you're both so gifted. I was amazed when he sang the solo part in church. I'd no idea he was so good. He should have trained as a singer. It's never too late, you know.'

Two tears rolled down Mercedes' face, which were quickly wiped away.

'We've been so happy living here. Ever since we came, people have liked us and that's worth a lot.'

'Why shouldn't they like two lovely people with such wonderful skills?'

'If only …'

'Mercedes! Cheer up. Let's go for a wander, see if anything comes up to Turnham Malpas standards, shall we?' And wander they did, arm in arm, along the upper gallery and then all the way round the ground floor, till finally they went out into the street.

'There you are, you see,' said Caroline. 'Our village entries were far and away the best, due mostly to your superb work.'

Mercedes turned to her. 'Thank you for keeping me company. I needed someone back there. Those two lovely children of yours are a delight. Take care of them as best you can; they deserve it. Ford and I can't have children and it's a running sore that never heals, so rejoice you've got them. They're very precious. Bye-bye.'

Unexpectedly, Mercedes kissed Caroline on both cheeks. It felt almost like a goodbye kiss. Then she squeezed the hand she was holding and … looked as though she was going to say something more but didn't.

Instead Mercedes quickly turned away and walked rapidly in the direction of the bus station. Caroline called out, 'Let me give you a lift …' but her offer was ignored.

*

Peter didn't get back until seven o'clock. He'd rung about five to say he was leaving for home and nothing more, so Caroline still didn't know where he'd been or what he'd been doing. She expected an explanation on his return, but it was an explanation she didn't get.

Peter walked in just as they were finishing their evening meal. He stood right behind Caroline's chair, held her shoulders and leaned over to kiss the top of her head.

'Darling!' Caroline looked up at him, smiling. 'You've timed it well. Sit down – you must be starving.'

'Lovely to be home. Been all right, Alex, Beth?'

'Got plenty of prep done, if that's what you mean,' Alex replied. 'Mum and Beth and me are thinking of going to the late film at the cinema. Want to come?'

'No, thanks. Need time to sort out my head for tomorrow. You go if you want. I shan't be much company anyway.'

Beth poured him a glass of wine. 'Where've you been, Dad?'

Peter hesitated. 'Church business.'

'Church business and no explanation? Top-secret church business, then? You haven't been asked to consider being Archbishop of York or something, have you? I'd love to live in York.' Caroline laughed.

'No.'

It suddenly occurred to Caroline that, judging by his closed, hurt look, he wasn't intending to say a word about where he'd been. She needed to be told, because her instincts had told her he'd been to see Suzy Palmer and she, as his wife, wanted to know. Her mind shrank from pondering about them together, even though her common sense told her they hadn't ... no, no, he wouldn't, not after all these years. So what had happened?

The twins went upstairs to get ready for the cinema and before she could ask him Peter said, 'I'll clear up. You get off, or you'll be late. Enjoy.'

'Enjoy? I doubt it.'

Peter sensed her eagerness for his explanation. He shook his head. 'I'm not telling you, not today, possibly not this year, possibly never. Suffice to say, the whole problem has been resolved. You have no need to worry any more and I mean that. It is my problem, my burden, not yours nor the children's, so please, worry no more.' His main course only half-eaten, he got to his feet, kissed her forehead, gave her a loving hug and began stacking plates in the dishwasher as though all was right with his world.

But the village knew full well it wasn't, because the lights had been on in the church for over an hour that evening and they never were at that time on a Saturday, so they knew their Rector had problems. But not one of those who made a stab at guessing what was troubling him got anywhere near the mark.

Chapter 20

Jake turned up at the Rectory one evening straight off the school coach. He'd followed Beth because she still wasn't speaking to him and he felt bereft. He'd never felt like this about a girl. If they didn't fancy him then he tossed them away without a second thought, but Beth ... he needed to get it sorted. This attraction he felt for her was grinding him down and beginning to affect his work, and when, in all his life, had he been unable to cope with schoolwork? Never. He'd called out to her when the coach stopped, but she'd disappeared without so much as a glance at him.

He saw her use her latch key to get in and hoped perhaps she would be the only one at home, as he knew Alex was coming back on the late coach. He rapped hard on the door. Immediately the door burst open and there she stood, tight-lipped and obviously angry.

'Beth!'

'That's me.'

'I need a word.' She hadn't found out about Janey, had she?

'Well, who's stopping you?' Beth was determined not to make it easy for him.

'May I come in?'

She opened the door a little wider. He stepped into the hall.

'Whatever I've done, I'm sorry. Very sorry. I don't honestly know what, though.'

'A smidgen of truth might help.'

Jake hesitated. Which truth did she mean?

'When I get home I usually have toast and tea. Would you like some?'

He nodded, and she led the way to the kitchen. There was hope, then. Obviously it wasn't the truth he feared she meant.

He sat at her invitation in one of the rocking chairs beside the Aga and enjoyed watching her assembling their feast. Somehow the thought of hot toast and tea with her felt like a privilege and was more than welcome. Since when had he liked the idea of tea and toast with a girl?

'How about the truth, then?' Beth said as she placed her Winnie the Pooh teapot on the table. But the toaster popped up and gave him more time to assemble his thoughts. Had Alex told her what he'd said in the changing rooms? It was likely seeing as they were twins. They'd be closer than most brothers and sisters. His face flushed. Surely not. As she passed him a plate with four neatly buttered and jammed triangles of toast on it, she stated rather forcefully, 'I know why Alex beat you up.'

Jake almost cried aloud with relief.

'It was shameful of you, Jake, to talk about me in that way, and not a scrap of truth in it, either.'

'It was shameful. You're right. Boasting, I was, and I shouldn't have done. Not about you.'

'Is that an apology?' Beth stuffed her mouth with toast while she waited for him to reply.

He got up and stood in front of her, obviously intending to lean over her and give her a kiss to heal things, but she raised a determined hand to check him. 'Don't you dare touch me, afterwards you might go round saying you've had full sex in front of the Aga in the Rectory kitchen, and I'm not risking that.'

She blushed at the words she'd used and wished she hadn't, but she had and she'd meant them, too. He wasn't getting away with it as easy as that. He might have kissability, but there were limits.

'*Touché*.' He stood looking down at her, and she looked back at him ... there was raspberry jam at the corner of his mouth and he couldn't work out his next move, she could see that, and it made him look particularly vulnerable. At that moment Beth loved him.

'Best sit down and finish your toast, then you can go. How will you get home?'

Jake glanced at his watch. 'Teatime bus.'

'There's a seat by the bus stop; you can wait there. It'll only be an hour and a bit.' She looked out of the window at the lowering clouds. 'It looks like rain.'

'I see.' Jake wondered what had happened to his charisma. It had never been so devastatingly unappealing to a girl before. 'I do apologise, Beth. I'm very sorry for what I did. It was unforgivable and you deserve more consideration on my part. I am truly sorry.'

'Is there anything else you need to apologise for?'

Jake's heart leapt with shock. Surely not Janey, too? He shrugged and said cautiously. 'Nothing ... that I know of.' His reply seemed to satisfy her.

To Beth he appeared truly humbled. All her instincts told her to kiss him to relieve him of his guilt, but something her dad had said held her back. Instead she got a piece of kitchen roll and wiped the jam from the corner of his mouth. She was so close she could smell the smell boys have after a day at school, and as she looked deeply into his eyes for one long moment, she realised he wasn't a boy like Alex was a boy. Jake was a man and, for a split second, she recognised, as Alex had said, you supped with the devil at your peril. But living dangerously had great appeal right now. Those dark eyes with their tigerish glints ... Oh God! She almost moved to kiss him, but drew back just in time.

'Time to go. Thanks for the apology.'

'Be seeing you?'

Beth shrugged.

'If I called at the weekend perhaps we could go for a cycle ride?'

'Saturday is Dad's day off and we're all going out for the day, so it'll have to be Sunday afternoon.' Having resigned herself to being a daughter of a member of the clergy once again, she added, 'Church in the morning, you see.' She pulled a face.

'Ah! I'll come at half past two?'

'OK.'

Beth shut the door behind him and found herself crying, though she didn't know why. She slammed round the kitchen, tidying up and sniffing back the tears, then picked up her school bag and raced upstairs to begin her prep. She wished her mother was home so she could talk to her. She wished she'd kissed him, then was glad she hadn't.

Apparently it was called being in charge but it didn't feel quite the right place to be at the moment.

But Jake arrived at the morning service just before it began. He squeezed into the Rectory pew, thanking Caroline for moving her legs so he could get past her to sit next to Beth. He took hold of Beth's hand, kissed her fingers and smiled at her. Alex signalled vomiting was the order of the day, but Beth gripped Jake's hand as though she would never let it go.

She was oblivious to the nudging and winking that went on in the congregation behind her at the sight of Jake turning up in the Rectory pew again, and the kiss he gave her hand did not go unnoticed. Bless her! they all thought. She's growing up and not half. But a chap from Penny Fawcett? They all collectively despised villagers from there, they weren't a patch on Turnham Malpas people, they weren't. Even Little Derehams was not much better. Still, if Beth liked him ... A plus was that he did know how to behave in church. He never made a slip with his order of service, and his singing voice sounded good.

The women in the congregation thought him handsome and really very attractive, but the men guessed he might be a bit of a devil . . .

Caroline played her part by inviting him for lunch, which he gratefully accepted. Peter was pleased to see him and they had a lovely time chatting about this and that, school and gap years, exams and university, and the world in general.

After helping Caroline to clear up, Jake and Beth set off for their bicycle ride, deciding to go as far as Little Derehams to visit the medieval prison Mr Fitch had restored and which was open on Sundays for inspection from two until four o'clock.

'Do you know, I've lived in Penny Fawcett for two years and never been to see it?'

'Shame on you. It won't take long. It's tiny but very atmospheric. Three people were hanged, drawn and quartered at the crossroads there. Harrowing really, just the thought of it.'

Sitting on a chair outside the medieval prison was Sheila Bissett. 'Hello, you two. Saw you in church this morning, Jake. Nice to see you there. Have a leaflet. You're my first customers today.'

'I didn't know you were involved in this,' said Beth, waving her hand at the prison building.

'Oh, I'm a casual. The two in charge are both away on holiday so I volunteer when that happens. I love it. Cruel times, but still we have our religious freedom because of people like these who died for it.' She smiled up at Jake and pushed open the door with her foot. 'Please go in. There's room, just.'

It scarcely measured six feet by four. A tiny barred window without glass almost at the peak of the roof was the only source of light, and with the door closed it was gloomy inside.

'Hardly room to lie down, is there?'

'Not for us, perhaps, but people were smaller then.'

Jake took hold of Beth's hand and she didn't object. 'I wonder if they were provided with a blanket or anything?'

'Read the leaflet.'

Jake held it up close to the barred opening and read. 'Open the door; the old bucket they used as a lavatory is still here.'

'Oh!' She pushed the door ajar and there it was chained to the wall, made of leather and looking incredibly ancient. 'Do you suppose it's the original one or one made for effect?'

Jake muttered, 'Close the door.' Then he promptly took her in his arms and kissed her. She made no objection and welcomed his closeness with a stirring of desire that thrilled him. This was the real Beth, the loving, sweet, beautiful Beth, and his feelings for her roared through his body, till Beth pushed him off and hastily opened the door.

'Thank you for being here to let us in,' she said to Sheila. 'It's very real in there with the door shut. Will you show Jake the key? You know, the real one they found in the ruins when it was restored?'

Beside her chair lay Sheila's well-known shopping basket and in it, in a leather pouch, was the key. For such a tiny building the key was huge and heavy, easily as long as Jake's hand.

'It's a very thick door, you see, made so's not to let them out by chance.'

'Thank you, Mrs—'

'It's Lady Sheila Bissett, Jake.'

'Ah! Right. Thanks anyway. We must push on.'

Disappointed that Jake showed no sign of being interested in the key, nor in feeling anything grim about the little prison, Beth shivered as she stood her bike up and sat on the saddle. She pushed off without giving Jake a glance. 'That place gives me the creeps.'

'Nonsense. It's just a heap of stones with a door. How can it give you the creeps?'

'All that pain and unhappiness, and us kissing in there as if …'

'As if?'

'We haven't a care in the world.'

'Well, we haven't, have we? Why should we allow ourselves to suffer for something that happened centuries ago? It wasn't our fault. It's history. You've got it all wrong.'

'Can't you feel the pain and the fear? You can't, can you? It means not a thing to you. Well, I'm going home now. Thanks for the ride. See you on the coach Monday.'

'Don't go yet, please ...'

But Beth cycled off, leaving Jake puzzled. All he'd done was kiss her, and what was wrong with that? Man kissing a girl, a beautiful girl, who needed kissing lots and lots. Somehow he'd behaved below the standard she expected of him and she was disappointed. Or maybe he was too down-to-earth about the prison when she felt so badly about it. Still, Janey would have loved being kissed in that pokey little place. She'd find it a laugh, would Janey, kissing inside a prison. He laughed as he pedalled home, thinking that maybe she might be free right now and at the same time despising himself for looking forward to seeing her.

Beth was furious with herself. She'd discovered their apparent incompatibility this afternoon in the prison and she wasn't the least bit pleased about it. At home Dad had disappeared into his study, Mum was in the sitting room reading the Sunday paper, and Alex, as usual on a Sunday afternoon, was in his room working. Well, Mum would have to listen to her.

'Mum?'

Caroline put down the paper instantly. 'Oh, good, someone to talk to. What have you to tell me?'

Beth wasn't entirely sure what she had to tell her. 'It's funny, we went to see the old prison and it gave me the creeps like it always does, all those people waiting to be hanged, all waiting to die or, almost as bad, for transportation, but Jake was unmoved by it. Isn't it odd when I like him so much?'

'Not really. We're all different. Even the people we dearly love can behave differently from what we expect.'

'Even Dad?'

Caroline, thinking of his absence all day yesterday, nodded. 'Even your dad.'

'Like yesterday,' Beth said, as if reading her mind. 'Where had he been?'

'He's never said, and he may never tell me.'

Beth went to sit down. 'Well, why don't you demand an answer? After all, you are his wife.'

'Because I know he doesn't want to tell me. So I don't ask.'

'Is it because he's a priest? Is that what stops you?'

'No, it's because he's my husband.'

'I'd like to know. I'll ask him, shall I? Perhaps he'll tell me.' She stood up, ready to go to his study, but Caroline said, 'No, Beth, don't.'

'But you want to know just as much as me. I will—'

'*I said no.*'

Beth collapsed back on the sofa again. 'If I was married to Jake and I wanted to know something *I'd* ask.'

'Well, you're not so ... you're not thinking on those lines already, are you?'

Beth laughed. 'No. He likes me very much and he can't get me out of his head, which is good news, but ... I like him very, very much indeed, so very much, but I'm keeping him at arm's length at the moment till I know better how I feel.'

'He's a good-looking boy—'

'He's a man, Mum, I'm sure about that. By comparison Alex is a little kid.'

This statement alarmed Caroline and before she could stop herself she blurted out, 'What makes you say that?'

'The way he kisses.'

'Ah! Right. Perhaps it might be—'

At this important juncture Peter came in. 'I'm going for a walk. Anyone want to come? I thought I'd drive to Penny Fawcett and walk that new ramblers' footpath they've opened up. Considering the fuss they made about it, somebody's got to make use of it. What do you say?'

'I'll come, darling, do me good. Beth?'

'Sorry, prep. Bye-bye.'

She watched them from the kitchen window as Mum waited by the back gate for Dad to bring the car down from the garage. As Mum got in the car they paused for a moment for a kiss, which wasn't just a little peck, and she wondered about them and kissing at their time of life. It always appeared to mean a lot because she could just see her dad's hand caressing Mum's shoulder as they kissed, and she loved the gentleness of his gesture … and heavens! They were *still* kissing, even though Mum wouldn't ask him where he'd been yesterday, and he refused to tell her. So you could disagree about important things and still love each other. Their togetherness illustrated to her the complete security she enjoyed. Compared to Jake, with his mother's fondness for any man going past the gate, she was the luckiest person alive. Poor Jake. The kindness in her heart brimmed over for him, and she couldn't help but love him all over again.

Chapter 21

Evie had promised to go to Culworth and collect their exhibits from the embroidery exhibition that very morning so they would be available for everyone to take home in the afternoon when the embroidery group met.

The only member not present at two o'clock was Merc, which surprised them all. Somehow she had woven herself into the village's fabric. They all liked her and were so proud of her embroidery skills that they boasted to friends and family about how brilliant she was and they meant to tell her that very afternoon.

'Did she tell any of you she wouldn't be here?' Evie asked, disappointed she wouldn't have a chance to say how proud she was to Merc's face.

Vera said no, she hadn't seen her at all this last week.

'I drove over on Wednesday morning 'cos I couldn't wait till the weekend to see our display and I met Merc,' said Barbara the weekender. 'She'd been to see the exhibition, she said, and was on her way home. She asked me about when the exhibits would be available and I told her, like you said, Evie, that she'd be able to take them home this afternoon. She nodded and went off.'

'Don't know how many times she saw that exhibition, because I met her Friday and she'd been then,' said Dottie.

Bel chimed in that Merc'd been in the Store on Tuesday and said she was going with Ford after lunch in the car.

'Mmm. Sounds like she's been every day 'cos Caroline told

me how proud she was when she went to see the exhibition on Saturday and that she talked to Merc then. But she thought Merc seemed very depressed,' Sheila said.

'But wasn't it marvellous, all our work looking so good? I was so proud,' Barbara said.

Bel agreed. 'I didn't think there was anything there that could beat our offering, and Merc's stuff absolutely put the icing on the cake.'

'She is very talented,' Evie said, 'and what's so nice, very modest about it, too. I had several people speak to me about asking her to do a commission for them. I was longing to be able to tell her. I've got their names and addresses for her.'

'She's never late, and now there'll be no racing tips if she doesn't come.'

There were sighs of disappointment all round.

'I had plans for my winnings,' Bel announced.

'You have?' said Vera.

'What?' asked Dottie, who'd enjoyed that weekend in London so much she could have gone again the following week.

The embroidering came to a full stop as they waited to hear Bel's plans.

'Well, I was thinking of going to a hotel I've seen advertised in a magazine. It does trips out for its clientele. You set off Friday night, champagne lunch on the Saturday, Christmas market in the afternoon and a theatre on the Saturday night, and a visit to the biggest fashion outlet in the North on the Sunday first thing before you drive home. Thought it would be just right for Christmas presents and that.'

By the time she'd finished speaking she knew they were all fascinated by the whole idea.

Barbara almost leapt across the table she was so excited. 'I'll go! Sounds great. Just what I need with it getting dark so soon now. It's so depressing. Cheer me up no end. How do you get there?'

'Well,' said Bel, 'they pick you up by coach if you have ten or more, and one of the pickups is Culworth.'

'No!'

'Brilliant! Barbara, you're our booking person – can you do it for us like you did last time?'

'Yes, but there's not ten of us.'

Spirits fell. Silence reigned.

Evie said, 'It doesn't have to be just this group. We wouldn't mind others coming, would we? Compatible people from the village.'

A spontaneous outburst of excited voices filled the hall.

'Ah! But just a minute. How much is it?'

This dampened their enthusiasm for a moment, but at that precise moment Zack appeared at the door.

Sheila shouted, 'Sorry, Zack, we've been too busy to make tea. What are you doing here anyway? You're not mowing now, surely?'

'Who's worried about tea? I've just been to Glebe House with a message for Merc from a neighbour of mine about her embroidery but there's no reply.'

They were puzzled by his extreme excitement over them not being in

'But,' said Dottie, 'they are free to come and go as they please, you know. They don't have to stay home in case someone calls.'

'That isn't it. They've gone!'

'Gone where?'

'Who knows? The side gate wasn't locked so I went to knock on their kitchen door, thought they might not have heard me, and couldn't help but see in through the glass. *They're not there.*'

Growing increasingly impatient with Zack's lack of clarity, Barbara said sharply, 'For God's sake man, explain yourself.'

'They've flitted. Gone. Left. Moved house. Is that plain enough?'

Moved house? They all sat appalled by this news. Speechless, shaken and incredibly disappointed. What on earth had happened? They'd been so happy here, what with Merc's embroidery and Ford's wonderful singing voice and his help with the youth club and those outrageous trips they'd done and one still to be finalised before Christmas. And that fabulous Elizabethan banquet. Now what were they going to do? No more betting tips! Most surprising of all was Merc leaving her embroidery behind. She'd never do that. No, he must be wrong.

Evie, shocked to the core, muttered, 'I don't believe it, Zack.' None of them did.

'It's true. There's not a stick of furniture left downstairs. I looked in all the winders.'

'Well,' said Sheila Bissett, getting to her feet, 'I won't believe it till I see for myself.'

'And neither will I,' they all said.

There was a rush to be first through the door, and the whole group marched down the church hall path to the road, past the church and Glebe Cottages, and turned up the garden path of Glebe House. Evie realised it was true before they reached the door, because two huge garden pots placed either side out at the front, which Merc had filled with flowers in riotous colours and tended with loving care all the summer long, had gone.

Grandmama heard the scurry of many feet and looked out to see what was afoot. She joined the crowd, and neither could she believe they'd gone. They all peered in through the windows, even into the room that had been Neville Neal's sacred sanctum, as well as the drawing-room, the kitchen and, the dining-room where the curtains had caught fire that time from Wee Willie Winkie's candle being carelessly left alight on the window sill.

'But I saw her only yesterday. She was in church, and so was he, in the choir. I spoke to her and she never mentioned a word about going.'

'They must have been in a terrible hurry, her leaving her embroidery behind.'

'When did they go?'

'Must have gone after dark. Late, like when they came. Remember how surprised we all were?' Zack recalled.

Well, I never! each of them thought. Now what? The biggest question in all their minds was *why*?

Craddock Fitch had a nasty feeling he knew *exactly* why, when he heard the news which had excited the entire village with its unexpectedness. Unusually for him, he'd gone to the Village Store just before closing time. Kate was away on an educational freebie and wouldn't be back until very late, it was the housekeeper's day off and Craddock felt too idle to potter in the kitchen trying to make the kind of meal he'd become accustomed to since marrying Kate. So here he was looking through the freezer for something to tempt his tastebuds and finding himself listening to the big story of the week, if not the year, which was still bubbling round the shelves as it had been since four o'clock.

He hurriedly picked out a chicken casserole (which he later discovered was a chicken curry) and fled. It had happened then. This thing had been preying on his mind ever since that fateful game of golf, and he was to blame. It had led to the hurried departure of Ford in a desperate attempt to hide all over again. He'd heard all about Ford's marvellous singing voice and sneaked a quick look at Merc's embroidery in the town hall. Embroidery, for heaven's sake! It was only his guilty conscience that had made him go, and very guilty he felt, too, but it was exceptional, even he could see that.

It was no good him thinking that Kate would never find out. She probably knew already, even though she was fifty miles away; her village grapevine information centre was second to none.

It seemed that Nigel Farrow had indeed put paid to Ford Barclay's love for Turnham Malpas. Damn and blast. Sentimentality never intruded on his business dealings but Craddock Fitch felt remarkably disappointed by Ford Barclay moving away. A man who, despite appearing insensitive and very down-to-earth, had picked out the fact that the two of them, Ford and Craddock, had pulled themselves up from the bottom of the pile, and what's more had told him so. He had rather liked that. How could he sort it out? Obviously Ford couldn't come back to live in Turnham Malpas no matter what, but at the very least ...

Well, that Nigel Farrow had plenty of dirt sticking to him, so it was up to him, Craddock Fitch, to dig something out and make Nigel suffer. After all, even though he'd set up the lunch and the round of golf and the idea of finding out if Ford was crooked, he hadn't meant to go this far. Not ruin the chap.

But why oh why had they disappeared in such secrecy?

That same night in the Royal Oak, the table with the settle down one side was the centre of the gossip.

'I mean, what can we do about her embroidery? Such beautiful stuff; Merc was so clever. It's nothing short of a tragedy,' Dottie said as she placed the next round of drinks on the table.

Willie had his own opinion. 'There must be a blooming good reason for it. This disappearance in the night, that's significant, that is. Who in their right mind moves house in the night?'

'You mean something illegal?' Sylvia asked him.

'What else can it be? Who sitting round this table would move house in the dark? None of us, not one. Therefore, it stands to reason they're avoiding the police. They don't want no one to find out where they are.'

'Now, Willie, that is ridiculous. He told us the furniture van had broken down and that was why they were so late when they first arrived.'

'That was *their* story,' Willie said emphatically.

Sylvia pleaded, 'There couldn't have been a nicer man than Ford, and as for Merc, she was a treasure, she truly was.'

But Willie persisted. 'They don't have thief written on their foreheads, you know. There is such a thing as gentlemen thieves.' Rather wistfully, he picked up his tankard to take a drink, then hesitated and said softly, 'I shall miss Merc and not half. She was a lovely woman. She doesn't deserve all this flitting about in a damn big hurry.'

'I'm sorry, but much as I liked Ford, he was no gentleman, was he? Not like Sir Ralph of blessed memory.' This from Barbara who, instead of going home straight after embroidery, had stayed on, hoping to find out the true reason for the Barclays' hurried departure.

'No, but he was lovely.' Dottie smiled, thinking of Ford and his generosity and the money she'd made betting on his tips. She'd miss that for certain.

'He was, and speculate as we might,' said Sheila, 'I've an idea we shan't ever find out why, so we might as well save our breath.'

'Is there anyone they gave their address to?' asked Bel, who'd joined them after finishing supervising in the dining room. 'Who's the most likely?'

Various suggestions were put forward and the most likely was felt to be the Rector, so Dottie was given the task of enquiring from him the following morning about Ford's whereabouts.

'Well, Reverend, we're all that disappointed, not to say shocked, about Ford and Mercedes, and we wondered last night, all of us in the pub, if you knew anything ... unless it's all confidential, of course. But it seems that awful. We all liked 'em, you know. Everybody's that upset.'

Peter could truthfully say that he was just as surprised as everyone else, and frankly he knew nothing. 'We'll all miss them. The choir, the embroidery group, the youth club ... the church.

They're a great loss even though they've been here such a short time. I'm sorry I can't help.'

It was only when he opened his post later that morning that he found himself to be the one in possession of the true facts. Well ... almost the true facts. There was a letter for him from Ford and Mercedes, and enclosed was a cheque, which was made payable to him for ... £10,000!

Dear Reverend,

You will be surprised to receive this letter and I am just as surprised to be having to write it. Mercedes and I have had to go to an unknown destination. Someone has found out where we live and they are hounding us night and day about the past, so we have to hide again. I can't tell you details. Suffice to say it is to do with my previous occupation.

We are being continually pestered by threatening phone calls and mysterious anonymous letters with sly references to our past, and I need to get Merc away before she finally collapses under the strain. She is heartbroken and so am I. We wanted to stay in Turnham Malpas for ever but it is not to be.

We know we can trust you completely so the cheque is in your care for you to deal with as you see fit. First, Merc's embroidery needs posting to us and it won't be cheap to do that. Love and thanks to Evie for all her support and that of her class. They were all great chums for Merc, and she loved every one of them.

Secondly, I want two thousand pounds to go to the youth club to complete the programme of events we set in motion. I would have loved to have seen more of them, but it isn't to be.

Thirdly, tell Craddock Fitch I hold no animosity towards him for what has happened. I honestly don't think he intended things to go this far.

Fourthly, the rest of the money is for the church to be invested or used as best fits the situation at the moment, and I leave that entirely to your discretion.

I'm not particularly religious, but the hours I spent singing with the choir have been the most wonderful in all my life, and your understanding and compassion towards everyone has helped convince me I should do better in the future than I have in the past.

Glebe House will be sold as soon as possible. I sincerely hope that whoever lives in it will love it as we have, and live there longer than we have been able to.

Please let the embroidery group know that this week's tip is Swindlerspride, 3.30, Sandown, Saturday. Thank you. Bless you and yours.

Sincerely,

Ford and Mercedes Barclay.

There was no address at the top of the letter but when Peter turned the last page over he found an address which was described by Ford as an 'accommodation address': *Frank Buchan, 29 Glyde Grove, Birmingham (no post code).*

Peter rang Turnham House immediately to enquire if Mr Fitch was at home. He was, so he called out, 'Dottie! I'm going up to see Mr Fitch. Bang the front door shut when you leave if I'm not back.'

'Will do. What about lunch? Shall I make some for you?'

'Yes, please. Thanks.'

On his way up the drive, Peter wondered what on earth Craddock had done to bring about the hurried departure of the Barclays. Was he truly instrumental in making them run, or was it simply an idea of Ford's? For that matter, what the blazes had Ford done?

Seated comfortably in one of Craddock's sumptuous leather chairs with the door firmly closed, Peter asked him outright what he had done.

Thinking Peter meant what he had done to make them disappear, Craddock told his part in the tale. 'But, Peter, believe me, I have plans in hand for the destruction of this supposed golfing friend of mine. I had a lot of respect for Ford. He sized me up and told me what he thought of me. I'm not accustomed to that, and I had to admire him for it although he made the biggest gaffe by assuming Kate was my daughter, which annoyed me beyond belief.' He grinned. 'Was I mad! I raged about after they'd gone until Kate fell about laughing, and her laughing always makes me see sense.'

'But what did *Ford* do to make them have to run away like this?'

'Ah! Well, he was obviously involved in some sleight of hand to do with scrap metal. Very dodgy business, is scrap metal, difficult not to get caught up in theft and what-not. He made his fortune and retired quick to Turnham Malpas, but this so-called friend of mine began sniffing around. They've obviously panicked.'

'He says he bears you no animosity at all; he believes you didn't mean to ruin him.'

'That's generous of him. I didn't mean it to go this far. Can I have his address?'

Peter shook his head. 'No. If you wish to write to him you'll have to give the letter to me and I'll address it and post it for you. He's given me two thousand pounds to complete the youth club's planned activities, and almost eight thousand pounds for the church. Amazing generosity.'

Craddock toyed with his silver letter-opener for a moment and then said, 'Tell him I've matched his contribution to the church, pound for pound.' He snatched up a cheque book and wrote out the cheque there and then. 'There we are. That decorating you want to press ahead with can be done now.'

'You must understand I didn't come begging.'

'You never do. It would be beneath you. I give this cheque willingly. You see, I feel a little guilty that I influenced his decision to run. Kate almost scalped me for what I did and I can't have that. I love her more than life itself. Daft thing for an old chap like me to be saying but I know it won't go further than these four walls.'

Peter stood up and reached across Craddock's impressive desk to shake his hand. 'You're a kinder man than you seem. Like me you're very much in love and it's a splendid state of affairs for a man to be in.'

With a wry smile on his thin, white face, Craddock replied, 'Don't you tell anyone. It wouldn't do my image any good at all.'

The businessman was back, and Peter took his leave. The following day Craddock put a sealed envelope through the Rectory letterbox, to be forwarded to Ford at his secret address, and that night he told Kate what he had done.

'Remember Ford and how angry I was about him thinking you were my daughter and that I was retired and living in rented property?'

Kate laughed. 'Of course I do. I haven't quite forgiven you even yet. Why do you ask me?'

'I've done something about it. Written him a letter, today.' He turned away and shook the ash from his cigar into the fire. 'They've gone to a secret address known only to the Rector.'

'Oh! Where?'

'It wouldn't be secret if we all knew, now would it?' He grinned at her.

'No, of course not. So what did you say in the letter? I hope it was full of apologies?' Kate looked up at him from the rug where she was sitting beside her cats.

'He's forgiven me apparently, says I didn't intentionally mean to hurt him and Merc by getting those damned scoundrels Nigel and Marcus to interrogate him and dig into his past.'

'Peter told you that?'

'Yes, it was in *his* letter.'

'So what did you put in *your* letter?'

Craddock walked across to the windows, drew back the

curtains and stood staring out at the dark sky, wondering if he truly deserved to be forgiven.

'Well?'

'Truth?'

'Of course. What else?'

Craddock shuffled with embarrassment. Finally he muttered, 'I'm buying his house for him, if he'll let me.'

'Buying Glebe House? Whatever for?'

'Because I shall keep it for Ford and Merc so ... when they want to come back they've somewhere of their own to go. I'll rent it out in the meantime. Can't have it standing idle not earning its keep, now can I? And what's more, I've resigned my membership of the golf club. They're a blasted lot of utter rogues there, and I'm having nothing more to do with them. Let's face it – I never have enjoyed golf. Stupid game, really.' Craddock turned to look at her at the moment she leapt to her feet. The cats scattered in shock at being so carelessly disturbed by their beloved owner, who apparently cared for nothing at that moment except Craddock Fitch.

'Darling, I am thrilled. They were so right for the village, weren't they?'

'Rather more right than perhaps I shall ever be. I didn't like the idea of them not being able to come back. Lovely people, and out of the same drawer as me, which was very pleasant.' His arms slipped round Kate's waist, and she kissed him and he kissed her.

'All right now, Kate?'

'Of course.'

Chapter 22

The next youth club outing was a weekend camping on the coast. There were ten of them, accompanied by Venetia and Kate, with Craddock in a nearby hotel as he couldn't face the inconvenience of living in a tent. It proved to be a fantastic opportunity for Jake and Beth to get to know each other better, or so Beth imagined. What Jake didn't know, until they were waiting for the minibus, was that Janey from Penny Fawcett had unexpectedly decided to go to even up the numbers – and that she was expecting to share a tent with Jake. Jake sat with Alex, feeling that was the easier though not the most exciting option.

At the campsite Beth and Janey paired up, as the others had come along with their own friends and it seemed the sensible option. Alex and Jake were left to share. Beth wasn't at all sure that she liked the idea of sharing a two-person tent with someone she only knew by sight. But she decided to make the best of it and appeared positive and cheerful about the arrangements. The campsite had excellent shower blocks and Venetia had brought along some marvellous top-of-the-range cooking equipment. All they needed now was good weather.

They arrived on the Friday night and by the time the tents were set up and they'd been to the fish and chip shop for a takeaway supper, there was no time to go anywhere or do anything except sit round the campfire, competently organised by Jake and Alex, and talk and drink their cans of beer and soft drinks. They were well wrapped up, and it felt to be a wonderful evening, with a breeze blowing off the cliffs, a full moon and friends. They couldn't ask for more.

Jake's amorous intentions were binned now Janey was there. He'd had fantasies of wandering along the cliffs with Beth and finding a nice hollow out of the wind … but that was definitely off the agenda. In fact, he was in a situation so hot he couldn't possibly have imagined it however hard he'd tried. He had his best girl's brother in the same tent as himself, and his best girl was sharing with his 'bit on the side', as his mother would have said. She'd have laughed, would his mum, but he wasn't laughing, not at all. It was frustration all the way. If Beth hadn't been there … If Janey hadn't been there … But they were and he'd have to spend a celibate weekend. Though he hadn't intended to go the whole way with Beth. The Reverend's wrath would be more than he could cope with. In any case, he was almost afraid to expect to go the whole way with her. She was so precious to him and nothing could be allowed to upset that state of affairs.

Alex crept into their tent and began getting ready for bed. God! Jake thought. Am I in a mess and it's all my own doing. Damn Janey! Served him right really.

'You know that Janey, do you, with her living in Penny Fawcett?' Alex said.

Oh, hell. 'Yes,' Jake answered, cautiously. 'Yes, I do vaguely. You'd best keep your hands off her, she's dynamite.'

'She looks hot stuff.'

Jake didn't have a handy reply ready. 'Yes, well, maybe you're right. That's what I meant actually. She is hot stuff.'

A torch shone at their tent door. 'Venetia here. You two OK? Alex? Jake?'

They both answered, 'Yes, thanks.'

'Good. Sleep tight. Breakfast at eight-thirty. Departure for the boat trip at nine-thirty.'

'OK. Goodnight.'

'Remember, Jake, you're on kitchen duty, so you've an early start.'

'Right!' Oh no, thought Jake. Is there no end to my agony? 'Don't suppose you'd like to do my kitchen duty, Alex?'

Alex was shuffling down into his sleeping bag, wishing it was about a foot longer than it was. 'No thanks! Goodnight.'

'Oh well, goodnight then,' said Jake, wishing he was anywhere but there. He pulled his wool hat down over his ears and his eyes and groaned.

In the next-door tent Janey wouldn't or couldn't go to sleep. 'Your brother is utterly gorgeous, do you know that? I like tall men.'

'I don't know about gorgeous. He's a self-controlled, clean-living, self-contained, verging on pompous individual, single-minded about his life and his career. A reliable, hard-working, industrious, self-disciplined so-and-so.'

'Oh. Right. Got a girlfriend?'

In the dark, Beth giggled. 'Not that I know of. He'd have told me if he had.' Then she began laughing uncontrollably.

'What's the matter?'

'The thought of Alex with a girl. I don't think he'd know what to do!' She laughed even louder and got several shouts of 'Shush!' from the other tents. Which made her giggle more and she couldn't stop. Then Janey started laughing and inside five minutes the pair of them were friends. Then neither of them could get to sleep for hours.

The whole weekend was fraught with claims and counter-claims, about who was on kitchen duty, who'd promised to go to the farm to get the milk, who hadn't got ready in time, who'd held them up by getting back to the minibus late, who'd kept them awake until the early hours talking and laughing, and by the time late Saturday afternoon came Venetia and Kate were exhausted and determined never to bring any of them camping again.

The second night Jake refused point-blank to share the tent with Alex because he claimed he snored, and Janey offered to share with Jake, as though sacrificing herself by doing so. Beth had been blinded with temper by the whole idea, and to Janey's fury Jake had agreed it wouldn't be at all suitable for them to share and he'd just tolerate Alex snoring. Venetia and Kate vehemently agreed. So they shared as first arranged, and Beth was livid and Janey greatly disappointed that her offer to share with Jake hadn't worked. What was the point of going away for a weekend to find oneself sleeping in the wrong tent? She said as much to Beth. 'I wanted to sleep with Jake. The two stuffy old biddies in charge can go to blazes as far as I'm concerned.'

Beth, her equilibrium disrupted by being out of her comfort zone, suddenly saw with the most amazing clarity what the situation really was. Why should Janey want to sleep with Jake if she apparently didn't know him ... she must know him! But Jake couldn't have another girlfriend beside herself. Could he? She must have got it wrong. Aware she could be stepping right into the most appalling row she said tentatively, 'I've got some chocolate biscuits in my bag. Would you like one?' That question seemed like a very good opening for the next ones she intended to ask.

'Oh yes, please. My plate tonight was filled with the most burnt fatty bits you could imagine. I'd love a biscuit.' Janey switched on her torch. 'There, can you see any better?'

'Yes, thanks.' She rooted about in her bag for the biscuits her mother had given her. She'd said that if things got bad, a chocolate biscuit could work wonders in desperate moments when camping. Well, she'd better be right.

They had two each and then Janey asked for another. 'I know it's disgusting and very bad for my spots, but please?'

Beth offered her the rest of the packet. She never got spots so she could eat as many as she liked, but if Janey got spots, well, she could have just as many as she wanted. There was a loud rustling and the sound of Janey chomping. Beth smiled to herself and asked, 'What's the talent like in Penny Fawcett, then?'

'The one and only bit of talent is Jake.'

'I thought he looked a bit of all right.'

'He most definitely is. He's the best there is, believe me, and I should know.'

'You should know?'

If it hadn't been so dark Beth would have been able to see the most beautiful smile on Janey's face. 'Oh yes. We keep it very secret otherwise his mother would be laughing like a drain. She's so vulgar you wouldn't believe it. He'd never hear the end of it and she'd tell absolutely everybody she knew. He's a darling and very, very sexy and wonderful at it. I can't get enough of him. Best one ever, is Jake.'

'Oh! Like that, is he? Must be marvellous to have someone as good as that. I didn't know you were an item.'

'Old innocent, aren't you, I bet.'

'Not specially.' Beth's stomach was heaving with distress. He'd never wanted to with her. Well, almost not wanted. 'He's OK, then?'

'More than OK. I just hope he never moves away. He wants to live with his dad, you see, but he works abroad a lot so he can't. If he went, I'd be devastated.'

'Of course you would.' Beth heard Janey shuffle into her sleeping bag as though settling down to sleep. She was glad. She needed time to think. That was why Jake had never been close to her the whole weekend. She just thought he was being discreet. More than discreet! Very slowly tears began to roll down her cheeks, they kept welling up and wouldn't stop, and the next hour was miserable and lonely and desolate. If her mother opened up the tent flap right now and said, 'I've come to take you home', she'd be saved, absolutely saved. She'd understand how this kind of betrayal felt, she'd know exactly. Beth fell asleep just as she was working out how she should behave towards Jake the following day.

She woke at first light, thinking she'd do just as she had done all the weekend – behave towards him as she did to everyone on the trip: friendly, chatty, helpful and well-balanced. Then she'd talk to her mum at home and decide on a plan of action. Well, the only action she was going to take was nothing. She wouldn't berate him about two-timing her, she wouldn't criticise him, lose her temper, nothing, because that was the only dignified way in which to retrieve her self-esteem. But it would be her who finished it. Not him.

She fell asleep again, and had to be woken by Janey just as breakfast was being served. Janey said she felt sick as a dog after finishing the chocolate biscuits before she went to sleep. Beth thought the biscuit saga had turned out rather well, then she remembered it wasn't Janey's fault, because she'd been two-timed, too, so though Janey didn't know it she also needed sympathy. For the rest of the day Janey and Beth were the greatest of friends, a state of affairs that caused Jake to become increasingly bewildered. Still, that was girls, off and on with their relationships, just like the rain.

The Penny Fawcett people were being taken home in the minibus after the Turnham Malpas people had been dropped off with their bags. At Turnham Malpas, while the luggage and the sleeping bags were being sorted out from under seats and out of the luggage racks, Jake spoke to Beth.

'Sorry I've not taken much notice of you while ... you know, but I thought it best.'

Beth looked him straight in the eye. 'That's all right, Jake. In fact, I think it would be a good idea if we cooled it for a while. You've got loads of work to do for exams in the summer, I've got lots of things on and I think it would be for the best.'

She almost felt his shock, but she kept a rein on her feelings and didn't allow it to upset her too much. She'd keep all that for when she got in the house.

'I'm sorry, did I hear you right? You want to finish? Why?'

'Just do, Jake. I've talked a lot to Janey this weekend and I realise it's all a waste of time.' It hurt to say that, but it was true. She had talked to Janey and in the process learned far more than she'd bargained for. 'Night-night, Jake.' She kissed his cheek and left him standing in the road. Alex picked up her bag for her, she clutched their sleeping bags, and the two of them walked across to the Rectory, Alex shouting as they left, 'Goodnight, everybody, thanks for a good weekend.'

Beth's heart hammered in her chest and tears were very close, but she held on until her mother, who'd been waiting on the doorstep since the moment she'd heard the minibus pull up, closed the door behind them.

'You've been lucky with the weather. Have you had a great time?'

Alex said, 'Marvellous, thanks. We've really enjoyed ourselves, haven't we, Beth?'

Beth replied by flinging herself into her mother's arms and bursting into tears.

Caroline raised her eyebrows at Alex but he shrugged. 'Put the kettle on, darling, I think we all need a cup of tea.' She walked Beth into the sitting room and closed the door behind them.

'Well now, Beth darling. Hush, hush. Tell me what the problem is.'

They were still in the sitting room when Peter got back from Evensong and Alex had no explanation for him. 'To be frank, Dad, Jake Harding came along and also a girl from Penny Fawcett, who used to be in primary school with Beth and me, and I have a sneaky feeling, though I could be wrong, that Jake is having it off with her and seeing Beth at the same time, and I think she's found out because the two girls shared a tent. She never said a word to me but she's just spoken to Jake before the minibus left and I thought Jake looked pole-axed, so perhaps she's finished it. She's telling Mum right now. Tea?'

'Yes. She's bound to be upset.'

'I know.'

'Just tell me, Alex, as far as you know, they haven't been having sex, have they, Jake and Beth?'

Alex shrugged. 'Don't think so. In fact, I'm pretty sure they haven't.'

'Just in case there are consequences, you understand.'

Alex said, 'Oh God, I hadn't thought of that. But I shouldn't be discussing this with you. You should ask *her*.'

'Indeed I should.' He opened the sitting-room door and closed it carefully behind him.

Beth and Caroline were sitting close together on the sofa, Beth still tearful and Caroline with her arm round her looking very composed. Peter raised his eyebrows and when he got a wink from Caroline in reply he began to relax.

Beth looked up. 'You were right, Dad. I've stayed in charge and I've finished with him. He was sleeping with Janey King from Penny Fawcett. You remember her from school, don't you? She was wearing a bra while still at primary school; you know who I mean. But sleeping with her and coming here for lunch at the same time? Well! Such duplicity! How could he? How *could* he? It's so humiliating.'

'I guess you didn't sleep with him, then.' He looked hard at her face, trying to work out for himself whether she had.

'I don't know how you could ask me that.'

'I didn't ask you. I *told* you you hadn't, didn't I?'

Beth thought for a moment and realised he was right. 'Then it really would have been painful. However, I've done what I've done even if it hurts like hell, which it does, but it was the only way. Is there any tea going?'

Caroline gave her an extra big hug. 'Yes, come on, your meal's all ready on the kitchen table.'

Beth's face lit up when she saw the food and the nicely laid table. 'Oh! This is marvellous. The food was disgusting, the company even worse, and it'll be a long time before I go camping again.'

Alex, tucking into his food as though he hadn't eaten for a fortnight, said, 'In that case, I'll book just one place on the narrowboat in the summer.'

'Ah! I'd forgotten about that. Better book two. I'll have forgotten how bad it's been by then.' She sounded cheerful enough but Caroline felt her underlying distress and recollected how painful the ending of one's first love affair could be. Thank God Beth had found the strength to finish it herself.

But it wasn't to be the end of it. The next evening Jake followed Beth home off the school coach and asked to have a word. Alex beat a hasty retreat to the kitchen and Beth showed Jake into the sitting room.

'Yes? What do you want? I meant it, you know, what I said last night. I truly did.'

'I know.' His face was alight with pleasure and she could have slapped him for it. 'I'm most awfully sorry about you finishing with me. I feel very disappointed with myself, but I've got some good news I need to tell you. I've come to say I'm relieving you of the problem of bumping into me because after Christmas, I shall be out of your way.'

'Why?'

'When I got home last night my dad had left a message for me to ring him. He's been promoted to a head office job at a wonderful salary, so he won't be travelling abroad hardly at all and I'm going to live with him, which means he won't have to have any contact with my mum.'

'What about school?'

'He's hoping to buy a house the other side of Culworth so I shall still be able to travel to school to finish my A-levels. You've no idea how pleased I am. I'm sorry, so sorry. I told Janey about you. She thought it funny the two of you were sharing a tent, but then she would. I didn't want you to know, you see.'

'Obviously you didn't.'

'I must have been mad.'

'Yes, that's right. But I think perhaps you get on with your dad better than you do with your mum.'

'Yes, I do. He and I – we're the same sort of people, well, almost that is ... I've no right to ask after ... anyway, I will: would you let me write to you sometimes? Perhaps see you in Culworth occasionally? It's been the best thing since sliced bread, knowing you and meeting your family. It's given me a chance to see what quality of life it's possible to have. Your dad frightens the life out of me, though. He sees right through you, doesn't he? He isn't in, is he?'

Having no idea where he was she mischievously answered, 'I expect he's in his study.'

'Ah! Well, I'll go, then.' He headed for the front door. 'Can't apologise enough. Janey's a different type of girl from you, very different, you see, but you ... well, you're special.' Somewhere in the house a door opened. 'However, I'll be off. She's finished with me, too, but perhaps it's as well. I shan't forget you, never will. Be seeing you at school things and such.' Jake hastily picked up his school bag, raised a hand in greeting, smiled that splendid smile of his and legged it out of the door.

Beth refused to allow the tears to flow. She'd done enough of that last night and she wasn't going to allow it to happen any more. They'd parted as friends and that was it, for ever. She wouldn't mind seeing him occasionally, but she rather suspected that they wouldn't meet in Culworth, and perhaps it was for the best. She had to smile at his hurried response when he heard the kitchen door opening, and smiled even more when she found her dad wasn't even at home. Anytime in the future there was a man to get rid of she'd have to remember he was her secret weapon. But her eyes filled with tears when she remembered Jake's wonderful kissability, then she recalled why he was an expert and cancelled the tears.

Chapter 23

That night, lying in bed after making love, Peter said to Caroline, 'It'll be odd when the two of them leave home, leaving us behind.'

Caroline rolled over towards him and smiled into his eyes. 'Jake's been to see Beth. He's going to live with his father after Christmas so they won't be seeing much of each other, not even on the school coach. That's a relief. I liked him but ...'

'She appears to have survived rather well, though.'

'But she's still hurting badly, I can tell. It could have been an awful lot worse, however.'

'Exactly. This love business is fraught with dramas, isn't it?'

Caroline stared at the ceiling, her hands locked behind her head. 'Yes. I'm in the midst of one now.'

'You are? Want to tell me?'

'I hope you're not in your Rector-with-sympathy mode, because if you are I'm not telling you.'

'No, I'm in husband-with-sympathy mode.'

'Good. When we make love which are you in?'

'Definitely husband mode.' He laughed and so did she.

'It's not a laughing matter.'

'What isn't?'

'My problem, Peter.'

'Well?'

'I've loved unswervingly since the day we met. Couple of hiccups, serious ones, but they've been overcome. However, the current one looks like being with me for life.'

Peter turned away from her and all she had of him was the back of his head and his long bare back.

'Well, you haven't answered me.'

'No.'

'It won't go away, Peter. You say there'll be no more of Suzy Meadows but you don't say why. Have you murdered her? Are you just waiting for someone to find the body?'

'That is flippant and unnecessary and not worthy of you.'

'No, Peter, you can't get away with a reprimand, it's too serious. I have a need to know and so have the children. You owe us that at the very least.'

There was a long silence and eventually she gave up her quest, turned away from him, snatched her nightgown from under her pillow and struggled to put it on lying down. He turned over to give her a hand.

Comfortable once her nightgown was not rucked up beneath her, she looked at him intently. She waited five whole minutes and then he spoke.

'It was so difficult. I went there to reason with her, naturally, a sensible adult conversation, leaving a door open in case the children changed their minds. An hour or two and then we'd have it sorted.'

'And wasn't it?'

Peter half propped himself up on his pillows. 'I'd sent a letter to her saying I was coming, that if it wasn't convenient could she please let me know, but when I got there she flung the door open, looking puzzled as though something was missing. "Where are your cases?" she said. She'd assumed I was going there that day to live with her. I'd no answer, I'm afraid.'

She heard him swallow hard so she slipped her hand into his to comfort him.

'There were no grounds for her to think so for one single minute, as you well know. Then there was a footstep in the hall and someone who looked like her except not so painfully screwed up, said loudly, "Come in, Peter. I'm Suzy's older sister, Paula. There's three of us. The other one is still in the States." I shook hands with her, but Suzy dragged hold of me and pulled me into the sitting room saying she'd got everything arranged, that she'd cleared a little snug and made it into a study for me with a desk her father had used, how wonderful it all was and telling the plans she'd made and asking when the children would be coming? End of term? In time for Christmas?

'It was then I knew she had to be told the stark truth, no trimmings, no going round corners, no trying to be kind because she'd simply ignore the bits she didn't want to hear. Her sister pushed her down into a chair and insisted she must listen to what I had to say. So I sat down too and told her I'd never said I was coming to stay. I'd come to explain the situation and it didn't involve me or the children going there to live. Finally, finally it sunk in. Then ...'

Caroline squeezed his hand tightly. 'Go on.'

'Then she exploded into a massive hysterical outburst, throwing herself about, screaming, crying, throwing things – books, ornaments, chairs, anything she had the strength to pick up. She was going to kill herself, she was going to kill me, she'd get the children no doubt about that ... Both Paula and I were appalled, and for the first few minutes watched in horror, just not knowing what on earth to do. It occurred to me that there was a similarity between her behaviour and the terrible twos behaviour of the twins when they threw a tantrum. She wasn't getting her own way so she threw a wobbly. Paula and I grabbed her and forced her down on to the sofa, holding her so she couldn't get up.'

In the soft lighting of the bedroom she couldn't see his face properly but Caroline heard him swallow several times while he regained control. 'Paula said, "Hold her, I'll get her tablets." She left me holding Suzy down, and went to the kitchen to fetch the tablets and a glass of water. Eventually we got them down her and she began to quieten. It took about twenty minutes and then she fell asleep. I looked down at her and she was pitiable. That blonde hair that Beth has inherited was streaked with sweat, her face was reddened and puffy with her tears, her dowdy clothes ... Skin and bone, she was. There was nothing appealing about her. I was horrified.

'That doesn't sound kind. She's obviously very ill.'

'I didn't feel kind. She'd tried so hard to ruin our lives, and for one terrible minute I could have done what you suggested I'd done. Then of course I was so afraid, thinking a psychiatric hospital would be the next stage. Paula got us each a stiff whisky and she sat down to tell me what would happen next.' He hesitated for a while, picturing in his mind how Suzy looked and wondering how he had ever come to have sex with her.

'Apparently Paula and the other sister run a private school in the States for seriously disturbed children, just a small one about six children at a time, and Suzy is going to live in the States with them and help in the school.'

'Frankly, Peter, she sounds to be just the right person for a job like that. She'll be able to match them tantrum for tantrum.'

This was Caroline at her most damning and Peter felt angry with her. 'Darling! That's not fair. Being busy teaching, with her sisters to care for her, could be the very thing she needs. They're doing their best for her. Apparently she adored Patrick – you know, her first husband – and when he killed himself it was a crushing blow. Her mother did everything for her little girls at the time because she was useless.'

Caroline knew she'd achieve nothing by being unkind about Suzy. He'd seen her as she actually was and been shattered by it so criticism of her was out, but it was obvious to Caroline the woman was mad. 'Where are your cases?' Huh! She despised Suzy for being so ridiculous as to say that to a man like Peter. As if Peter would just walk away from his responsibilities to the church and his God. 'So how did she come to marry Michael Palmer? Did her sister say?'

'Apparently they were as bewildered as anyone could be. He wasn't right for her at all, Paula said. He was too kind, too soft, too lacking in oomph. He needed her to lean on, not the other way round and Suzy finished up despising him.'

'I rather thought so. Well, I've heard enough.'

'I need to talk some more.'

Resigning herself to his need to talk, she replied, 'OK.'

Peter turned to look at her, this woman who was the light of his life, the beat of his heart, his springboard, his courage, his joy. This woman who lay beside him every night of his life and whom he loved with an abandonment he'd never thought possible to experience. 'Guilt, you know, that's my problem. Because of one moment of weakness on my part this human being has been reduced to that pathetic bundle. All my fault.'

'I would like to point out, my darling, that it takes two to tango. You're a very, very attractive man, though you don't appear to know it. Remember Louise Bissett? Venetia Mayer? They threw themselves at you just as she has done. There could be others, I'm sure. Ah, yes. Anna Sanderson for one.'

'The Reverend Anna Sanderson, do you mean? Now that is rubbish.'

'No, darling, it isn't. It's the truth, except, being a very honourable member of the clergy, she kept it well under control.'

'I don't believe that for one second and you're distracting me—'

'Distracting you from strapping yourself to the stake and being burned alive, do you mean? Lay it to rest, and put your hair shirt away, too. It's over. Done with. She's going to be taken care of thousands of miles away from us, and at last the children can stop worrying about her popping in unexpectedly. And so can you.'

Peter lay quite still, thinking about what she'd just said. Was she right? Or had she arrived at a place of contentment that he could never reach? With her help, maybe he could reach it. Finally put behind him the guilt, the sorrow, the burden it had all become, for it had never lessened as the years went by.

'Just think, Peter, about the pluses. You've proved yourself capable of fathering children and for a man that's incredibly important, and something you would never have known otherwise. We've both got the children we needed, me especially, since I was unable to conceive . Maybe your moment of weakness, as you call it, was ordained from above. All part of God's plan for you and me.'

'Now look here, you can't—'

'No, *you* look here. I'm well aware I have not got your depth of understanding of God and his mysterious ways, but if it pleases me to look at it like that, why can't you?'

The long silence which followed at least proved to Caroline that he hadn't entirely dismissed the idea.

Very, very softly Peter asked, 'In your heart of hearts, is all your gut-wrenching pain as nothing now?'

She had to strain to hear and her heart jumped with joy.

'The answer is yes, very much so. It just doesn't hurt any more. What's more important is we're here, together, loving one another. And it is no longer a matter of contemplation, discussion, for agonizing over, chewing over, remembering at moments of stress between us, nor, most importantly, when we're making love, because you may not know it but it never leaves you, even then.'

'It doesn't? Not even when ... I didn't realise.'

'So as it is now midnight, let's start the new day and our new life by making love all over again on the new basis we've just established.'

'I don't know if I can feel totally free of guilt like you feel free of hurt.'

'Oh, Peter! Do you *enjoy* feeling guilty?'

'Not one little bit, actually, but I can't help it.'

'Well, I'm totally free of hurt now. I see what's the most important and that's you and me loving each other and having our very own two children.'

'I suppose if that's how you feel then I don't need to feel guilty because of your hurt, not any more, and I promise, most especially at moments like these, I shall be, as you say, completely free in my soul. And this is your husband speaking, not your priest.'

He turned towards her and took her hand in his, then raised it to his lips and kissed it.